Do The Write Thing

Do The Write Thing

14 WINNING STORIES
BY IRELAND'S
NEWEST WRITERS

POOLBEG

Published 2007
by Poolbeg Press Ltd
123 Grange Hill, Baldoyle
Dublin 13, Ireland
E-mail: poolbeg@poolbeg.com
www.poolbeg.com

1 3 5 7 9 10 8 6 4 2

A catalogue record for this book is available from the British Library.

ISBN 978-1-84223-302-3

Typeset by Patricia Hope in Caslon 10.75/15.5

Printed by
Litografia Rosés, S.A., Spain

Contents

Jacqueline Ashmore lives in Dublin with her husband and a family of cute, adorable, mischievous, entertaining, fun-loving, sun-worshipping felines.

Educated at the University of Keele, she has worked as a special adviser at the Department of the Taoiseach and is currently engaged in corporate development for UCD's School of Business.

Eton Road

Jacqueline Ashmore

DEDICATION

For Jasper, my little treasure.
Forever in my heart.

APRIL 1998 – MAY 2007

Eton Road

THURSDAY 29TH JUNE 2006

Gerry heard his wife coming down the hall as he reached for the marmalade and thought, Oh my God, here we go again – "the dreaded question" rears its ugly head: "Does my bum look big in this, is it too tight? Now tell me the truth, Gerry, I want to know!" Every bloody morning it's the same rigmarole!

Every morning Anna went through the same ritual. She tried on various outfits and then asked her husband Gerry a variety of questions, but what Anna really wanted to know was not "Do I *look* fat?" but "*Am* I fat?" The truthful answer was "Yes, you are!" but how could he ever say that to her? Over the last few years, Gerry had learned a variety of tactful ways of saving his wife's feelings and also stopping her from venturing out in outfits that highlighted the fact that she was wearing clothes that were meant for someone at least three-stone lighter.

Anna Maguire worked as a doctor's receptionist and could wear whatever she liked as long as it was smart and business like. Out of work, Anna had adopted a uniform of jeans and T-shirts in the summer and jeans and sweatshirts in the winter, with trainers all year round. With each pound in weight gained, Anna's self-confidence slipped away, along with her dress sense.

Anna Maguire was, as the saying goes, "fair, fat and forty" – well, to be honest, she had celebrated her forty-second birthday two months before. She and Gerry had been married for twenty-two years and they had two children, Michael aged twenty and Robert aged eighteen. Michael would start the third year of his degree in Business and Law at UCD this coming September, and Robert, Leaving Cert results permitting, would start the first year of a Media Studies course in DCU.

When Anna's fortieth birthday had loomed into view, Gerry toyed with the idea of giving her a gift of a membership to the local gym, but his mate Joe had talked him out of it, insisting that the breakdown of his own marriage could be traced back to the gym membership that he had given his wife for her fortieth birthday. Whether it was true or not, Gerry didn't know, but he wasn't taking the risk, as he loved his wife. So he had sensibly settled on a gift of a one-carat diamond and gold pendant, similar to one he had seen Anna looking at in one of those many magazines she regularly brought home from the waiting room at the doctor's surgery. It was expensive. But the jeweller had assured him that no woman ever complained that she couldn't wear a one-carat diamond pendant because it made her bum look big. He'd sold hundreds over the years, he assured Gerry, and never had one dissatisfied customer. And just to make sure there were no difficulties with it fitting around her neck, which wasn't as slim as it used to be, Gerry had done the sensible thing and taken the jeweller's advice to go for the twenty-one-inch chain.

Now, two years and three birthdays later, if there was one thing Gerry Maguire knew without question, it was that diamonds really were a girl's best friend. And jewellery, as long as you stuck with earrings of any sort, pendants with long chains and long necklaces, could be a husband's best friend when shopping for a size-conscious wife. He had learned, from his now trusty jeweller, never to buy bracelets, as they may not fit around a plump wrist and this only leads to tears. Rings are not a good idea either, even if they are a perfect fit when they are first purchased. They can also lead to tears when they no longer fit due to plump fingers – and this can never be blamed on "shrinking in the wash" or as "a result of dry cleaning" as with clothes, although "water retention" is always worth a try for focusing blame. And so, over the last few years, as Anna's weight increased so did her collection of jewellery. Anna's birthday, Valentine's Day, their wedding anniversary and Christmas saw Gerry pay a visit to "his jeweller", as he now regarded him and with whom he was now on first-name terms – and why wouldn't he be with all the money he spent? – to seek his advice about adding to Anna's jewellery collection.

All the special occasions were now celebrated with Gerry producing jewellery boxes of varying shapes and sizes and Anna never once had a complaint. And most importantly of all, Gerry never had to answer "the dreaded question" when Anna tried on her gift of jewellery. The jeweller was right – a woman never questioned if her bum looked big in diamonds, so to speak! There was, of course, that awful diamond encrusted G-string on sale in Brown Thomas of Grafton Street. It was selling for €23,000 just before Valentine's Day. The story was all over the papers, as some eejit had bought it for his girlfriend.

Twenty-three K, thought Gerry when he'd read the story, and you can be sure that at some point the eejit's girlfriend will ask him "the dreaded question" – it's fools like him that give men a bad name.

Only at Easter did he give both of them some leeway and buy the traditional Easter egg, fearing that if he didn't Anna might accuse him of believing her to be too fat to be eating a chocolate Easter egg. If there was another thing Gerry Maguire knew it was that he could never be too careful where the issue of weight and his wife were concerned.

"IT", as it became known by Gerry and his two sons, arrived in June 2006 – Thursday 29th June to be precise. "IT" had arrived at Anna's mother's house earlier that week and been redirected by her and "IT" popped into the mailbox of Number 85, Eton Road, at around 7:45 a.m., just as Gerry was reaching for the marmalade.

"IT" arrived in a card-sized envelope, with the crest and name of Anna's old school displayed in colour on the upper left-hand corner and her maiden name and mother's address on the envelope. "IT" was an embossed card and read as follows:

INVITATION

The Board and Management of the School cordially invite

Ms Anna Matthews and Guest

To attend a Gala Evening in the School Hall to celebrate
The class of 1982 – Twenty-fifth Anniversary Reunion

On Friday 29th June 2007 at 7:30 p.m.

Please RSVP before 29th September 2006 to:
Tel. 088-6987963
Or e-mail: classof82@olbs.ie

"IT" was an invitation to her twenty-fifth year Class Reunion. Anna had left school twenty-four years earlier, aged eighteen, having completed a "satisfactory" Leaving Cert. By the time of the Class Reunion in 2007, twenty-five years would have passed since she last saw her classmates, and she would be forty-three years and two months old by then.

Panic set in – she didn't want to turn up at the class of 1982 reunion: it wouldn't just be those in her class but everyone in her Leaving Cert year! Some of her former classmates had, as her mother put it, "done well for themselves", the implication being that she *hadn't* done well – her mother had an annoying habit of managing to say things without actually saying them! One went on to become a TD and would be up for re-election in the 2007 General Election, which was due to take place just before the Class Reunion. Another was a model, now turned boutique owner, a couple of them were teachers, at least one was a university lecturer, Marie Doyle was a nun – and even she had managed to win an award for her work with the homeless. Bloody hell, how can I possibly compete with that lot? thought Anna.

Anna knew all of this about her former classmates by logging on to the school website and accessing *Class of 1982 – Where We Are Now*. Anna had never sent any of her details to be added to the website, and her school newsletter was still sent to her mother's home address: her mother just readdressed it to Anna's house and popped it in the mail again, just like she had done when "IT" arrived. But although Anna didn't exist on the website, she had over the years kept an eye on how everyone else was doing. Some people had even added their photos along with their details. None of them looked older than forty-two – in fact some looked a lot younger – and none of them appeared to be overweight, quite the opposite. Anna didn't feel that she had anything to boast about career-wise, and whilst she had once been happy with her looks, this was no longer the case.

Another thing that bugged her was that no one had ever posted a *Where Are You Now?* notice for her on the website. So, obviously, her former classmates had no interest in contacting her nor ever gave her a thought.

For a full week Anna wavered between yes, she was going to attend, and no, she wasn't. She was going. She wasn't going. She hadn't seen them for twenty-four years and by then it would be twenty-five years. She wouldn't recognise anyone. She was going. She wouldn't have anything in common with them any more. She wasn't going. On and on it went like a verbal game of tennis. Should she go or shouldn't she go? "What do you think, Gerry?" Anna would ask her husband on an hourly basis.

"IT" began to overtake "the dreaded question". Gerry knew that behind Anna's indecision, to go or not to go, was her insecurity about her appearance, coupled with the fear and belief that she didn't measure up to her classmates. She was fretting about how she would be viewed, if not judged, by them.

Bloody hell, thought Gerry, a trip to the jeweller's isn't going to sort this one out! This is major league. And for once Gerry was lost for knowing what to say and what not to say.

At age forty-two and two months, Anna Maguire was eleven stone in weight – three stone overweight for her 5'2" height – forty-two pounds – one pound for every year of her life. Anna had always been a size eight to ten until she turned thirty-seven years old. Then her figure didn't just head south – it went north, south, east and west.

But in the end it was another man who decided if Anna would go to the Class Reunion or not. While watching an episode of *Dr Phil* that focused on "Take Control of Your Life and Turn It Around in One Year", Anna made the decision that was to change her life. The episode had shown how Mindy from Montana had lost sixty pounds in weight in one year and turned up at her ex-fiancé's wedding – he'd broken off their engagement because he said she was "too darn big". If Mindy from Montana could reinvent herself in one year and accept an invitation from her ex-fiancé to his wedding, then "Anna from Eton Road" could shed those forty-two pounds and turn up at her own Class Reunion.

"You have everything to gain and nothing to lose – except the weight," declared Dr Phil. "Get out there and take control of your life. Be the person you really want to be."

Gerry wasn't sure if he should be grateful to Dr Phil and Mindy from Montana or not at this stage, but at least a decision had been made.

JULY 2006

Once the decision had been made by Anna, with the help of Dr Phil and Mindy from Montana, she set about reinventing herself with a determination and a dedication that Gerry had never seen before. Anna considered herself too fat to go to the gym, Shapes and Sizes, that was located in the same complex as the doctor's surgery where she worked.

"I can't possibly let anyone see me in this state – I

look like a beached whale. What if I met someone I knew, say one of the neighbours? I'd die of embarrassment, Gerry, honest I would," said Anna.

And so it was that Gerry set about clearing out the room over the garage and, with the help of the Argos Catalogue, kitted part of it out as a mini-gym for Anna. Anna's gym consisted of an exercise bike and one of those new twist-steppers.

"Keep it simple, love, no point in getting in over yourself," advised Gerry, convinced that Anna's get-fit campaign would be short-lived.

Surprisingly, for the first time in her life, Anna managed to stick to a calorie-controlled diet and an exercise routine. It wasn't a diet in the sense that it had A Name. Anna simply cut out the bad food that she was eating, bought herself a calorie-counter book and noted the amount of calories that she was consuming every day. She started out exercising three days a week and over time built up to six days a week. Every night she fell asleep listening to the Paul McKenna *Think Yourself Thin* CD. At Gerry's insistence she took Sunday off. "Even famous temples close for maintenance, love," insisted Gerry. Anna took the saying "Worship your body like a temple" as seriously as if it was the famous Konark Sun Temple or even the Golden Temple in India.

In the beginning, Anna was so busy concentrating on her exercises that the world outside of her "gym" didn't exist. But after a few weeks, while she was pounding away on her exercise bike and twist-stepping, Anna started to take notice of what was going on outside of her house. A whole world passed by her door every day and, without meaning to, she began to take notice of the comings and goings of her neighbours and their visitors.

The first person to come to her notice was her posh next-door neighbour Luisa Montgomery. Luisa lounged out in her back garden every summer's day, supposedly topping up her tan, and during the winter months stayed indoors out of the cold. "You poor thing," Luisa was fond of commenting to Anna, "I don't know how you do it, day in and day out, going to work and caring for a husband and two boys as well. Still, I suppose if you need the money . . . I think you're great, I couldn't imagine having to go out to work every day!" Luisa always insisted that her husband, whom she referred to as "my Andrew", "wouldn't hear tell of me working – he says a husband's place is to provide for his wife and family", followed closely by, "and it's not as if we need the money". Over the years, Anna had come to hate the sight of Luisa spread out on her sun-lounger from early morning during the summer months – sometimes even before Anna had left for her job at the doctor's.

Over a short while Anna began to notice that Luisa went out every evening at the same time – 10:00 p.m. – and that the car was missing for hours after that. One early morning, by chance, Anna happened to look out of her window and to her surprise saw Luisa arriving home. She noticed that Luisa dropped something as she got out of her car. On her way to work, Anna discovered that it was a Tesco staff ID marked *Louise Mooney, Shelving Staff – Balbriggan Branch*, and interestingly it had a photo of Luisa Montgomery on it.

Hmm, interesting, very interesting, thought Anna, as she popped the ID into her bag to show Gerry later.

"So why is she using a different name?"

"Tax and insurance, love, simple as that," explained Gerry. "Obviously, the name 'Luisa Montgomery' is a 'poshed-up' version of her real name, Louise Mooney – clever really, same initials but sounds better when you're trying to be something you're not. She'd have to use her real name to get her pay – chances are her bank account is in her real name."

"So all this time when she's being making me feel bad about having to work and how they 'don't need the money', she's been working as a shelver in Tesco's in Balbriggan," fumed Anna.

"Well, there's very little chance of any other night worker in Tesco's Balbriggan recognising her as Luisa Montgomery from Eton Road, love. And there's even less chance of anyone from around here turning up in Tesco's in Balbriggan when there's a Tesco's ten minutes' drive away from here. Mind you, that could always be rectified. Doesn't the Balbriggan branch do twenty-four-hour opening on a Thursday and Friday night? Sure maybe we could take a wander out there some Thursday or Friday evening. We could pop into the Balbriggan Bay Hotel for dinner and then on our way home drop into Tesco's to pick up a few things. What do you think, love?"

"I think, Gerry, that you are devious enough to be an honorary woman! Let's do it!"

"Right. Whenever you want."

"So when Mrs 'We Don't Need the Money'

Montgomery spends hours supposedly sunning herself as a lady of leisure in her back garden in the summer, she's probably asleep after doing a night's work in Tesco's. Wonder what else she's hiding?"

"Probably a fake tan as well, I should think."

Over the next few weeks, Anna upped her exercise regime to include a thirty-minute morning exercise session. She quickly worked out that her neighbour did the 11:00 p.m. to 7:00 a.m. shift. She noticed that Luisa, or "The Fake" as Gerry had now taken to calling her, arrived home every morning at 7:45 a.m. having left the previous evening at 10:00 p.m. It was approximately a forty-five-minute drive to Balbriggan – then parking the car and changing into her uniform would account for the extra fifteen minutes.

Anna began to wonder what secrets her other neighbours harboured behind their double-, and in one case triple-, glazed windows and doors. Over the coming weeks and months, other stories about her other neighbours emerged. Each one as interesting and as intriguing as the next.

AUGUST 2006

Scarpetti's award-winning hairdressing salon is situated on Dawson Street, the same street as the Mansion House. Scarpetti's is very exclusive, very expensive and very hard to get an appointment for, as there's a waiting list, a very long one. For very special clients Scarpetti's will open late on the evenings of the many, now highly fashionable, fundraising balls that frequently take place in the Mansion House or in the exclusive hotels scattered around the expensive Grafton Street or upmarket Merrion Street, home to Government Buildings.

Scarpetti's is owned by the flamboyant Ronaldo Scarpetti – hairdresser to the rich and famous. His clients think that he is both Italian and gay – two things which he openly encourages as being true. In fact, his real name is Ronnie O'Shea and he was born and raised in a very small village in Sligo, which he left at the age of sixteen to go and train as a hairdresser in New York. Ronaldo is happily married with a wife and three children. In fact, Ronaldo is as straight as a piece of hair that has had the attentions of a straightening iron on it for a full five minutes. His female clients love him and confide their many secrets in him, thus proving the saying that "gay men make the best friends for a woman".

Shortly after she decided that she would attend the Class Reunion, and had her home gym up and running, Anna decided to turn her attentions to her hair. She hadn't been to a hairdresser's in years: she coloured her hair herself and got her sister Una to trim it for her when she felt it needed it – about twice a year. She was a "wash 'n' go" person, only blow-drying and using her straightening iron on special occasions. Occasions which would see Gerry produce a jewellery box.

Anna read about Scarpetti's many times in the glossy magazines in the waiting room of the doctor's surgery.

Not realising that there was a waiting list, and a very long one at that, Anna turned up early one Saturday morning and asked if she could speak to someone about her hair and what she could have done with it. Luckily for her, Ronaldo overheard her talking to the receptionist and liked the idea of dealing with a non-celebrity for a change.

Over the next few months, Anna visited Scarpetti's every Saturday morning for her appointment with Ronaldo. He liked Anna. She was not like his usual stuck-up clients and he understood what she was trying to do, to reinvent herself, and she had now less than one year to do it. Anna liked Ronaldo and, finding him easy to chat away to as he "hmmed" and "aahed" over what best to do next with her hair, she told him about what she saw when she was exercising. Ronaldo found her stories entertaining and a nice change from the usual self-obsessed prattle of his celebrity clients. Sensing a true celebrity in the making, Ronaldo told Anna that she should write down her stories. At first Anna laughed at him, but when he told her that's how Miriam Garfield, the famous author, started out, she decided to take his advice and typed up the story of Luisa Montgomery. With her permission, Ronaldo showed it to one of his clients, the famous, or should that be infamous, Irish literary agent Lulu Baxter-Guinness. LB-G, as she was known, had a reputation for being difficult, but Ronaldo knew that, just like his, this was a manufactured image that for all sorts of reasons suited her.

OCTOBER 2006

On Friday 20th October 2006, after a lovely calorie-conscious meal in the Balbriggan Bay Hotel, Anna and Gerry dropped into the Balbriggan branch of Tesco's, supposedly to pick up a few bits and pieces. And Anna met her "we don't need the money" neighbour stacking shelves – with bottles of fake tan.

"Fitting, very fitting," remarked Gerry, "that The Fake should be shelving fake-tan lotion, don't you think, love?"

Later that month, Lulu Baxter-Guinness read the story about Anna's neighbour, Luisa Montgomery The Fake.

"Delicious, just delicious," murmured Lulu, as Ron snipped the tiniest of pieces from her perfectly coiffed hair.

"What's that, sweetie?" asked Ron.

"The story about how Anna and her husband Gerry dropped into the Balbriggan branch of Tesco's on the pretence of picking up a few things, and Anna finally confronted her "we don't need the money" neighbour stacking shelves – and the fallout from that!" Lulu laughed. "I just love it! I felt that I was actually there, I could even smell the bread baking from the on-site bakery!"

"I know, you're right, it's just yummy," said Ron. "Particularly the bit about Anna taking a picture of The Fake on her mobile phone when she was stacking a shelf with bottles of fake-tan lotion!"

"Does she have any more stories like this one, do you

know, Ron?" asked Lulu as she reached for her freshly made cappuccino.

Ron knew that it was the little things, like the lattes, cappuccinos and freshly baked pastries, and not just his highly trained staff that helped make his salon the top hairdressing salon in Dublin and the salon of choice for many TV personalities, female politicians and, of course, people like Lulu Baxter-Guinness. The years he spent working in top salons in the USA taught him that everyone likes that little bit extra, and the rich and famous particularly love a freebie. Though, in reality, he always included 5 per cent extra in his final fee to include any 'freebies' they might have availed of during their visit.

"Oh yes, she has others. There's a real gem about another of her neighbours who earns a living by, how shall I put it, the oldest profession in the world, without ever leaving her house. And another called 'Enough to Make a Cat Laugh' which is a total hoot – you'll just love it, Lulu, it's a total scream and all true according to Anna." He laughed. "I'm only glad that I don't live on Eton Road or I'm sure she'd have a story about 'the real me' and that would never do."

"Get them for me, Ron. If they are as good as this one you could be looking at a great big thank-you from me," said Lulu.

"Consider them in your hands," replied Ron, already wondering if the big thank-you from Lulu would be another long weekend away for him and his wife Amanda. Over the years, he had managed to put some now very famous authors her way. Lulu was always very grateful, and he and Amanda had spent many a romantic weekend away in five-star hotels in exotic countries as a thank-you from Lulu.

Anna typed up another two stories and gave them to Ronaldo to pass on to Lulu. One was about another of her supposedly wealthy neighbours – Sophie Gere, who like Luisa also didn't work, as yet again "Darling Mattie would never agree to me working outside of the home." Sophie had always managed to imply that "her Mattie" and Richard Gere were distant cousins. But, as Anna discovered, while Sophie mightn't "work outside of the home", she certainly earned a living inside of the home through the many men who visited her while "Darling Mattie" was at work, and particularly when he was working abroad – possibly catching up with "his cousin Richard". Sophie was a hooker, a call girl, call it what you like.

Lulu laughed out loud when she read the story of Finnegan the cat, who got his revenge on an obnoxious, inconsiderate, fast-driving sports-car owner who dared to try and deliberately run Finnegan down one evening. Finnegan proved the saying "Never trust a smiling cat" and was solely responsible for a major fight between the owner of the sports car and another of Anna's neighbours. It resulted in both of them being arrested by the gardaí. Rumour had it that two separate court cases were pending, one for criminal damage and one for assault and slander, but again, that was another chapter in Anna's now-emerging book.

"Well, Ron," Lulu was the only one of his clients to call him Ron, "I think we have a winner here. These stories are excellent, and the fact that they are based on fact is super, although Anna will have to change the names to protect the innocent – or should I say the guilty?"

"Can't say I don't know how to pick 'em, sweetie," whispered Ron.

"Yes, I must say you do have an eye for a winner, darling!" laughed Lulu, already mentally calculating her fee as Anna's literary agent. Lulu Baxter-Guinness recognised a winner and, more importantly, a money-spinner when she saw it, and she wasn't about to let this one slip through her perfectly manicured hands.

To cut a long story short, or indeed to make a short story out of a book, Lulu offered to represent Anna as her literary agent if she could come up with a total of nine complete short stories all linked together through Eton Road. Anna couldn't believe her luck. Lulu Baxter-Guinness was the most famous literary agent in the country. "Now, sweetie, we really have to think further than your hairstyle," sighed Ronaldo. "When LB-G offers to act as your agent, you are on the road to TV appearances, book signings, the whole kit and caboodle. So keep working out – remember 'if you wanna lose it you gotta move it' – and watch what you eat, darling. It's not true what they say about the camera adding ten pounds, actually it adds twenty. And remember LB-G needs another six stories out of you as soon as poss, darling, so keep those eyes and ears wide open."

Over the next few months Anna continued to lose weight

and had her hair done weekly by Ronaldo and with the help of a variety of "procedures", as Ronaldo referred to them, improved her overall appearance. She had some Botox done in a private clinic in Haddington Road.

Through Ronaldo, Anna met Amelia Davidson, who also just happened to be one of his clients. Amelia was a former model and ran a small exclusive boutique in Blackrock. She also ran one-to-one personal image consultations, and like Ronaldo she had a long waiting list of famous people.

"Lose the glasses, sweetie," advised Amelia.

And so it was that Gerry found himself holding Anna's hand as she underwent laser eye surgery in the exclusive and expensive Blackrock Clinic.

"Worth every penny, sweetie, you look years younger," enthused Ronaldo, and for once Gerry had to agree.

Amelia helped the rapidly slimming Anna choose a new wardrobe. She showed her what suited her now slimmed-down figure and constantly improving image. Along with the new hairstyle, ditching the glasses, Botox every few months, Anna invested in some facials, quit chewing her nails with the help of some gel nails and then, to top it all off, she got her teeth whitened.

Spurred on by Lulu Baxter-Guinness's interest in her stories, Anna set about watching her neighbours with eagle eyes as she cycled and side-stepped the pounds away. She kept a voice-activated dictaphone on the windowsill so that she could keep notes of what was going on in Eton Road. Every evening after her exercise routine, Anna typed up her dictated notes, and before long she had enough material for not nine but twelve short stories, including one titled "The Class Reunion", which was to be the opening chapter of Anna's book. The second chapter was entitled "What The Fitness Fanatic Saw".

FRIDAY 29TH JUNE – CLASS REUNION DAY

Anna couldn't attend the Class Reunion, as she was appearing on the *Seoige & O'Shea* show that afternoon to plug her forthcoming book. That same evening, she would also be appearing on the last *Late Late Show* of the season.

The week before the Class Reunion Anna posted a photo of herself on the *Class of 1982 – Where We Are Now* section of her old school website and included a message.

> *Hi Everyone!*
> *Sorry I can't be with you on this wonderful occasion. Twenty-five years since we all graduated with our Leaving Certificate, who can believe it! I had hoped to be able to attend but the date clashed with some TV appearances I am making. I hope you all have a wonderful time.*
>
> *Love, Anna M*

The "Love, Anna M" was scanned in and looked absolutely fab. Anna had practised signing "Love, Anna M" for hours until she was happy with it.

The photo of Anna looked fabulous. It was one taken by a professional photographer for the back cover of her book and was also her official photo to be used for all her publicity. Much to Anna's delight, LB-G had approved her using it on the school website.

"I don't know what you're more excited about, love, the appearance of your photo on your old school website or the one of you on the back of your book," remarked Gerry.

The footnote after Anna's message read, *"Anna Maguire will be signing copies of her debut novel* Eton Road *in bookshops in September – check out a bookstore near you. Anna is currently working on her second novel entitled:* Carrot Cake Isn't a Vegetable!*"*

Eton Road wasn't a work of fiction – but then who was going to tell? Certainly not Luisa Montgomery or Sophie Gere, and Finnegan's silence could always be guaranteed with a few fish-heads.

The last thing that Anna Maguire asked her husband Gerry before she left him in the green room in RTÉ to join Gráinne Seoige and Joe O'Shea for her first ever interview was: "Gerry, are you sure my bum doesn't look big in this? Now tell me the truth, Gerry, I want to know!"

"Women!" sighed Gerry. "As hard to change when it comes to worrying about their looks as it is to break a diamond."

Elizabeth Bradley was born and raised in Dublin Inner City. She went to Australia at the age of eighteen for six months and stayed for twenty-six years. Now she resides in Spain for six months of the year, working as a property consultant. For the remainder of the year she lives with her mum and dad in Kilmore West, Dublin. Her greatest influence is Brendan Behan and her dad who said: "If it is to be, it's up to me."

Dead Ends

and

New Beginnings

Elizabeth Bradley

Dead Ends
and
New Beginnings

I t wasn't the plane banking for twenty minutes, nor the two Americans seated beside me drawling on about the forty shades of green that had my stomach turning inside out.

As we circled Dublin airport my thoughts kept drifting to what my parents' reaction would be to my unexpected arrival.

I was normally quite the chatterbox with strangers on planes. But the Americans sitting beside me must have asked me a hundred questions since we had left Heathrow. In typical Yankee style all the questions were of a personal nature. Are you married? How long have you lived in Australia? Where is your husband? Do you have any children? Why did you leave Australia? On and on until I eventually had to feign a headache and then sleep.

By the time we landed in Dublin airport I was as

agitated as a washing machine and my head was on a full spin cycle

I had travelled sixteen thousand kilometres from Australia but these next five kilometres to my parents' house were proving to be the hardest.

I didn't know what I was going to say or how I was going to say it

I didn't know much about anything any more.

I was in a constant state of turmoil. The doctor called it acute anxiety. I called it hell on earth. The disappointment of waking every morning was overwhelming. The crying for half an hour before my feet even touched the floor had become a ritual which engulfed me to the point I couldn't function normally.

My days consisted of unanswered phone calls and staring at a TV that wasn't even switched on.

Joy was no longer a part of my life. Even the songs on the radio triggered memories of my once full life: Shania Twain singing "Looks Like We Made It" seemed to mock me; the Lighthouse Family's "Lifted" well and truly caused an avalanche of tears.

My mother-in-law had advised me to find a new road because the one I was on was a dead end.

So here I was at the top of my parents' road and the taxi driver asked me if I was all right. I didn't realise I had been crying. I told him I always got emotional when I came home, which wasn't too far from the truth. In the eight years I had lived in Australia this was to be my third and final trip.

I asked the driver to stop short of Mam and Dad's

house, which was at the end of the road. He stopped four doors up, outside Mrs Ryan's. There were two little black girls and a redheaded girl playing in the garden. I guessed the little redhead was Kitty O'Meara's – she lived next door to Mam and she was also a redhead. The girls were playing with a doll's house. This caused another flood of tears from me. I too had played with doll's houses and dreamt of having the perfect house and the perfect life, as all little girls do. I watched as they packed away their dolls and their furniture and wished that I hadn't had to do the adult version of it.

I was surprised when the taxi driver insisted on carrying my luggage right up to the front door and ringing the bell. I suspected he wanted to see Mam's reaction – I had told him it was a surprise visit.

The surprise was entirely on us. I had forgotten Mam's Sunday morning routine which consisted of her soaking her false teeth, top and bottom, in a glass filled with a mixture of bleach and washing-up liquid, followed by her shaving off both her eyebrows.

Where her eyebrows used to be now had two white strips of Sudocream and although it was now one o'clock her hair remained unbrushed since she had got up this morning.

On Sundays she usually got the dinner on before having her shower.

My threatened tears turned to hysterical laughter and I was quickly followed by the taxi driver, who doubled up with laughter as Mam stood there doing her goldfish impression – mouth moving but nothing coming out.

Mam finally got me into the hallway, which wasn't easy as my legs were crossed to stop myself from peeing my pants. Through his laughter I heard the taxi driver saying to Mam: "Jaysus, missus, you have made my day!" He staggered back to his car and it was only then Mam realised we had been laughing at her appearance. A small gang of kids had gathered at the gate to see what all the laughter was about. The poor taxi driver couldn't get his keys into the lock – the tears streaming down his face had left him temporarily blinded.

Mam quickly closed the door and I fell into a chair at the kitchen table still laughing.

Mam stood in front of me, arms folded, waiting for me to stop laughing. She was just about to give out to me when the cabbage boiled over. She ran to rescue it, muttering that the dinner would be ruined. The kitchen was now filled with steam and the smell of burning cabbage water.

The laughter finally gave way to guffawing tears and all Mam could say was that all laughing ended in tears.

Mam put the kettle on. Tea was Mam's answer to all dilemmas.

When the tea was made and pushed into my hands her first words were "Sweet Mother of Jaysus, what has happened to you?"

I was incapable of coherent speech. Mam wasn't very good with hysterics so off she went to retrieve the hidden chocolate biscuits from behind the couch in the lounge room. We all knew her hiding places and had known for the past twenty years. This gave me the chance to get rid of the bubbles that were now coming from my nose. It always amazed me how actresses in movies never had this problem and they certainly didn't make the guttural noises I was making.

I wasn't a very attractive crier and, boy, had I had plenty of practice lately!

In the distance I could hear Mam talking – she was known to talk to the furniture, the walls, the doors and even the carpet.

Mam arrived back in with the biscuits and surprisingly a bottle of Jameson Irish whiskey. It surprised me because Mam was a teetotaller of the highest order and didn't allow alcohol to be consumed in the house.

"I spoke to your dad and he said you're to have a strong whiskey to calm you down." As tea was Mam's answer to whatever ailed you, whiskey was Dad's.

"Your dad is on his way back from the village," she said.

Dad normally watched a local soccer match on Sunday morning before heading to the village for a few pints with his mates until about three o'clock, when his dinner would normally be ready and waiting for him.

Mam poured a frighteningly large tumbler of whiskey and handed it to me. I had to tell her I couldn't drink it straight. She tutted before heading to the bathroom to retrieve the hidden lemonade. This was hidden in the breadbin which was in the bathtub. Why there was a breadbin in the bathtub was never questioned or explained.

Mam was such a creature of habit: in the twenty years

we had lived in this house her menu had never varied. Monday was chicken, Tuesday was pork chops, Wednesday tinned steak and kidney pie, Thursday was stew, Friday was fish and chips, Saturday was a fry and Sunday was corn beef in summer and a shoulder of bacon in winter.

Mam was sitting opposite me chain-smoking and filling me in on all who had died in the area. Poor Mrs Boyle who had thirteen children and an alcoholic husband; he should have died not her, according to Mam. Mrs Ryan (Dolly) whose dementia got worse after poor Paddy died. It was my dad who had found poor Paddy dead in the gutter outside of the local pub. People walking past thought he was just a drunk sleeping it off and when Dad came out at closing time Paddy was well dead (massive heart attack). It was left to Dad to tell Dolly that Paddy wouldn't be coming home; Dolly only lasted another six months before joining him in the big pub up in the sky. The council bought her house back off her children which was why it now housed the Nigerian family.

I asked Mam what were they like. She said the kids had fit in well with the local children but the parents kept to themselves – all she knew about them was that they drank red wine. Maisie in the corner shop had told her so.

I heard Dad's key turn in the door. He came straight into the kitchen and stopped abruptly. I guess my appearance told half the story: my normally round face was gaunt and sunken, my long curly hair lay like a wet towel down my back, the dark circles deadened my normally bright eyes and even my freckles were pale. My tears started again on seeing the distressed look on his face.

He enveloped me in a bear hug, shushing me and patting my back, as dads do.

Mam disappeared into the bathroom to discreetly blow her nose. Mam wasn't very good at consoling people – she usually ended up in tears herself.

Dad poured both of us a Jameson, adding lemonade to mine and tutting that it ruined a good drop.

Mam emerged red-eyed and put the kettle on again.

We moved to the sitting room, me sitting beside the fire, Mam and Dad opposite on the couch. Dad was twiddling his wedding ring round and round. He was in danger of giving himself a Chinese burn. Mam was polishing the same spot on the coffee table over and over.

This took me back to eight years ago when I had asked if I could go to Australia with my friend Geraldine. I had broken up with my first love Michael after two years – he had wanted to settle down; I wanted to travel and see a bit of the world. I had told Mam and Dad about Michael's new girlfriend. Michael only lived three streets away and seeing him with someone else really upset me. A tearful Mam reluctantly agreed to let me go, whereas Dad was very encouraging, as this was something he would have liked to have done himself. Two months later I left for Australia. The plan had been to stay for six months to see if I liked it.

Within two weeks I had a job and Geraldine and I had our first flat. Geraldine got very homesick and returned after three months; me, I loved the freedom and independence and wasn't ready to give it up.

I made a lot of friends in the hotel I worked in and it was these friends who set me up on a blind date. Within a month of meeting John I knew we would marry. I was besotted with him, which was probably why I ignored any obvious faults he may have had. He was a newly qualified accountant. When I met his family that was the seal of approval that I was seeking. They loved Irish people – like just about every Australian person they were of Irish extraction; their grandparents had migrated to Australia to start a new life almost sixty years before. As time went on it was just accepted that we would marry. I don't actually remember a proposal as such, just an acceptance that this was right, it felt right.

After six months I took him back to Ireland to meet my family.

My parents instantly took to him. Although they knew they would lose me, they gave their approval and we returned to Australia an engaged couple. We bought the ring in the Happy Ring House in O'Connell Street and followed it with an impromptu engagement party in the Golden Sun Chinese restaurant.

His family were thrilled.

But trying to arrange a wedding proved to be a major stumbling block, the main question being which country to actually have the wedding in. Of course my family wanted the big wedding in our local church in Dublin; his family wanted the typical laidback Aussie wedding. My solution was this: we couldn't please everybody so we should book a registry office wedding and not tell anybody except our two closest friends, who would be our witnesses.

So that's exactly what we did.

Informing both families after the fact proved difficult. My family took it worse. I had deprived them of a big ceremony. His family were more accepting – Australians didn't go for formal ceremonies the way the Irish did.

We settled into our flat to live the blissful life that all newlyweds do.

We had a plan and that was to save for our own house. I took on a second job. John was newly qualified and his wages were minimal but, as soon as he had some practical experience and his reputation was established, his wages would double.

He worked very long hours and well into the evenings and most weekends but his pay still didn't come close to covering any of our expenses. I was too tired to let it bother me. I knew eventually things would improve.

When we moved into our new house three years later it was the happiest day of my life, and having to continue in both jobs didn't bother me in the slightest. I was really keen to furnish the house. My pay actually paid the mortgage and the household bills; John occasionally got bonuses which paid for things like our lounge suite, washing machine, dryer, occasional holidays and finally two tickets for my parents to come for a three-week holiday.

While my parents were there we really pulled out all the stops to ensure they had a great holiday. Their trip happened to coincide with the spring carnival race season so we took them to all the major race meetings, which was every second day.

Dad wasn't much of a gambler but I explained to him how seriously Australians took their racing, to the extent that Melbourne Cup Day was known as the race that stops a nation and it was actually an official bank holiday.

They were impressed with our house and our lifestyle but concerned about my working two jobs and John's long hours. I explained that once John opened his own practice I would probably only work part-time and then we would concentrate on starting a family.

They returned to Ireland content that I was living the good life.

Now, the good life well behind me, I took a big gulp of my Jameson and through sobs and anger I told them of the embezzled funds, the gambling, John losing his job, the subsequent court case, the order of restitution to repay the embezzled funds – one hundred and thirty thousand dollars all of which had been gambled away – the court costs of twenty-eight thousand and finally the eight months imprisonment in a minimum security prison farm.

I finished the last of my drink. I knew this next part would be the hardest for them to understand. Dad refilled both our drinks. I couldn't even look at Mam and Dad, I was burning with the shame of it all.

John was eventually granted weekend leave after three months. His family had been very shocked and disappointed in him and, although his mum and dad went to visit him, they were his only visitors. He stayed with his parents when he was on leave. I couldn't bring myself to visit him there or at the prison, even though it was an open prison farm. He was allowed to ring me twice a week. He was receiving counselling for his gambling problem and eventually his counsellor asked to see me. I reluctantly agreed. He explained that like alcoholism it was a real illness and had to be treated as such. John had excellent prospects of being rehabilitated and he stressed how important forgiving him was to his rehabilitation.

How I felt about being lied to wasn't even mentioned. I still loved him and I believed him when he told me prison had cured him of ever gambling again and I believed him when he said he would spend the rest of his life trying to make it up to me.

On his release I let him stay in the spare bedroom. We had been granted only twelve months to repay the debt and the house had to be sold. I could see how demoralised he was when we were packing up the house, and it was then I decided to give him another chance.

We rented a two-bedroom flat and started all over again. John was deregistered as a practising accountant for five years so he had to settle for a clerical job.

I still worked shift work at the hotel, but overnight shifts paid much more so I switched my hours to work to 7 p.m. till 7 a.m. five nights a week to make ends meet and pay off the rest of our debts.

John seemed to be enjoying his job and said it had

great future prospects. His brother had lent us a car so things were going very well. John was still going to counselling one night a week and I started trusting him again and finally let him move back into our bedroom and into my life.

For eight months things were good and when my pregnancy was confirmed we were over the moon.

John said he would push for a promotion at work and in his spare time he would do private tax assessments from home to earn extra money so I could ease up on my workload.

This was the fresh start we needed; even his family seemed to have forgiven him. Two weeks later we were on our way to tell his family the good news about the baby, and as we were driving along a young boy on a bike pulled out of a side street. John had to slam on the brakes to avoid hitting him. I was thrown forward and if I hadn't had my seatbelt on I would have hit the dashboard. The boy didn't even look back; John was beside himself with anger and concern for me.

I assured him our baby was OK – the seatbelt had squashed me a bit around the stomach but I was all right. We continued on to his parents' house where there was much backslapping and congratulations. Life was looking really good again.

I drove home because John had one too many drinks; he fell asleep on the way home and I had a hell of a job waking him up when we got to the flat. I eventually got him inside and went out to the car to get my bag. Then I noticed a bundle of papers under the passenger seat.

Even as I bent to pick them up my instincts were on full alert. I picked up the papers with shaking hands, knowing without really looking what they were. Racing form guides.

John's jamming on the brakes must have dislodged them from their hiding place.

I put the papers back under the seat. I wasn't sure how to deal with this and decided I needed time to think it through.

For the next week I didn't say anything – he took my silence as raging hormones associated with pregnancy.

I rang the estate agent to check that our rent had been paid and no, it hadn't been – the same with the electricity and the gas bill. Because I worked shift work it was easier for John to pay the bills during business hours as that was when I slept.

A week had passed since I found the papers and I was no closer to a decision on what to do. I think I was hoping he would tell me that he had had a setback and it was a once-off.

I came home from work and crawled into bed. I had been feeling really tired lately.

I woke up with the worst stomach cramp I have ever had. It took me a while before it dawned on me that this was no ordinary cramp. I made it to the bathroom and that's when I saw all the blood. I rang John at work and the receptionist said he was having the day off to take me to my gynaecologist. I mumbled something about pregnancy affecting your memory. I knew then it had all started again, or had it ever stopped?

I rang John's mum. She had been a midwife for twenty-five years – she would know what to do about my bleeding. I didn't have a car any more and I didn't think my situation warranted an ambulance. She advised me to get back into bed and she would come over straight away. She arrived within twenty minutes and, as soon as she saw how much I was bleeding, she rang for an ambulance. I heard her mention the word haemorrhage to the dispatcher and knew in my heart my baby wouldn't make it. I told her I had rung John at work and what the receptionist had told me. I knew by the look on her face she understood the implications of this and where he was likely to be.

She sat with me, holding my hand, our silent tears mingling as we waited for the ambulance, and we both knew this was a day of great loss.

Two weeks later it was my in-laws who drove me to the airport and out of their son's life.

"Try another road," she had said, "because the one you are on is a dead end."

The whiskey and the jetlag were now kicking in and my eyes were burning from all the crying. Mam crossed the room and pulled me up from the chair. She held my face in her hands and kissed me on the forehead and told me everything would be OK. Dad had his head in his hands. I knew he was finding it difficult to take in – the wind had been knocked out of him. I was the daughter with the big house in Australia with matching his and hers cars. The one he used to boast about to his mates.

I dissolved into tears again and Dad was very quickly beside me patting my back and shushing me again.

Mam took me upstairs to her room. I felt like an overused tea bag – all the life had been drained out of me. I felt like I had all those years ago when I had broken up with Michael – back then Mam had also taken me up to her room. She took out the TLC pillow as we had always called it.

This was just an ordinary pillow with a floral pattern but it was only ever used when you were sick or in need of some tender loving care. It now smelt of Olbas Oil, which indicated whoever used it last had either a head cold or the flu. I wondered if Mam had any special oils to mend a broken heart and a broken life.

I was asleep as soon as she tucked the duvet in. I felt her taking my shoes off, I felt her kiss my cheek, I heard her pulling down the blinds and then I sank into a dreamless sleep for the first time in weeks.

When I woke I felt weightless. I wasn't sure where I was. For a couple of minutes I lay there. The first thing I became aware of was that I wasn't crying and then that I was very hungry. I sat up and looked around the darkened room. I could smell lavender and saw that as usual Mam had the washing draped on the three radiators. I could hear muffled voices coming from the sitting room. I felt the comfort of being home and was actually happy to wake up and be alive.

I came out of the bedroom and made my way downstairs. I was listening to the muffled voices when I realised I could hear more voices than just Mam's and

Dad's. It was my sisters Caroline and Patricia. They didn't normally visit on Sundays; they had their own families now and did their own family thing on Sundays. I continued on down the steps and just in time I remembered that the fourth step from the bottom was the one that squeaked, alerting whoever was downstairs that someone was coming.

I sat back on the fifth step and listened for a while. I couldn't hear anything they were saying, just the low hum of conversation.

I could hear the kids on the street playing kick-to-kick football. They were probably the children of the kids I used to play with. I sat on the steps feeling like I had never actually grown up. I realised my child would never play kick-to-kick outside my Mam's as my sisters' children had. The overwhelming sense of loss was back with me.

A sob must have escaped me because next thing I knew my sisters were beside me on the fifth step.

We hugged and cried in silence. Mam had obviously filled them in on what had happened.

Mam and Dad were standing at the bottom of the stairs. I could see in Mam's eyes that she too was remembering when the three of us were frequently caught sitting on these steps long after we had been sent to bed.

My sisters and I went downstairs together.

Nobody talked about what had brought me back home. We reminisced about all the trouble we used to get into and how we used to sit on the stairs trying to listen to the TV.

Patricia told me my first love Michael had never got over me and he was still single.

His mother had passed away and he had bought her house three streets away. Patricia and Caroline were nudging each other and behaving like the kids we used to be.

Who knew what the future held, but I certainly felt like living again and knew with the love of my family I would get through this.

∽

Patrick Brosnan grew up in Cork City and graduated from UCC in computer science. He has worked as a software engineer in England and Ireland. A course in creative writing sparked Patrick's interest in the subject and he is currently working on a novel. He is forty-seven and lives in County Wicklow.

Star of
Baghdad

Patrick Brosnan

Star of
Baghdad

Suha was in the shed at the bottom of the garden when her world ended. The missile's thunderous blast rattled and shook the little building but it remained standing. The girl stumbled outside to see the blazing shell of what had been her smart Baghdad home. Moments earlier, she had been inside watching the TV with her family, before stepping outside to return her diary to its hiding place. Now she gazed in disbelief until the heat of the flames on her face made her cry out. Running out the back gate and along the little lane, she came out into the street hoping, by some miracle, that her family had escaped but there was no sign of them.

Neighbours at their gateways stared open-mouthed at the scene. Suha made towards the inferno but people had approached and one man held her back. She struggled furiously with him and broke free. She looked again at the burning ruin and the frightful truth dawned on her.

She had to get away. Turning, she raced down the street, dodging the outstretched arms that would have stopped her.

Suha left the familiar landmarks of her neighbourhood behind, and still she ran. The streets were wider now and lined with shops and tall buildings. She had never crossed a busy road on her own before, and cars rushed at her only to swerve past at the last moment. People thought the sight of the little girl running odd, but Baghdad was a strange place now since the coming of the Americans. She ran down a side street, finally collapsing on the pavement, shaking and gasping for breath.

When she looked up, the derelict house across the road, its windows broken and the roof half gone, seemed to beckon her. The front door had long since been removed and, warily, she forced herself inside. In an upstairs room she threw herself down on the pile of old blankets she found heaped in a corner. There she begged God to end her life so she could, once again, be with her family. Her agony was like a giant insect eating her from the inside out. She writhed and wept and slowly learnt how to numb the pain.

For more than a year Suha survived, begging at a nearby market by day and sleeping in the house by night. The terrible memories of that day she buried in the deepest part of her young mind. She was not to know that the missile had been a tragic mistake nor that the many friends and relatives she had left behind in her neighbourhood would have gladly taken her in had she ever returned.

If I am honest, that day I was just another trigger-happy

GI. It had been a few weeks since I had seriously mixed it with the bad guys and I just wanted to blast off a few rounds. There was really no need to shoot at the shape up in that room that seemed to be watching us – we were done with the search – but I did it anyway. Everyone ducked; then they looked at me, querying. There was nothing in the window now, so I just waved them back to the gunships, feeling sheepish.

For 3rd Platoon, Delta Company, it had been a routine street search based on a tip-off that there were weapons hidden in the area. We were always jittery leaving the Green Zone, and the Mansour district was a particularly unappealing, insurgent-infested destination. However, we had not encountered any enemy as we combed the row of little houses.

I was keeping lookout from inside a garden at one end of the road. The stench of garbage and raw sewage from the open drain nearby choked the still air all around me. My uniform stuck to my skin under the Baghdad sun but in my mind I was already standing under a cool shower back at the base.

The guys doing the search banged on doors and kicked in any when they got no answer. The people told them that gunmen might take over a house from time to time but never left any weapons. As always it was impossible to tell the truth from the lies and every room was searched. Gardens were examined too, using metal detectors and shovels. No caches were found, just a few AK-47s, legally held. We were just going back to the Humvees and I had to go and lose the head.

Then it hit me – there had been a cry from the room, a child's scream. Had I just shot a kid?

"Hey!" I shouted, but the guys ignored me, eager to make the safety of the vehicles. I hesitated. Then I ran to the open doorway of the house and charged in. This was crazy – Baghdad was no place for heroics. Running up the stairs I tried one room – empty – then another.

Her sad little face looked up at me. Propped up against the back wall, blood oozing from her shoulder, the girl could not have been more than ten. Above her on the wall ran a neat line of bullet holes. Mine.

"Oh no," I whispered.

For a few moments I stood there, frozen. Then I ran to the window. Through the broken pane, I saw the gunships disappearing down the road. The bastards had left me, and I might not survive if I tried to catch them.

Her soft moan made me turn around. The girl's eyes were shut now and her head was slumping forward.

OK, they'll come back for me when they realise I'm missing, I thought. In the meantime I'll do what I can for her.

I moved her slowly so that she was lying on her back. She was very light, just skin and bone. The bullet had entered below the collarbone and there was blood all over her front. I ripped open the flimsy dress at the shoulder. I pressed the pad of a dressing firmly against the wound and rolled the bandage around the shoulder a few times before tying it off. There were a few old blankets in the corner of the room which I used to make her more comfortable. I sat down by the window to keep an eye on things outside.

Only then did I realise how much my hands were shaking. If I was caught here by the militias . . . I did not wish my parents' last sight of me to be my beheading on the Internet.

When I joined the National Guard some years previously, I never dreamed I would end up in a real, shooting war. All I wanted were a few weekends a year playing with guns in the woods. Now here I was, Joseph Patrick O'Shea, alone in a city where Americans were not too popular.

My family was Irish American with a little Native American thrown in. Our name came from my great-grandfather, Raymond O'Shea, who had come over to New York from County Cork in the late 1800s. Carpenter by day and, so legend had it, burglar by night, the attentions of that city's police force encouraged him to move on. His money ran out in Pittsburgh so he stayed, found an Irish girl and started our line. And just like him I too was a carpenter by trade, though an honest one. Right now I would have given anything to be back in the States fitting roofs and hanging doors.

The street was returning to normal after Uncle Sam's little visit. The odd car passed by, and the low tones of men talking nearby floated upwards. The cool air of the room kept the Mesopotamian heat at bay, which was a help to me in my thirty-odd pounds of body armour. The house looked abandoned; the rooms were mostly empty save for some trash.

The sleeping girl's face was peaceful under her black, unkempt hair. Her purple dress looked old and worn.

What was she doing alone in this dump? She looked like a beggar. Did she sleep in the pile of blankets in the corner? I was reminded of a story that my mother would read to me as a child, "The Little Match Girl".

Her worldly possessions were gathered on a tea chest next to me: an old plastic comb, a small, cracked mirror, a bottle of henna dye and a single fake pearl earring.

The minutes ticked by. When would someone notice I was missing? Maybe not till the platoon got back to base, maybe not even then. Christ.

I cursed the war. The arguments for invasion had always sounded lame to me. Before it started we would hear a different reason every week from the president, like he wanted to invade but could not decide why. Now here I was, risking my neck out here while he practised his golf swing back in the States.

The girl shifted underneath her blankets. Slowly she raised her head and spat a sticky, brown mixture onto the floor. Blood trickled down from underneath the dressing, which, by now, was soaked red. She looked up at me and started. I reassured her, though I knew she would have no English. She calmed down and even tried to smile. Then she fell back, exhausted and breathing noisily. She was a mess. I had to do something.

If she did not get medical assistance soon she would not survive and I would be responsible. If I took her outside she might get help but I would die on the streets, or worse. Having fired the fatal bullet, I could not live with myself if she died – I knew that – so we would have to go and look for help. The thought of what the insurgents might do to me was just too big to deal with right then, and I pushed it aside.

Things to do in Baghdad when you're dead, I thought stupidly.

Gathering up my stuff, I picked up the girl gently and left the room. I had to leave the rifle behind; I did not wish to draw more fire onto us – my bright desert camouflage would do plenty of that. I hesitated at the front door for a long moment. Then I stepped outside.

I strode out into the heat and down the street back the way I had come. In the distance a few people chatted. No one had noticed me yet. I kept walking.

Behind me a boy's cry pierced the air, *"Ameriki! Ameriki!"*

Everyone stopped to look at me. I passed a few people standing in doorways who looked at the girl first and then eyed me suspiciously. I could have given her to them but they just did not look right.

I kept walking, panic rising in my chest. The atmosphere in the street had changed. Something was about to happen. There were more shouts and noises. Doors opened and then a window.

When it came, the bullet slammed into my shoulder. The armour saved me but the impact knocked me, in slow motion, to my knees. Somehow I kept hold of the girl. A frightened couple peered out at me from inside a doorway. I held up the child to them. "Take her!" I pleaded, but they did not move.

Another bullet crashed into my armour. The gunman was playing with me. Nausea rose in my throat; my legs were giving way. The man in the doorway rushed out, shouting something. He grabbed the girl from me and ran back inside.

Free of my cargo, I got to my feet and turned around, the blood thumping in my ears. Two guns were trained on me from an upstairs room across the street. There were other men in the room behind the shooters. Someone laughed. I could have gone for my pistol but I would not have got far. It was then I heard the woman's voice in my head.

I had first met Sally Schultz a few years earlier when I was going out with her older sister, Patti. Sally seemed young and immature and nothing special. She was not around much anyway as she worked in Philly and was only home occasionally. After about a year seeing each other, Patti and I split up acrimoniously, and I thought I was finished with that family. However, within weeks I got a call from Sally, who asked me to meet her at a local bar. I was too shocked to say no. That night she looked great and we talked for hours. She had changed a lot in a year. There was something calm and dignified about her now that seemed to complement my wilful Celtic genes. From there things just took off for us. She quit her job and moved back to Pittsburgh. We were married the weekend before I left for Iraq. Some honeymoon, huh? That was three long months ago.

Now her voice seemed loud and clear in my head. "*Run!*" it screamed.

Just then a young man went past on a scooter. He saw the guns at the last minute and lost control of the bike.

Everyone was distracted. I saw myself turn and begin to pound down the sidewalk. I had been the fastest man on every football team I had played for, and the street corner was just a few hundred yards away. There were cars parked along the kerb and I lowered my head behind them as I ran. Bullets exploded all around me.

The shooting stopped and I heard the screech of car tyres behind me. As I reached the corner the vehicle swung round in front of me and mounted the sidewalk. An AK-47 poked out of the window aimed straight at my head. Exhausted and dripping sweat, I stopped and stared at it.

The roar of the heavy machine gun filled the air. The car and its occupants jumped then disintegrated as I looked on. When the shooting stopped it was just a smoking hulk and the occupants gone to Allah.

I heard familiar voices.

"Don't shoot, I'm an American!" I yelled, before rounding the corner.

It looked like the entire force of Delta Company had turned out to get me back. There was a stunned silence, and then delirious cheering broke out. I was hugged and cursed and slapped and kissed. The guys were as relieved as me that I was OK. I climbed up on the lead Humvee and shook hands with the beaming gunner who had saved my life, before finding a welcome place inside. They told me afterward that I chattered like a monkey but I do not remember much about it. I was just happy to be alive.

Back at base, I had to brief the lieutenant on my

adventure. When I had finished he paused for a moment, and then he exploded. Abandoning the platoon like I had done was the stupidest thing he had seen in his career, he told me. And shooting an Iraqi child was the best way to recruit more insurgents. There was more along these lines that I do not remember, except that any kind of medal for my little stunt would be out of the question.

I knew it was a waste of time pointing out that I had tried to save the life of an Iraqi citizen or that I had lured an insurgent cell to its doom.

At the end he said he felt like sending me for court-martial. Instead I got a few days' sick leave. I protested, as I did not want to mope around, but he assured me that I would need some time to think about what I had been through.

As the adrenaline wore off, I tried not to think about the girl and when I did I told myself that she would be looked after in hospital. Besides, I had risked my neck to save her and could not have done any more.

That evening I rang Sally. She had just gotten up. We made small talk, laughing at the sound of one another's voices. I did not talk about what had happened. At the end we imagined holding one another and I did not want it to end.

The next day I was sitting under a tree by a pond in the heart of the Green Zone. Birds were singing and, apart from the distant popping of gunfire, I could have been at home in Lincoln Park. It was after lunch and I was writing up a few e-mails on my laptop. Suddenly I felt myself back in the room looking at the girl, covered in blood and gasping for breath. What had I done to that poor child? Was she dead now? My stomach felt like it had been kicked. I leaned sideways and retched onto the grass. I lay there sweating, my body heavy, my arms weak.

In the days that followed, my guilt was a dark creature that sat brooding in the corner of my mind. Ever present, silent and unforgiving, it would invade my thoughts at every opportunity. I would try to push it away but it was always too strong and I would quickly tire of the effort.

The fear of being attacked by insurgents was the only thing that could distract me. We had seen a lot in a few months and images of vehicles and men hit by RPGs and roadside bombs haunted our thoughts and dreams. Inside the Humvee, over the din of the music and the engine, I clutched my rifle and kept a sharp lookout.

From time to time I would get sweaty flashbacks of the grinning insurgents pointing their guns at me. Or I would feel again the impact of the bullets hitting my armour and imagine the next one hitting my face. The shrink at the base explained to me, in great detail, how I was suffering from "combat stress". He offered me the choice of psychotherapy and drugs at the army hospital in Kuwait or a mild sedative. Up to that point I had not thought that the Kuwaiti experience of crowded tents and shrieking sand could get any worse. I took the sedative.

Sally could tell there was something wrong and, one evening, wheedled the story of the girl out of me.

"You idiot, O'Shea!" she hissed when I was finished. "How could you have abandoned your platoon like that? It's a miracle you're alive!" Anger did not come easily to her and I had never heard her like this before.

"I shot a little girl, Sally," I pleaded. "What was I supposed to do?"

"What about me?" she retorted. "Did you consider your wife at all when you were charging round Baghdad on your own?"

Her fury, eventually, spent itself. She was shaken and close to tears. When we were saying goodbye, I promised her no more Tom Cruise-style heroics.

She thought about what I had said, though, and over time she came to see why I had done what I had done; on subsequent calls, she would always ask for news of the girl but I had none to give.

The insurgent was on his belly, hugging the shadow of a parked car as our Humvee turned into the street. Leaning into his RPG, he squinted through the cross hairs and fired. We skidded to a halt as one of our front wheels exploded. Then a blizzard of bullets smacked into the vehicle on both sides – ambush!

The fading light of the late evening had seen us hurrying home after dropping off a pair of snipers on their night mission. A convoy of one is extremely vulnerable on the streets of Baghdad but we were in constant contact with the Apache helicopter that tracked our progress high overhead.

Shrapnel from the blast had sprayed the gunner, who

slid off his seat and down into the cabin. Our radioman alerted the Apache but none of us knew how long the car's armour would stave off the grenades and RPGs that would, inevitably, come our way. On an impulse, I made to climb up to the turret. Hands pulled me back – it was a suicidal move under this fire. I tore the hands off me and dragged myself up onto the canvas seat.

There were a couple of gunmen firing at us from a palm grove, adjacent to the road. Bullets bounced off the gun-shield as I heaved the big Browning round towards them. I was terrified but there was something else there too, something I only realised afterwards. The nearest man was quite close and I could see his broad, sweating face clearly. My gun could have stopped a charging rhino in its tracks. As I pointed the barrel at him his eyes widened and he stopped shooting; he lowered his gun, turned and fled. As I continued to swing the gun around his companion also fled. Behind me houses began to explode as the Apache's rockets found the rest of our attackers.

Back in the base my exploits elicited a mixture of disbelief and admiration from the other guys in the platoon.

"You should get a bronze star for that, Joe, easy," said one, "or maybe silver."

But I felt no satisfaction. I was a fake. I knew why I had jumped up in front of all those bullets. I wanted to die. I had shot a little girl; she was probably dead now. I deserved to die for it. I was lost in a dark hole with no way out except death.

Later, in desperation, I asked an Iraqi police chief that I knew to find out what had happened to the child. There was daily slaughter in Baghdad and the hospitals were chaotic but he said he would try. He never got back to me.

One sultry June morning, our convoy was heading out to guard the building of a forward operating base. As we neared our destination there was a huge boom and our vehicle lurched forward. For a few stunned moments nobody moved. Then someone said the guys behind us had been hit. Our driver radioed for assistance while we went out to secure the scene.

Hidden in a pothole in the road, the huge bomb had scored a perfect hit as the Humvee passed over. It had been cut in half, the rear section propelled twenty yards back up the road. The inside of the front part was a mass of torn metal and human remains. Of the eight men that had been inside six were dead. Only the driver and the gunner were still breathing, and we did what we could for their shattered bodies till help arrived.

Afterwards at the base, some men grieved on their own, others in little groups. I saw one man sobbing quietly as he lay on his bed. Walking over to him, I knelt down and gently placed my hand on one of his. He said he had been packing up the personal effects of one of the dead soldiers and thinking how he wished he could be there to comfort the man's family.

For a few days I forgot about the girl.

I was watching a movie in the palace when the sight

of her bloodied little body began to mingle with the scenes on the screen. I went outside and sat on a seat in the shade. For once I did not push the thoughts away. The girl merged with the ghosts of my dead comrades so that I could not tell them apart.

Some days after that I was visiting an injured soldier in the infirmary when an Iraqi nurse, a friend of mine, came up to me and asked to talk. She said she could tell me about the girl. I stared at her for a moment and then led her over to a table where we sat down.

Friends of hers, who worked at Yarmouk Hospital, had told her of a strange thing that had happened there on the day of my brush with death. A young girl had been brought in. Her name was Suha. She was wearing a purple dress and a blood-soaked field dressing clung to her shoulder. It was a busy day at the hospital but the doctors did what they could for her. She was put in intensive care, as she had lost a lot of blood and was severely malnourished.

Sometime in the night Suha became restless and woke up. She called out and two of the nurses came over to her. Her lips were moving. Her voice was weak and the nurses had to bend down to hear her.

"God has blessed me," she said. "Today I was shot. I was shot and I was dying. Then God sent an angel to me. He was tall. His skin was fair and he had blue eyes. He knelt and gave me water. He was so gentle. He bandaged my wound. He spoke a language I did not understand, the language of heaven. Then he carried me out of the house and gave me to someone who brought me here.

My heart is so full of joy I'm afraid it will burst. Praise be to God!"

Suha's face was blissful and she stared at each nurse in turn. Then slowly her eyes closed. The little figure sank into the bed and the life went from her. Tears sparkled in the nurses' eyes and they sat with her a while, holding her hands as they grew cold.

I thanked my friend and went outside. It was getting dark but I found a bench and sat down.

At last I knew.

"Suha," I whispered a few times, marvelling at the sound of the name. I had thought all along that her chances of survival were slim. A weight of sadness enveloped me as, in my mind, I listened again to the nurse's story.

Gradually the feeling turned into a more comforting presence. My mind slowly cleared like a pond after ripples fade away. It felt like I was outside it looking in. All the different emotions that had been pulling at me during the last few weeks drew apart and separated in such a way that I could see them clearly. I saw my guilt and how pointless it was and this very thought seemed to make it shrink in front of me. Life was the only thing that was precious and there was no point wasting it by dwelling on past mistakes.

In the bliss of Suha's last moments, I felt that everything bad that had happened in her short life had been forgiven. Her joy was like the river that rushes down from the mountains after a rainstorm, sweeping aside everything in its path. And I, her angel of death, accepted her mercy. I had been given a second chance.

I looked up at the darkening sky. Without the night there would be no stars. Without death there would be no life.

I rose and phoned Sally, hoping to catch her in. She was and I related the nurse's story to her.

"Oh Joe!" she said at the end, her voice choked.

Silence hung between us for a long time.

"Sally," I said at last, "when I get back, I'd like us to start a family."

ॐ

Kate Dempsey has had pieces on BBC and RTÉ radio, including a short story in the Francis MacManus competition. Her poems are published widely. An early version of her first novel was shortlisted for the London Book Fair Lit Idol. She lives in Maynooth and loves Jaffa Cakes (the orange ones).

The Essential Ingredients

Kate Dempsey

The Essential Ingredients

I was getting ready for a nice bath, looking forward to a long aromatherapy soak and an early night, when Becky rang.

"Mum. Thank goodness. I have an emergency," she said.

Becky had "emergencies" on a regular basis. They could range from a broken nail just before she went on camera, to a mouse behind the sofa, to Mark, her son, having a sore throat.

"What's wrong?" I said. "Is Mark sick? You know I worry about him, Becky. He's very scrawny for his age."

"No, Mum. He's fine. And he's not scrawny. He's just not going through a growth phase at the moment. And his name is Marco."

I wasn't going through a "Marco" phase at the moment but I let that lie. "What variety of an emergency is it?"

"The childcare variety."

Mark had been reared by a long line of au pairs stretching from here to Prague for most of his nine years. The current one, Anya or Olga or something, was from Latvia and had a sweet temperament. Becky worked unpredictable hours. She was something in the media. I wasn't sure exactly what. Whenever she started to explain, I couldn't prevent my mind from wandering. She had a soporific voice made for daytime TV. She had recently sat in for Gráinne on *Seoige & O'Shea*. The producer had been pleased with her performance and wanted to send her to Majorca to film a light-hearted holiday slot.

"It's very exciting. Robin was right about working on that show."

"Robin?"

"My agent. Surely you've met him? Tall guy, curly hair, flamboyant, you know?" I remembered meeting him at Becky's house. He talked three times the speed of anyone else but seemed to end up saying three times less. "He said that show would be the start of something big. He said I 'demonstrated an astute ability to steer my interviewees to the point'. And I quote."

The au pair, who turned out to be called Eva, had gone back to look after her sick mother.

"Poor girl. And such a long way from home."

"I said she could go home for a while on compassionate leave. I had to after the kerfuffle in the press about how badly some of my dear co-workers treat their staff. The media are sniffing around for their next victim – it's not going to be me. I can just see the headlines, 'Star Presenter in Secret Slave Shocker'."

I jumped at the chance to have Mark for a week. I put the phone down already planning what we could do together. He loved the zoo and we usually took a trip to the beach, whatever the weather. And we always baked. October was perfect timing for baking our Christmas cake. From what I could tell, he lived on fish fingers and oven-baked chips at home so some home cooking would be good for him. I sighed and went to run my bath.

It's always the fault of the parents. I had raised her and parenting skills should be learned in the nest. I knew she loved him in her own way, but Becky wasn't a good parent. Certainly her analyst put the blame on me for Becky's lack of maternal instincts. She'd seen one for a while, an Austrian with a ginger beard. It was the thing to do at the time.

That half-term week, I wanted to keep Mark for myself. I wanted to install him in his own room with piles of cuddly toys and a spaceman duvet. I wanted to feed him healthy food at regular meal times, plump him up like a turkey in December. But I knew it was only temporary. I bit my lip and tied the apron strings twice around his skinny body.

"Aren't you forgetting something?" I asked.

He scratched his head vigorously. I made a mental note to check him for nits.

"What?" he asked.

"What's the golden rule?"

"No shoes on the white sofa? Don't touch Mummy's handbag? Bailey's is only for adults?"

"No, pet. The golden rule in my house."

"First wash my hands." He flashed his gappy smile at me and skipped out to the bathroom.

I rolled up his sleeves and put the scales on the kitchen table so he could weigh the raisins, huge and plump in his thin hands. He stuffed a fistful in his mouth when he thought I wasn't looking. While I creamed the sugar and butter, we had a long discussion about the raisins' origins. I romanticised a little, describing them drying on the flat roofs of the farmers' houses.

"They shrivel up in the sun like a granny," he said.

"Thanks a bunch." I resolved to use my moisturiser more often and sent him to fetch the heavy atlas. We looked for California. He could find England, Italy and Latvia but he looked for America somewhere south of the Mediterranean so I threw in a subtle Geography lesson. We traced the line the raisins had taken from the American landmass across the Atlantic to Ireland.

"What do they teach you in that school of yours? Can you read that?" I pointed at Australia.

"Of course I can read but I'd rather draw. Oisín says I should concentrate on my artistic side."

I rolled my eyes. Oisín was his teacher and, in my opinion, verging on the insane side of wacky. We found Majorca but he went very quiet so I hurriedly ransacked the cupboards. We measured the spices and followed them to Sri Lanka and parts of the West Indies and the unrefined Muscovado sugar to Mauritius. The glacé cherries came from France and the eggs from a farmer down the road. The crystallised ginger was a product of

Australia, the organic Brazil nuts, rather satisfyingly, came from Brazil and the baking powder from Ballymount. The whiskey, I made sure, was Irish. It is essential to use the very best ingredients. By the time the cake was in the oven and the kitchen was filling with cheerful smells, the atlas pages were smeared with mixture and the cupboards had given up their global secrets.

"We've been to the egg farm already," he said. "How far away is Ballymount?"

"Not far."

"Can we go?"

"What for?" I picked some mixture out of his dark hair. It was curly like his father's. Becky's was the same as mine, sludge-coloured and wavy, although she spent hundreds of euros and days of her time at salons, ensuring that it looked sleek and naturally blonde. I had let mine go grey years ago and kept it short. Becky was always telling me it made me look far older than my years. Then she would start going on about how my clothes made me look like a shapeless lump and I would stop listening.

"Can we go to Ballymount? Just to see. Please?"

He aimed his dark eyes at me. They were his father's too. He was a dancer from The Sudan. I had only seen photos. He had moved in with Becky and moved out again just as quickly. He turned out to have not one but two wives back home in Khartoum. Becky hadn't even known she was pregnant but she didn't seem to mind. The best accessory next to a handbag that year had been a baby, plus it showed her caring side.

"OK. We've nothing on tomorrow," I said. "But I don't think there'll be a lot to see."

The next day we set off early and got to Ballymount as the rain cleared. The factory was in a sprawling industrial estate. It was grim, all grey concrete and garish corporate logos, which Mark compared with the baking-powder tin. We peered through the chainlink fence for a while but the bitter autumn wind soon blew us away. We found a pub a few minutes away and retreated inside to warm up. It had dusty green seats and maudlin background music but the menu on the blackboard looked promising and we ordered an early lunch. Mark put the precious baking powder on the table and wolfed down his scampi in a basket, dunking them in a glob of ketchup.

"Don't put baking powder on your chips," remarked a tall man seated at the next table. "Gives you the wind." He was an ex-military type with a ramrod-straight back and a smile that showed he still had most of his own teeth, which gleamed as shiny as his blazer buttons. He told us he had worked as a guard in the factory for years.

Mark explained about the cake ingredients.

"That must be an old tin," the man said. "They don't make it here any more. It's gone to Tunisia."

Tunisia certainly sounded more appealing than the bitter weather in Ballymount industrial estate.

"But you used to make baking powder, didn't you?" said Mark. "Could I have your autograph?"

Mark had been given an autograph book for his birthday and carried it everywhere with him. He showed the man the odd assortment he had collected. It included some of Becky's friends, my local egg farmer – a retired rock star with gold records in the chicken coop – and the footprint of one of his chickens. Becky had signed the first page with a flourish and the man was delighted to be in such good company, noting in beautiful copperplate handwriting that he was the Baking Powder Man in Ballymount.

"Where shall we go next, Granny?"

"Tunisia sounds appealing," I said. "This cold is bad for my old bones."

"Could we go for the weekend?"

"No, pet. It's too far away. And remember, your mum's home on Sunday."

He muttered something I couldn't catch and stored the autograph book carefully in his pocket.

On Sunday, he was spruced up and ready to go three long hours before Becky arrived. We filled the time listening to music on the radio. He had recently picked up an interest in the pop charts and wanted me to dance with him.

"I'm too old to boogie, pet. You dance for me."

The doorbell went as he was showing me the moves to "La Macarena".

"Precious, did you miss me?" said Becky, wafting in on a wave of Chanel No. 5.

Mark stopped dancing and thundered into her arms, let her kiss his head and started to tell her about the cake ingredients and the trip to Ballymount.

"Ballymount," she said. "How adventurous!" Her plucked eyebrows strained to rise but the Botox in her forehead kept it as smooth as Barbie's. She was striking rather than beautiful, according to the TV guide; she had her father's high cheekbones and the Roman nose that was her trademark. She told us all about Majorca and the cute little beach she had found.

"I really needed the break. Not that I got much time to myself with all the filming and the attention. It turned out to be a complete Irish enclave. Loads of people recognised me. I was forever signing autographs but I said it would be fabulous to go back there in the summer, or perhaps September. August is way too hot."

"September? What about school?"

"School? Oh, surely it's much better for Marco's education to spend time in Majorca than go to silly old school?" She tickled him under his chin.

Mark flushed. He took a step back behind her and started picking at a scab on his elbow. He was a scabby child. He had told me how much he was looking forward to seeing all his friends again on Monday. His school was the progressive type. So much so that they didn't learn to read until they were seven. Not that he wasn't clever, just lazy, and a "learn as you please" school didn't suit him, in my opinion. I said as much but Becky didn't agree and told me I was being old-fashioned.

"His reading skills are rudimentary and his maths is appalling. Can't I have an opinion about my grandson's education? You have to face up to reality, Becky. He needs a more academic school. I made a few calls . . ."

"Who died and put you in charge of his education?" she said. "Leave it, Mum. It's not your concern. He's concentrating on his artistic side."

"Oisín says I'm gifted at drawing," our budding artist said.

"Are you, pet?"

"His teacher is nurturing his creative skills," said Becky, "and what's with that zip-up cardigan he's wearing?"

"You only sent two thin shirts with him and they got dirty. They're washed and ironed in the suitcase."

She rolled her eyes. "Keep your coat buttoned up, Marco. There may be photographers outside."

"We made the Christmas cake," he said, buttoning his jacket obediently. "I did the weighing all by myself." He ran out to the kitchen to fetch it.

"Ah, Christmas," Becky said, glancing at me. "We've had a change of plan. We're going skiing for two weeks. A whole gang of us, kids and all, so there'll be someone for Marco to play with. A terribly chic resort in France. It's absolutely essential for my career, Mum. There are some mega-influential producers going along. This might be my lucky break. You don't mind, do you? I'm sure you have loads of other people wanting you for Christmas dinner – I mean, wanting to have you, not wanting to eat you." She did a false giggle that she used as cover when she was embarrassed on TV. I did watch her programmes from time to time.

But I was dumbstruck. Christmas without my grandson? Without my daughter? The plan had been for a small family get-together. I had the free-range turkey on order already. My farmer only kept a small flock. I had been planning it for months. Last year had been so relaxing, so enjoyable, just the three of us.

"Well," I managed to stammer. "Marian did ask . . ."

"Great. That's settled then. I was dreading having to tell you – now I know I needn't have worried." She glanced uninterestedly at the cake and dragged Mark away, throwing a "Thanks for looking after him" at me over her shoulder.

When I closed the door behind them, the cold kitchen suddenly felt too large for one old lady.

As Christmas grew closer, I decided not to go to Marian's. She was my dear friend but really I could only take her company for a couple of hours at a time. She was so opinionated and wouldn't listen to anyone who disagreed with her point of view. It quite wore me out. I resolved to have a quiet Christmas at home with lovely food and a nice bottle of wine. I went through the TV guide and marked the films I wanted to watch.

Becky hadn't wanted any Christmas cake. "Don't waste it on me, Mum," she said. "I get millions of hampers my fans insist on sending. I end up throwing half of them away."

I suggested she donate them to charity to show her caring side and went home to whip up the royal icing.

She rang on Christmas Eve. Marian had just left me, full of cake and vintage port.

"Mum, Mum! We have an emergency, a complete disaster," Becky started when I picked up the phone.

My relaxed state of mind evaporated. A disaster was worse than an emergency and I knew they were flying to France that day. A quick succession of disaster visions flew through my mind: road accident, airplane crash, terrorist bomb, brain haemorrhage . . . I had got as far as a hostage situation when Becky cut into my whirring thoughts.

"And then they have the nerve to say that they won't let him on the flight. I mean, we have first-class tickets. I paid through the nose for them at this time of year. I can't believe their altitude, I mean attitude."

"Wh-wh-who?" I stuttered, coming back to the present.

"The pigging airline. I told them I know the chairman. I'm sure I met him once. 'Who do you think I am?' I asked them but it made no difference. Stupid cow."

"No, Becky. I mean who won't they let on the plane?"

"I said 'I'm Rebecca Casey from *The Holiday Show*,' and that blue-rinse harridan had the nerve to . . ." She stopped. "Sorry?"

"Who won't they let on the plane?"

"Marco, of course. There's an English-speaking doctor in the resort – there had better be – but they won't listen. I'm at the end of my tether, really I am."

"Slow down. What does he need a doctor for?"

"Why the rash, of course, Mum. Weren't you listening? The trolley dolly, sorry 'flight attendant', says it may be catching and he can't fly. If only it hadn't spread to his face, they'd never have known he had it."

"A rash. Is he ill?"

"He's fine. Really. Just scratching a bit. And the rest of the gang were on an earlier flight so I'm on my own. Even the au pair's gone. I have no one else to call on. Will you come?"

"To the airport? You're stranded?" I did a quick calculation based on it being Christmas Eve. "I'll be there in forty minutes. Don't worry, Becky."

When I got there, Mark was shooting down enemy aircraft on a Playstation – not the most suitable game for an airport lounge, I thought. His head was lowered and his bony shoulders were hunched up like a buzzard. His scrunched-up face relaxed visibly when he saw me and I caught tears welling up in his tired eyes.

"Are you OK, pet?"

He sniffed and wiped his nose on his sleeve. "Fine. Can we go now?"

"In a minute. Let's have a look at you." I checked him over. It was the chickenpox, a mild dose by the look of it. Marian's grandson had had it recently and even his eyelids were pocked but I didn't remember Becky ever having it as a child.

"Nothing to worry about, pet. Finish your game and try not to scratch."

He went back to his missile launcher.

"Are you Rebecca Casey's mother?" asked the airport minder.

I nodded.

"She's wearing well, considering," he said, rearranging the piece of tinsel draped over the phone that constituted the Christmas decorations.

I hoped he hadn't said the same thing to her. Becky was coy about her age.

"Where is she?" I asked.

He looked at me curiously. "I thought you knew. She went on the flight. To France. You're to take the boy."

"The Boy" looked at me and hunched his shoulders again. "Mum said we were going to have Christmas together and she had to go to France for work." He lowered his voice. "She gave the man a hundred-euro note when no one was looking. Is that OK?"

"Yes, pet," I said, glancing at the airport minder, but inside I was seething. Becky had virtually abandoned him. How could the child I had raised turn out so egocentric? After Christmas we would have a few words.

We drove home in record time. When I am wound up, my anger transfers itself to the accelerator. Luckily the roads were clear; all the gardaí must have been home eating Christmas cake so we weren't stopped. I put Mark in the bath and added some new Tunisian baking soda to soothe the itching. I reassured him that Father Christmas would know he was here and not in France, yes, even if there was no snow. We both knew he was too old to believe but it soothed him and I put him to bed. I unearthed the parcels I had been saving for New Year and found a couple of packages hidden in his suitcase, filled an old walking sock with sweets and knick-knacks and hung it on the end of his bed.

We had the best Christmas I can remember since Becky was Mark's age and my husband was alive. In the morning, we opened our presents and I took him to the children's mass. He hadn't been to church since his First Communion and was swept away by the rituals and the Christmas story. Religion didn't play much of a part in his school or home life. We joined in with the carols and each child took a toy up to be blessed. I have never seen such an arsenal of toy pistols, machine guns, tanks and regiments of Action Men and Barbies. Mark played with his presents and we ate too much dinner, lit the fire and fell asleep watching *The Wizard of Oz*.

His rash was almost gone by the empty day after St Stephen's Day.

We were cutting a slice of the Christmas cake that evening when the phone call came.

"That'll be Mum," I predicted.

It was Robin, Becky's agent. He sounded distraught. "I am so sorry to be the one to tell you, Mrs Casey. There's been an accident . . ." I didn't have a chance to run through the disaster visions in my head, "a fatal accident."

Becky had let go of the chair lift to scratch a rash on her stomach and somehow had fallen thirty feet to her death. Ironically she had caught Mark's chickenpox.

I put the receiver down gently and stared at the cake knife I still held in my hand. I couldn't take it in. Was it one of Becky's jokes? She once had me convinced that she was going out with Colin Farrell.

It wasn't until I noticed Mark staring at Becky's photo on the news that I really believed it. The announcer actually looked shocked and I remembered I'd met him at one of Becky's parties. Mark turned round and stared at me, his face as white as icing. I put down the knife, switched off the television and told him what I knew, wrapping my arms tightly around him as I had for Becky when she was little, as I had when she lost her teddy when she was six, as I had when she argued with her best friend aged eleven and as I had when she was crying in pain during labour. I stroked Mark's arm with a shaking hand, then I ran out and vomited my dinner on the hall floor.

The media interest was immediate and overwhelming. They camped outside my house, ringing the bell and calling incessantly. They compared Becky to Jill Dando, the UK presenter, although, apart from their hairstyle, there were few similarities that I could see. Mark and I went about in a daze. I kept thinking about the last time I'd seen her, about our last conversation on the phone. I showed Mark photos of Becky when she was small and he spent a lot of time staring out of the window at the television vans. Robin organised everything and we flew out to France the next evening in our new black clothes. I was too numb to take in much bar three double gin and tonics but I kept my head for Mark's sake.

The ski resort was tranquil after the horror of Dublin, with only minimal media in attendance. Robin flapped around like a worried goose but got everything organised despite that. Mark was withdrawn but he seemed to understand everything. They had "done" death in school, he told me. Becky's ski crowd met us at the hotel, solicitous and tearful. We discussed the funeral and, because we were all there already, decided to bury her in that beautiful town rather than brave the extended media interest back home.

"Mum loved mountains," said Mark, giving the suggestion his blessing. "And snow. She always loved snow."

Robin handled the considerable paperwork with the French authorities. The service in the tiny chapel was exceptionally beautiful with a choir, mountains of tasteful flowers and an elegant congregation. Some of her media friends changed their Christmas plans to attend. *Seoige & O'Shea* sent a vast pink wreath but the media kept a respectful distance. Becky would have been furious to miss it all. I sat in the front pew with my arm around Mark. Robin gave a most moving eulogy and we all cried. Then Becky was buried in the frozen earth and we stood around holding each other against a stunning backdrop of the snow-covered Alps.

Mark and I holed up in the resort. I spent some time talking with her friends. Mark collected all their autographs but didn't say much. Robin took him skating a couple of times to give me a break. We moped around, picking at our food and simmering in the hot tub until our bodies were crinkled and rosy. One day merged into the next. It was a few days after New Year, and the ornate tree still glimmered in the lobby, when Mark made a suggestion.

"Glacé cherries," he said. "They came from France." He opened his autograph book and showed Robin the signature of the Baking Powder Man. "Let's go and get the glacé cherries."

This was the most animated he had been since the phone call and Robin and I decided it would be some kind of therapy to follow up. The town was in Provence, two, maybe three hours away and not too far from the airport. I had been thinking about returning home. School would be starting and there were legal details to sort out. I thanked my lucky stars I had insisted Becky made a will when Mark was born. She had left him well provided for.

We hired a car and headed south. The glacé cherry factory was in an industrial park, uncannily similar to the one in Ballymount, though much sweeter-smelling. We mooched around, then went for lunch in a local café. It was all typically French: delicious food, tiny tables and clouds of smoke, despite the smoking ban. Mark got lucky again. The proprietor owned several hectares of cherry trees and his daughter worked in the processing plant.

"Can we go and see?"

I looked at my watch. If we were going to make our flight, we had to go in twenty minutes.

"Oh, there will be no time," said the proprietor. He wiped his hands on the cloth dangling from the back of his trousers. "The fireworks, they begin at seven."

Mark's eyes lit up. "Fireworks? Tonight?"

"But of course. Epiphany, you know."

"What about school?" I said to Mark.

"Surely it's better for my education to spend time in France than go to silly old school?" He smiled a pale smile.

I remembered Becky saying "Who died and put you in charge of his education?" to me and had to wipe my eyes rather suddenly.

We stayed in the town long after the celebrations. Mark picked up some French words and made sketches around the town. The café proprietor showed him how to cook cherry tarts. After that, we took a flight to Tunisia and found the new baking powder factory. The industrial estate looked, once again, disturbingly similar to Ballymount. I faxed various power-of-attorney documents to the solicitor before we flew out to Mauritius. Well, what is the point of having money if you don't use it?

Mauritius looked nothing like Ballymount and we stayed there for six weeks. Mark added local sweet cake recipes to his autograph collection and illustrated them. He was quite handy at sketching. By the time we reached Australia he had quite a collection and there were nights he slept right through. When we arrived in the Jamaican spice plantations, he was an avid and fluent reader and had grown a foot upward and outward. None of his old clothes fitted any more and we both bought a whole new wardrobe. In Brazil, he persuaded me to learn the rumba with a devastatingly handsome instructor called José. In California, Mark lived on a surfboard and there were some days when the knot of grief in my stomach loosened for a while.

"Please, Gran," he said at one point, "call me Marco. It's my name."

He was right. It was.

I let my curls grow and dyed my hair honey gold.

When we felt up to it, we flew back to France. We planted irises on Becky's grave and organised the headstone, nothing too holy. Someone had left a bunch of red roses.

"I'm glad we buried her here," said Marco. "It's peaceful. You can get down and talk and there's no one to see."

He stayed at the grave for an hour, just chatting, telling Becky everything we'd done that year. I went away and had a little cry to myself, then Marco taught me how to skate.

At Hallow'een, we visited the distillery in Cork and picked up our last recipe for barm brack. Then we went home with suitcases full of the ingredients and a stack of sketches. It was time to bake this year's Christmas cake.

⅋

Ciara Geraghty lives in Donabate, County Dublin. She has two children, Sadhbh and Neil, and one husband, Frank. Ciara began writing three years ago and is currently working on her first novel. Favourite Fantasies include swinging on a hammock in a warm breeze with staff who bring books and baked alaska and beer. Pet hates include queuing and chips without salt.

Waiting

Ciara Geraghty

Waiting

She looks at the clock again: two minutes after six. He should be here by now. She worries at a cuticle with her teeth. It tears and bleeds, a thin red line curving around the top of her nail. She wipes it with a tissue. It doesn't hurt.

The children are in the front room watching cartoons in Irish on TG4. They are oblivious to the language barrier, soaking in the images through wide eyes.

"Sit back from the telly!" she calls in at them.

They don't move. She walks into the front room, her head turning this way and that, scanning everything as she goes. The clock on the mantelpiece is one of the two things her mother left her. The clock and the wedding ring. The ring is too big now so she wears it on a thin chain around her neck. When she is waiting, she fingers the thick band of the ring, turning it slowly.

The clock is ten minutes fast. It always has been but

Clare never changes it. It's best to have things done too early than too late.

Everything is in order. The children's faces are shiny and pink. She washes their faces and hands every day at 5.45 p.m. Except Sunday of course. Seán doesn't work on Sundays.

She picks up their hands in turn, inspecting them. She notices the nails. The pinkness of them. She runs her fingers over them. Smooth and rounded at the top. They are her hands. Turning them, she smiles at the palms, small and fleshy. She burrows her nose into the folds and breathes them in, like flowers. Of course, there are objections.

"Stop it, Mam! You're tickling me!" Grace says this, trying not to laugh.

"I can't see the telly, Ma!" This offering from Oisín, the TV addict.

Oisín's glasses reflect the light from the screen, the images glancing off the rims in garish technicolour. She wraps her arms around his warm, sturdy five-year-old body and slides him back from the telly. His only reaction is to crane his neck past her arm. Grace, lying on her belly, acknowledges her mother's presence by pushing herself back from the telly with her hands. She is small for a ten-year-old.

"What time is it, Ma?" she asks, in her low, careful voice.

"It's just after six. Your father should be home any minute," Clare answers, her eyes travelling over her daughter, looking for stains, rips, unravelling threads.

There are none and she steps back into the kitchen.

It is spotless, the table set for two. She runs her hands across the linen tablecloth, checking for creases. There are none.

She feeds the children at 5.30 p.m., with the promise of ice cream if they are quiet during his dinner. Although Grace is always quiet. Too quiet for a ten-year-old. In Grace's narrow face, Clare sees herself. Oisín is different. He talks with his mouth full. He even laughs with his mouth full. He pushes the food onto his fork with his fingers, no matter how often Clare tells him not to. His smile is infectious, especially since he lost his two front teeth. Now, he has a gappy smile, pink with gums. He is as messy as Grace is careful.

Clare crawls under the table after the children have eaten and picks up the bits of food that Oisín has let fall. He's a great grubber. But he's not careful. Clare worries about him. Where Grace sits, the floor is spotless.

The farming report has started on the radio. That means it's ten past six now. She looks at the kitchen clock. Just to be sure. It's ten past six now. The oven beeps, startling her. The sound is shrill in the quiet of the kitchen. She eases the oven door down and looks inside. The heat pushes at her face and she breathes it in, liking it. The kitchen is suddenly full of the smell of dinner. It smells homely, like *Little House on the Prairie*. This make her smile although she's not sure why. She sets the dish carefully on a cutting board on the counter. Steam rises from it in curves.

There is a roar from the driveway. She recognises it

and hurries towards the door, smoothing her hair. She stops and runs back, remembering the radio. She flicks at the switch and it's suddenly silent. Her fingers untie the knot in her apron and she shovels it into a drawer and runs out into the hall. The lights of the SUV are still on, interrupting the gloom of the hall. She has time to check her appearance in a cracked mirror over the hall table. For a moment there is quiet as she stares back at her reflection. People used to say she looked young for her age. She tucks a stray strand of greying hair behind her ear and pinches her cheeks to encourage some colour into her wan, worn face. She notices the deep creases along her forehead and recognises them. They are the same ones her mother had. They are the lines of women whose life is measured by the insistent turning of the sharp metallic hands of the kitchen clock.

Seven forty-five a.m. She hears the front door being wrenched open and slammed shut. She gets up then. In the winter she can see her breath in front of her down in the kitchen. It is a galley kitchen and pokes out like a finger from the back of the house, narrow and long. She makes porridge for the children. In a pot. Seán doesn't like microwaves. She loves the thickness of it. The way you have to pull the spoon through it. She pours honey over the top of the porridge, writing the children's names in golden threads over the dimpled surface. They love that and she loves hearing their giggles in the cold quiet of the morning.

Seven fifty-five. She makes their lunches for school.

Oisín loves tuna and doesn't believe her when she tells him it's a fish. He hates fish. Grace eats everything. Hollow Legs, Clare calls her, running her fingers through the fine strands of Grace's hair. A piece of fruit in each lunch box. A triangle of cheese in bright foil. The children laugh at the picture of the cow on the front, with great dangling earrings. It seems strange to Clare, making lunch before eight o'clock in the morning. But she loves this time in the house. The day stretches out in front of her, like hope.

Eight forty-five a.m. She wraps herself in a coat that is now too big for her. She walks them to school. Oisín runs in front of them, sometimes skipping, sometimes singing. It is Grace who holds her hand, watchful. On the way home, there are knots of mothers, talking. Clare wonders how they know each other so well and hurries past their laughing, her head down.

The long hours between breakfast and lunch when her children are in school and she is alone. She scrubs all surfaces, never wearing rubber gloves. Her hands reek of bleach. She spreads them out against the smooth wood of the hall table. Her fingers are pink and pulpy, swollen and lined with water. He likes everything to be cleaned by hand: the dishes, the clothes, the floors. There are some jobs she likes better than others. She hates washing the windows outside. Mrs Murtagh next door might come out to chat. Mrs Murtagh has three children, all grown up and gone now, and a husband who died on her. That's the way she puts it. He died on her, like he did it on purpose. Mrs Murtagh tells Clare secrets and expects the same in return.

What does your fella do? That's a grand jeep he has for himself. Is it for work?

Would you think about putting a bit of cobble-locking on the driveway?

What ages are the children now? I never see them. The poor pets.

Clare's hands tighten around the cloth. She says as little to Mrs Murtagh as she can without appearing rude. An interfering old bag, Seán calls her. He hates her and is suspicious of her. He is suspicious of everyone on the road, ever since the incident with the police. Seán never found out who called them. Clare thinks that makes it worse. Now everyone is a suspect. Clare cleans the windows as rarely as she can.

She listens to the radio. The DJs shout out the time after every song they play so she can keep track without having to watch the clocks. She'd like a mobile phone so she could text in an answer to a quiz sometimes. She'd never phone in. She'd hate to phone in. But texting. That's different. She likes the anonymity of that. Seán has a mobile phone. He hates it. When it rings during dinnertime. Or when he's watching the news. Or if it doesn't ring when he's expecting it to. Then, the darkness of the screen is like a stain, reminding him that someone has let him down.

Lunchtime to dinnertime. Trying to keep the children occupied through the endlessness of the afternoon. He doesn't let them play outside on the street. Oisín and Grace press their noses against the windowpane and watch their school friends run and yell, their faces red against the wind. She pulls them away, wiping their breath from the glass with a Windolene wipe. When the house is as clean as it has to be, she reads to them. Grace can read by herself but she loves when Clare gathers the pair of them to her on the worn couch and reads aloud from *Charlie and the Chocolate Factory*. Clare gives Willy Wonka an aristocratic English accent which makes Grace giggle. The sound echoes off the shiny floors and helps Clare to breathe.

Seán is struggling to find the hall-door key. She can hear him swearing under his breath. She turns from the mirror and the door swings open. The skin on her face stretches tight when she smiles. His work-stained T-shirt struggles to contain his bulky body. His tan lies in half-moons across his thick neck.

It's 6.15 p.m. He is jovial, bending to kiss Clare on her mouth. She stands on her tiptoes to reach him. He parts her lips with his, his tongue cold and wet. Clare knows he's had three pints. Maybe four. She can measure him in pints.

"Where are my children?" His voice is louder than it needs to be in the narrow confines of the hall. He surges into the front room and she follows, a shadow. He grabs Oisín from his slug-like position on the floor and throws him skyward. Oisín's glasses fall and he starts to cry, huge tears rolling down his pudgy pink cheeks. Seán drops him onto the couch where Grace shushes him.

"What's he cryin' for?"

"He's just tired, that's all."

"What, has he been out working since the fucking crack of dawn?" His voice is getting louder and Clare puts herself in the space between her husband and her son.

"Come on in for your dinner. It's shepherd's pie. Your favourite." Her hand is on his elbow, gently coaxing.

"What?"

"And I got us a bottle of wine. Half price in Lidl's." Clare trips over her words. She snakes her hand behind her back and pats Oisín's blond curls. The cries ease as she hides him behind her thickening waist.

"Wine? On a Tuesday?" He is playing along now, playing the game.

She takes his elbow and leads him into the kitchen, closing the double doors behind her. She settles him into a chair. Out of the corner of her eye, she sees Grace and Oisín settle back together on the couch, watching the telly. Oisín's thumb is in his mouth now and he leans against Grace. She lets him. Clare wishes, not for the first time, that she'd had a big sister like Grace when she was small.

Seán seems to fill the kitchen with his presence. He is talking loudly. About the Poles on site. Or the Nigerians. Or the Romanians. He employs them because they're cheap. They're lazy, he says. He can't remember their names. Weird names, he says. He can't pronounce them.

He sits down and she pushes the bottle opener into the cork, feels it give against her twisting hand. She pours him a glass and he smells it before drinking. The glass is half-empty when he lowers it and she fills it again, not looking at him.

"What's for dinner?"

She tells him again, fills his plate with it and carries it carefully to the table.

He eats quickly, nearly finished by the time she sits at the table and pours herself a small glass of wine.

He looks tired, she acknowledges, pale beneath his all-weather tan. His wedding ring catches the dying rays of sun, glinting with a white light. She remembers pushing the ring up over the knot of his knuckle. She had felt relief then, glancing down at her father in the front pew, uncomfortable in an ill-fitting suit. She wore her cousin's wedding dress, a little baggy around the neck, sliding past Clare's protruding collarbones. The sandals were also her cousin's and Clare's long, slender toes slid out over the tops, bracing themselves against the hardness of the ground as she emerged from the church in a hail of confetti. You were allowed have confetti then. Sean's father had strewn his Ford Cortina with gold ribbons and balloons, his childish, spidery scrawl barely legible in the dancing light of the afternoon sun. They honeymooned for two nights in Killarney. It was the first time either of them had been on holiday. In the daytime they walked for miles and sometimes he took her hand at particularly rocky spots. In the evening, they sat on the end of the pier and ate chips out of brown-paper bags, sodden with grease, licking their fingers and laughing out loud when they belched. She saw a seal one of those nights, its sleek grey head bobbing in the water like a buoy. She screamed and pointed at it but when Sean looked it was gone, sunk under the water like it had never been there. Clare could have sat there forever, watching the sun sink into the sea, transforming the grey water into a palette of pinks and oranges. But Seán was always anxious to leave, checking his watch, worrying about closing time.

In the pub at night, she watched him getting drunk as she sipped on a soda water and lime. She recognised the various stages from days spent in the pub with her father when she was a child. At first, gulping pints and wiping the froth from his mouth with the back of his hand. Looking around him. Never really talking to her. Alcohol-fuelled bonhomie seeping from his pores, his face a red shiny mass of smiles. Meeting people at the bar and bringing them back to the table to introduce them to his new wife.

"This is the ball and chain." Stout staining the new growth about his upper lip. Claire smiled shyly from beneath her fringe and shuffled over in her seat, sandwiched between two men intent on being the best of friends. Later, ominous complaints when newfound friends disappeared when it was their turn to buy a round.

"No wonder they didn't hang around." Seán bent his face towards hers. "You haven't said a word – you've been nursing that drink all night"

He hated that she didn't drink back then. Now she did. She drank wine, not liking it, sipping it. Preferring it to his disdain at her abstinence.

"Why aren't you eating your dinner?" Seán's voice

cuts across her.

She raises her navy blue eyes to his dark brown ones. She sees him as a stranger might for a moment. He is attractive in a swarthy, compact way. His hair is still full and mostly black, shot through with flecks of grey at the temples, lending him some dignity.

It's not all his fault. She knows that. She should have said something earlier. Maybe before the children were born. Or before they got married. She was just so desperate to get away. Maybe she should have taken better care of her hair. Or her face. Or just been more like her sister, Kate. Kate who lived in New York City with another woman. Kate who told her not to marry Seán. Kate who wore jeans long before women wearing jeans became fashionable. Or acceptable. Kate who hadn't been home since their mother's funeral. Kate.

Sounds from the neighbourhood float in through the open window. A dog barks insistently; the steady shriek of a car alarm slices the air. The high-pitched squeals of children anticipating the summer holidays. The dying rays of the sun pour in through the kitchen window, leaving her dull-headed and heavy with heat.

"I was just thinking about our honeymoon," she answers lightly. "Eleven years ago tomorrow."

He grunts in response, absorbed by the weather forecast flashing across the small screen sitting on the kitchen counter.

"Fucking rain tomorrow. I promised Ma I'd look at her roof. Fucking typical!"

Something catches Clare's eye and she glances

towards the double doors of the front room. She stiffens when she sees Grace's nose pressed against the glass. She is mouthing something. Seán is still talking, his voice getting louder as he stabs at the gravy on his plate with a piece of white bread. While his head is bent to his plate, Clare holds her daughter's face with her eyes, warning her with a slight shake of her head. She sees Grace moving towards the door, her small hand lifting to open it. Beads of sweat form above Clare's upper lip. She can taste it. Her mouth is dry. Seán doesn't seem to notice.

"Is there any more?" he asks, holding his plate out to her.

She jumps up from the table, her elbow sending her fork and spoon skidding off the edge. She tries to catch them but they slip past her hand and fall onto the tiled floor, rattling and rolling.

Seán puts his hands against his ears, colour staining his face, rising from his neck.

"Jesus, Clare, you're so fucking clumsy!"

"Sorry, Seán, they got away from me there." She is at the counter now, heaping his plate with seconds. She looks over to the door and Grace is still there, at the window, like a statue. Clare puts the plate carefully in front of Seán and sits back down at the table. She picks up her wineglass, smiling at him. But Grace is still coming into the room, moving towards them, making no sound. She has her worried face on and doesn't look at her father. She moves over to Clare, bending her head to whisper to her.

"I'll talk to you later, Grace," Clare says in a low voice. "After dinner, OK?"

"What does she want now?" Seán scratchs the back of his neck furiously. She can hear his wide, thick nails rasp against his skin. He swats an imaginary fly away from his head and breathes out heavily through his nose, like a horse.

"Don't worry, Seán – Grace can talk to me later, OK?"

"Christ, can a man not have his dinner in peace?"

Still Grace doesn't move. She speaks instead.

"Ma, I need twenty euro for school tomorrow. It's for our school tour." Grace's voice is an urgent whisper and Clare curses herself for not paying enough attention when Grace spoke anxiously about the school tour last week.

"Grace, I'll sort you out later, OK? Just let your father have his dinner." Clare is pushing the girl away from her towards the front room.

"What the fuck are you whispering about now? Can a man have no peace in his own house after a hard day's work?" Seán scrapes his chair away from the table, his knife raised.

Clare's hand jerks, the back of it hitting against the wineglass beside her plate. The glass teeters unsteadily on its stem and wine sloshes against the edges. For a moment Clare thinks it might be OK. Then, as if in slow motion, the glass tips too far and falls on its side before it rolls and rolls to the edge of the table. The sound of the glass shattering against the tiles is like a cat howling in the night. Blood-red stains seep through the impossible whiteness of the linen tablecloth and drip noiselessly onto the floor. A puddle of wine gathers in her lap. She can taste flecks of it on her lips.

Seán is on his feet, moving towards her. She sees his lips moving, spittle gathering in the corners of his mouth as he strains to contain his rage. He can't contain it. She knows that. She hears nothing. She feels relief. She is giddy with it. The noise of the world rushes back at her and she is up, pushing her chair back, skidding on a puddle of red wine, nearly falling. Out of the corner of her eye, she can see her young daughter cowering against the wall, watching them. Again.

The doorbell rings and for a moment, neither of them can place the sound. It sounds ridiculous, like an ice-cream van in the desert. Clare and Seán freeze, his fist raised, her hands in front of her, palms facing him, like a lollipop lady, halting traffic. She holds him with her eyes and lowers her hands slowly. The bell rings again, more insistently this time.

Still Grace stands there, saying nothing. Her stillness is like a sound moving between them.

"Seán, the door," she whispers breathlessly as if she's been running up a hill for the longest time.

Seán blinks his eyes several times, looking around him as if wondering where he is. Clare recognises the look and waits. His fist unclenches and lowers. He moves back from her, scrabbling at the waistband of his jeans, hoisting them up over his hips. He pulls his hand down the length of his face, straightening his features. Grace can move now. She closes the door of the sitting room behind her.

"I'll get it," he says.

His voice is quiet now. The voice she remembered

from years before. The voice of the man she thought would save her from her father's house. The voice he always uses afterwards. When he's sorry. He uses the backs of the chairs to support him as he moves towards the door.

She sits again, her legs trembling.

It's his mother. She sometimes calls at this time of the day. When he's not home, she frets about him working too hard, just like his father before him. When she's in the mood, she releases her tight curls from a wool hat and unwinds an endless scarf from around her thin neck revealing folds of jaded skin that sag under her jaw. Then she'll accept a cup of tea – leave the tea bag in, love, please – heaped with sugar and two Fig Roll biscuits. When she is settled in her chair and the steam from the tea has lent a pale flush to her cheeks, she'll tell Clare kindly stories of Seán as a youngster. Clare has heard these stories many times but she never gets tired of listening to the comforting ramblings of the old lady. Seán is all she has left. Her husband died years ago. It is a widely known fact that he died from cirrhosis of the liver but this is never acknowledged by the remaining members of the family. His two daughters took the boat when they were barely out of their teens and little has been heard of them since. His mother never mentions them.

"Look who's here!" Seán bellows with a wide smile that she can see from the kitchen. He gently escorts his mother down the hallway. The pair of them stand under the arch of the doorway, arms around each other, wide smiles like boats across their faces.

Clare stands up abruptly and feels the wetness of the wine on her legs. She rushes to explain herself, her words falling over each other as she reaches for a cloth.

"Clare, love, don't worry. I'll clean that up." It is Seán speaking and she can hear the confusion in his voice, wondering how they ended up like this. His face is stained with shame and a part of her feels sorry for him.

Mostly, she just wishes things were different.

"Please, Mrs Murray, sit down." Clare ushers her mother-in-law to a high-backed chair. "Seán, pour your mother a glass of wine and I'll go and change."

As she ascends the narrow staircase, Clare can hear the old lady feebly protesting against the glass of wine that she will sip for the next two hours. When she gets near the top, she sits on a stair, the wine cold now against her thighs. When she takes her trousers off, she will soak them in cold water with a little salt. She can hear Mrs Murray open the door into the front room, hoping for her grandchildren. The children will be brought out from the front room by Seán and greedily admired and fussed over by their only living grandparent. Soft cheeks will be pinched; round bellies will be tickled. Grace will hang her head and hide behind her hair. Oisín will settle himself in the warm bulk of his grandmother's lap, hoping for sweets which will inevitably be produced.

Clare will make good strong coffee which Seán will obediently drink under his mother's adoring eyes. The family will collectively breathe in and breathe out. Clare will hug her long arms about her thin body, her knees tucked under her chin. Mrs Murray will repeat herself again and again and Clare and Grace will catch each other's eyes and share a smile that no one else can see.

When Clare's hammering heart slows to a steady dull thud, she will acknowledge that there will be peace in this house tonight. She will hug Mrs Murray close when she leaves and bid her goodnight and a silent thank-you. She will leave Seán to fall asleep in front of the telly in the front room, sprawled on the couch. She will put her children to bed, tucking the bedclothes so tightly around them they can barely move. She will hold them close to her and shut her eyes and breathe in the warm, sweet smell of them.

She will go to bed and set her alarm for 7.45 a.m.

She will hear the door being wrenched open and banging shut behind him.

And life will go on.

Eileen Keane lives in Newbridge, County Kildare. She began to write five years ago and her first short story won the Cecil Day Lewis Fiction Award in 2003. She is working on a novel. She has been a teacher, artist and printmaker for many years. This story was inspired by a letter to the problem page of a Sunday paper.

Tryst

Eileen Keane

Tryst

"Rosie, for the last time will you finish your supper and stop dawdling? It's after nine o'clock already."

Mark raised his voice irritably. He was giving the kitchen a quick tidy up, looking forward to sitting down in peace when he got her off, watching Sky Sports while reading through the day's papers. Daniel was already out for the count. Tonight was Julie's night out with the girls and his night for bedtime stories and suppers and harassing children to get to bed.

"Ah, Rosie, look at the table! I thought I told you to tidy up those school books ages ago?"

"OK, OK, I'm doing it," Rosie said resentfully. "Oh, I need some cardboard and an egg carton for school tomorrow."

"For Christ's sake! Bedtime isn't the time to be thinking of those things!"

He opened the fridge and emptied the remaining eggs into the tray. "What do you mean – cardboard?"

"A cereal carton."

He looked in the press. "Well, I'm not giving you one of these unless there's a nearly empty one."

They were all more than half full. Then he remembered the recycling bin. There were lots of empty cereal boxes in there.

"That's really handy," he muttered to no one in particular. He selected two. "Do you want to bring an extra one in case one of your friends forgets?"

Rosie smiled at him.

As he packed them into her schoolbag something fell onto the ground. A piece of paper. No, a bag. Expensive-looking design, *Samantha's Secrets* in gold lettering on a black background. Black and gold handles. Must have got stuck in the empty cereal packet. He shooed Rosie up the stairs, picking up the bag at the same time.

"Night, Dad, love you. Come up to me in a while, won't you?" The routine of the goodnight kiss and the hug. She always wanted him to tuck her in, tried to prolong his sitting there, to put off the moment of lights out.

He turned on the television and opened a can of beer before bringing the bag and some empty milk cartons out to the recycling bin. He studied the bag. Lingerie? She must be planning something. She usually got her bits and pieces in Dunnes. Wore those kind of sexy things when they were single. Got sense after the kids. What was she up to? He had seen that shop somewhere. Yeah, over in the mall. Hardly that exclusive-looking place? He groaned mentally, subconsciously lifting his eyebrows, throwing his eyes to heaven and nodding his head. So much for a relaxing weekend.

Christ, she must be getting desperate. She had a much higher sex drive than he had. When was the last time? He frowned in concentration. He could hardly remember. Must be ages ago. He felt guilty. Terry's fortieth, that was it. Half-drunken fumbling, a few cursory attempts at foreplay, keep her happy, then sleep at last. He felt even more guilty as he remembered. That was at least two months ago. He had been under so much pressure at work, hadn't been thinking of much else for the past while. He was nearly always too tired anyway. Ah, she could hardly expect it to be like in the beginning – the honeymoon stage. A man needs to relax. He was happy with a quick cuddle. She worried that he didn't fancy her. Of course he did – but after twelve years of marriage, all the same, it wasn't exactly at the top of his list. He scratched his crotch reflectively, staring at the bag before dropping the lid of the recycling bin and shuffling inside.

Two months though, surprised she hadn't made any moves. He never initiated sex, left that to her once he realised she wanted it far more often than him. Fine the first year or two when he couldn't believe his luck. Regular supply whenever he wanted. Adolescent boy's dream. The novelty began to wear off the second year though. Foreplay. That was all fine when you were still at the infatuated stage but then it began to seem a bit tedious. A three-minute job would have suited him fine. He even fell asleep a few times in the middle of it and then had to endure the tension and silences for days, had to spend a whole evening trying to make it up to her. Worn out by the time it was over. Tried flowers the next time but that just made her all the more eager. Married couples move on from all that surely? Like pizza. He remembered the first time he had it. On holiday in Italy when he was ten. Mother won the holiday. Couldn't remember what for. How they turned up their noses at first when the ma said they should try the local food. Huge trays of it. Different flavours. The shock of it! Like tasting a piece of heaven. She learned to make it when they came home and he became obsessed. She wasn't famed for her culinary ability but he devoured it anyway. Almost unheard of in the country in the late seventies. When the first pizza place opened in Rathmines he couldn't believe his luck. Several times a week. Brought every girlfriend. Then the frozen ones appeared and next thing everyone was eating pizza. Couldn't stand them now. One every six months would do him.

A bit the same with sex. Still – two months! He felt a faint stirring of desire. Might be nice. Sexy knickers. Women thought that all men went for that sort of thing. Wear a pair of lacy see-through bits and he was yours to do what you wanted with. She had tried it before. Sexy nighties. Lipstick on at bedtime. Cuddling up to him. His favourite dinner. He always knew when she was thinking about it. He smiled to himself as he flicked the channels. He'd know by her when she came in. How had she lasted this long, he wondered, before getting absorbed in a thriller.

He was dozing when her step in the hall brought him back to consciousness. Her hair was newly styled, glinting with chestnut highlights, and though her face reflected her tiredness she was still beautiful, he thought fondly. It was ages since he'd looked at her properly. She made some tea and they talked for a few minutes.

"You haven't forgotten about the dinner with Marge and Jim on Saturday night?' she said, as she headed for bed.

So that's it, he thought, Saturday night! She'd get all dressed up and wear the new stuff underneath and be all set for seducing him later on. Dinner with friends always got her going, the wine and conversation. Women loved to talk. If the way to a man's heart was through his stomach then the way to a woman's must be through the tongue! He'd play along, though – after all, two months was a long time, even for him. He wouldn't mind himself. It was only fair to her anyway. Go to bed now, have a good sleep, go to bed early tomorrow night, then he'd be all set.

He smiled to himself as he made his way upstairs, where Julie was already asleep, her hair just visible over the top of the quilt.

"Yeah, we must do it more often, our place next time."

It was 1 a. m. on Saturday night – or Sunday morning rather. The dinner party had been a resounding success. Julie's eyes sparkled as she discussed it on the way home.

He smiled indulgently. She looked beautiful tonight, her cheeks pink from the wine, her face animated, full of wellbeing. He was feeling a bit merry himself, mellow and satisfied. Wine usually made him sleepy but the conversation had been particularly lively, as Mark and himself had a few brandies each after dinner, Julie smiling and sticking to coffee.

Wants to keep me sweet, he thought to himself. Well he was all ready for her. As he watched her driving, desire began to course through his veins, fuelled by the alcohol and mingling with the sense of happiness and anticipation. He tried to stifle a yawn as she glanced at him speculatively.

"I'm not tired," he hurried to reassure her. "It's just the brandy and the relaxing. You don't seem tired yourself?"

He waited for her to make a suggestive comment, but she just carried on chatting about the night.

"I'm not a bit tired now," he said, smiling suggestively as he put the key in the lock, but she was examining the top of the planter pot, plucking some stray weeds.

"You couldn't be up to those weeds," she sighed disgustedly. "Can't relax for a minute or they take over. God knows what the rest of the garden is like."

Inside she dropped the weeds in the bin and put the kettle on. He wondered if he should put his arm around her, show her he cared, but he felt awkward now, at a loss suddenly. They had got out of the habit of closeness and she seemed miles away.

"Are you sure you want tea?" he said, using that low

suggestive tone that she said used to drive her wild once.

"I'll have a quick cup," she said, not looking at him. "It's not that late anyway. Fancy a cup?' She glanced at him briefly.

"Well, okay so," he said. She was being very casual about it, he thought resentfully. Probably some game. Wanting him to make the first move. He had got out of the habit though. He accepted the tea awkwardly, trying to catch her eye again. She picked up the weekend review section of the paper.

"Think I'll bring the tea up with me. No point mooning around here."

When he went upstairs she was propped up on the pillows with her glasses perched on her nose. When he was in the bathroom he heard the click of her reading light going off and felt desire rise in him again. Maybe she was wearing it under that cardigan she draped around her for reading. Still she was behaving a bit strangely. A new approach. Keep him guessing. Well, it was working. He came out quietly and slipped into bed beside her, turning towards her expectantly. Her eyes were closed, her regular breathing showing that she was in fact fast asleep.

"Julie," he whispered incredulously. Frustration made a hard knot in his stomach. He rolled onto his back and began to masturbate, feeling peeved. What was the lingerie about so? It had been two months, for Christ's sake. Well, if that's the way she wanted it. He imagined her in red and black lace and, as the rhythm of his manipulation grew faster, abandoned that and reverted to his usual fantasy of domination and leather collars and whips, finding relief shortly afterwards in an explosion of brief but intense pleasure. Just as well, he thought peevishly as sleep came, if she had been on for it he'd still be up there slaving away.

Next morning she was up and about long before him and by the time he woke the appetising smell of the Sunday-morning fry wafted up to him and he could hear her singing in the kitchen. Getting out of bed quietly, he opened the drawers where she kept her underwear and quickly scanned the contents. Nothing that seemed new or unusually fancy. He checked the labels on some of them. All Dunnes or Marks. So what was the bag about? He observed her covertly as he ate breakfast. She seemed to be in great form.

Later when she took the children swimming he decided to get the papers and on an impulse headed for the shopping centre instead of the local paper shop. The lingerie shop was tucked into a quiet section of the mall, not a place he passed often. He paused in front of it, holding the front of the paper as if he was absorbed in the lead stories. Christ, the prices! Some right-looking stuff though. Seriously sexy. Nothing cheap in there. Maybe she was buying a present for someone? But here? Anyway she'd have shown him. She never kept secrets from him – she just wasn't the secretive type. Always rattled on about whatever was in her mind. Maybe he'd just show her the bag and ask her. Bound to be a simple explanation.

Strange though, the sex thing. The more he thought

about it the more it puzzled him. She used to be constantly pestering him. He hadn't noticed that she had stopped. When? Which of them had started it that night after the fortieth? He puzzled over this for a few moments but it was no good. He couldn't remember. He was well jarred that night anyway. It could have been him.

Maybe it was the menopause. She was thirty-five. What age did women get it at anyway? The "change" they called it too. Well, she seemed to have changed. He'd have to read something to find out. Hardly yet though. The jokes at the golf club, sorry he hadn't listened more carefully. Older men complaining the wives didn't want it as much. Gave them an excuse for "playing away". They thought this was hilarious, using the term constantly any time they were going away for a weekend. Playing away. He couldn't be bothered. His marriage was different.

A new idea startled him. Maybe Julie. . . He folded the paper, frowning at first, then his features relaxed into an amused grin. Not Julie! The postman was an ugly bastard and the milkman was a woman.

Even if she'd wanted to she didn't have the time. She worked mornings as a secretary in an accountant's office and had to pick up Daniel from junior school as soon as she finished. The only time she went out was with the girls once a week. Had she said something about going to see a play with Clare tonight? He must start paying her more attention. He had been taking her for granted for the past while, he realised. He didn't even know her friends from work, had never asked her about her

Thursday nights out with the office crowd. He was usually in bed when she got home. Right, he'd start taking more notice of her, show an interest. She was probably saving up the underwear for a special occasion. That was fine. *I can do special*, he thought to himself smiling, mentally congratulating himself on his perceptiveness.

Julie kissed and hugged the children before leaving to meet Clare at seven thirty.

"You'd think I was never coming back!" she laughed. "Now be good and go to bed on time for Daddy."

Mark had been unusually chatty this evening, Julie thought, as she parked the car behind the Moat Club. Good, Clare's Fiesta was there already. They'd have time for a glass of wine and a chat before the play started.

It was late when she let herself back into the house, nearly twelve thirty. It was one of those nights when everyone she knew seemed to be in the pub. She was still rerunning conversations in her head when she let herself in, surprised to see that Mark was still up. He usually went to bed early on Sunday nights.

"Had a good night?' he asked, immediately getting up and putting the kettle on.

She told him about the night, surprised and gratified at his sudden display of interest. He knew Clare well. When they were still single they had made a foursome with Clare and Dermot.

"So," he said at last, "where are you off to on Thursday night?"

She looked at him sharply. "You know I always go out

with the crowd from work."

"No, I mean what pub are you going to?"

She looked flustered suddenly, hesitating for a moment before the words spilled out resentfully. "I don't know yet. What difference does it make anyway?"

He did not look at her as he answered, staring into his cup as if there was something infinitely interesting at the bottom of it. "No, it's just I have a late meeting on Thursday. I meant to tell you earlier. We're going to have to get a baby-sitter. Anyway the meeting should be over by about ten so if ye were going to Reagan's I could call in for a quick drink on the way home and meet your friends. I hope you haven't told them anything terrible about me," he joked. "Don't worry, I won't stay long. I know ye want a good old gossip when ye get together."

She turned away and rinsed her cup at the sink, trying to hide her confusion. "I don't know. We sometimes go there but one of the girls was talking about a new pub over on the far side of town that she wanted to try. I'll find out on Tuesday."

"Oh, it was just an idea. Maybe you'd prefer if I didn't."

"No, it's not that," she said distractedly, "it's just that some of them like to move on to another pub if they don't like the crowd, so I couldn't be sure. I'll let you know anyway." She smiled briefly at him before putting her cup away and heading for bed.

Damn it, damn it! she kept repeating to herself as she got ready for bed, hurrying so that she could pretend to be asleep when he came up. All the questions all of a sudden. She had been caught totally off guard. She would have to be careful. She was never any good at lying. He had never shown any curiosity before, so it had been easy to deceive him. What would she tell him about Thursday night? She'd have to make sure he didn't think he could just turn up. Her Thursday nights had saved her marriage, she often thought. Before there was tension, frustration, a constant anxiety, watching him, stalking him almost, wondering why he didn't fancy her and need sex the way she did. She would not be able to help herself from trying to get his attention, wearing sexy nighties even though she knew he despised that type of thing, feeling let down and inadequate when he did not want her. After she began the affair with Paul the tension had gone and she could relax. Now she could let him initiate sex occasionally.

Occasionally was the word. She wouldn't want to be depending on him. It was easier to restrain herself now, releasing all the pent-up frustration on Thursday nights or occasional Monday afternoons in a mad sexual frenzy. She smiled to herself. Paul wanted her though. She still hadn't got used to the intensity of his desire. Everything had worked out so well really – she still couldn't believe it. You heard all these horror stories about the Internet and chatrooms and the danger of meeting people that way but there were plenty of people like Paul and herself to whose lives it had given a whole new dimension.

It had started out as just a frustrated reaction to Mark's immersion in the papers or the telly every night, a bit of harmless flirtation to fill a gap in her life. With

Paul it had been a way to while away a few hours in a hotel room, as he had to travel several times a week to meet his clients in other counties. They were totally honest with each other from the beginning. They were both happily enough married or at least still committed to their respective marriages. It had never been about anything more than sex really for either of them. Sort of marriage therapy really. This way everyone was happy, they reassured each other regularly.

She had chosen the hotel for their first meeting as it was on the far side of town but yet a safe place to meet a stranger. Although nothing too obvious had been said via the chatroom each knew exactly or thought they knew the reason for their meeting. They were quite disciplined about it, never divulging the details of their other lives, keeping to the excitement of sex with a partner who wanted to experiment as much as the other, to push back the boundaries of how many orgasms or erections or mad sexual gymnastics they could manage in the hour on Monday when he was passing through on his way to the city and on Thursday nights when he had to stay over to complete his business in the area before going home for the weekend.

She could relax and enjoy Mark's company now, even forgive him for his low sex drive. Maybe she should make more of an effort though. Had she become too complacent? She had gone from harassing him for sex several months ago to rarely making the first move, allowing him to take the lead. But that was a rare occurrence. Perhaps the sudden show of interest in her social life was an indication that he was feeling the effects. He couldn't have found out anything, could he? She thought of the box high up at the back of the top shelf of the wardrobe where she kept her Thursday bits and pieces. No, it would never occur to him to search her stuff. If he couldn't find something he'd just wait and ask her. So it wasn't that. She'd have to test the waters.

The restless feeling started in her lower belly and her breath quickened as she heard his step on the stairs. He was surprised when she was still awake, and this time she did not pretend to be asleep or hold back her desire when he slipped into bed beside her.

"It's been a long time," he said happily and he responded with some of the vigour of their first days of marriage. Afterwards, instead of falling asleep as usual, he leaned on one elbow, playing with a lock of her hair.

"Time for sleep," she said. "Monday tomorrow."

"Remember that fancy underwear you used to like one time?"

"That you made very obvious you had no interest in?" she said, a hard, cynical note creeping into her voice.

"Yeah, but you haven't been buying any of it again, have you? It's just that I saw a bag in the bin."

She froze. How could she have been so stupid?

"Mmm," she said, her mind working furiously. "What bag?" She could not read his expression in the darkness. "Wouldn't be much point in my wasting money in a shop like that, would there? Ah, you mean the Samantha's Secrets bag. Now I remember!" She started to laugh.

"Hannah at work, she bought some really sexy underwear on her break. She has a new boyfriend, much younger than her, and she's going all out to impress him. Anyway she put the bag in the bin and I found it when I was looking for something to put bits and pieces in when I was leaving the office. So no, you needn't worry, I'm not making elaborate plans to seduce you. Now, goodnight, it's a long day tomorrow."

It was nearly nine when Julie left the house. She was wearing a short skirt and a fitted leather jacket and knee boots. All dressed up but for whom, Mark thought cynically. His heart was beating fast as he watched her getting into the car. He wondered if he would be able to follow her without being noticed. How could he ever explain if he was caught? But he had to be sure, otherwise he would never be able to regain his peace of mind. The relief that flooded through him when she turned towards him on Sunday night hadn't lasted much longer than his erection. He had felt the way she stiffened when he asked her about the bag, noticed how she played for time before coming up with that story. It just didn't ring true. Sex should have been enough to allay his suspicions – it was probably all in his mind but he just had to be sure, see who she was meeting and what they got up to. Then he could go home and relax. He was being silly really, he thought, as he tried to stay far enough behind her not to be seen.

Her jealous husband, stalking her! If anyone saw him! The traffic was just heavy enough. He hadn't asked her again where they were meeting and she had avoided the subject completely. That was odd too. She took a left turn on a road leading out of town. Where was she heading? There was nothing much on this road. Ah, the Royal Hotel. Strange place to be meeting the girls. He had almost forgotten about this place, hadn't been in it for years, but it had had major renovations in the past year so maybe it had become trendy. Or maybe there was something on there.

He pulled in to a secluded corner of the carpark where he had a good view of the front entrance. She strode in quickly, checking her watch, smoothing her skirt and hurriedly reapplying some lipstick. They worried more about what "the girls" thought than anything else, he had figured out over the years. Since most men never noticed what women wore, and most women knew that, it followed that though they fooled themselves that they wanted to look nice for their blokes or to attract one, it was really to keep their so-called friends at bay. Knives out. Tear each other to shreds. Or some sort of competitive streak, show the others up.

His problem now was that he had not been in the Royal since it was done up. Didn't know the layout, whether he could chance having a look around without her spotting him. Probably too risky. He'd wait. Maybe they'd go somewhere else after a while anyway if what she said was true.

An hour later he was stiff and cold and dying to go to the toilet. He decided to chance it. He looked through the glass doors before going cautiously inside. The toilets were just opposite the entrance to the lounge, big glass panels in the lounge walls giving him a quick view of the interior. The toilets were empty and when he was finished he opened the door just enough to scan the lounge. A group of girls on the far side in a corner, another nearer, too young though, various couples, men in suits. No sign of Julie. A man came out of the lounge and Mark tried to look casual and innocent as he slipped out of the bathroom, his back prickling with tension as he felt that at any moment she might walk out of the ladies' and recognise him disappearing through the door. He did not relax until he was in the comparative safety of the car again. He could wait. She had to come out sometime, and then he would have proof of the ridiculousness of his suspicions and go home and relax. All this because of a bloody bag!

It was after midnight when Julie made her way quietly down the corridor from the residents' rooms. Her body was still tingling with excitement. Every part of her felt alive, sated, fulfilled. Soon that would give way to tiredness. She was anxious to get home, but first she had to change her underwear. She couldn't risk leaving the lacy lingerie set on though she was tempted. She turned into the main foyer of the hotel and went into the ladies' opposite the main lounge. Her nipples were sore, throbbing, and she savoured the feeling. She leaned against the door of the cubicle, closing her eyes and smiling to herself for a moment before beginning to change hurriedly. Paul had wanted to watch her getting dressed, followed her back into the bathroom. Usually he sat on the bed smoking while she dressed quickly in the bathroom. She had not wanted to shatter his illusions, see her getting dressed in her plain white sensible bra and knickers, so she had put the plunging peach-coloured cami set back on. She couldn't go home like that though, certainly not at the moment. She rolled the peach silk into a tight ball and stashed it in the inside pocket of her handbag.

A young couple were linking each other through the doors of the lounge and, as Julie came out of the ladies, she saw Stacey, an old school friend, through the open door. Glancing up, Stacey caught her eye at exactly the same moment so even if she wanted to she could not have avoided her. She was with a noisy group of friends. They were just finishing their drinks and were all a bit merry, Stacey doing hurried introductions while they tried to catch up on each other's lives. A few minutes later the group spilled untidily out of the hotel, Julie and Stacey standing chatting for a few minutes as the others dispersed to cars, arguing over which nightclub they were most likely to bag a man or preferably several men in.

Mark nodded to himself in satisfaction as he started the car. He was stiff, sore and frozen, but his mood was ebullient as he nosed out and drove around the back of the carpark. She was still there talking when he left. Now to get home and make her a nice cup of tea. He'd buy her some flowers tomorrow, maybe some chocolates. He thought briefly about the lingerie shop. No, that would be overdoing it a bit. How could he have doubted her? He clicked his lips in self-satisfaction and began to whistle, drumming his fingers on the steering wheel and looking forward to the match on Saturday.

Patricia McAdoo completed the MA in Writing at NUIG and wrote a children's book, *Claddagh, The Tale of the Ring*, published by Galway Online. She was short-listed for the Francis MacManus Short Story Award. From Cork, she now lives in Moycullen, County Galway, and is married with three sons.

Fallow Time

Patricia McAdoo

Fallow Time

The moment it was out of my mouth, I knew my timing was off. I blame the in-flight movie. I blame the whole thing on *Dead Poets Society*. That film always throws me off course in some way. Everybody else seems to remember all that "seize the day" stuff but the part that gets to me is where they stand on their desks and say to Robin Williams, *"Oh Captain! My Captain!"* because they're prepared to make a stand for something important.

"You're *what*?"

This wasn't my mother speaking. No, my mother was just sort of staring at me, her eyes tired and droopy, like an old cocker spaniel. This was the airhostess, for God's sake. She was just standing there, with my mother's gin in her hand, supposedly doing her job but with her other hand on her hip like she was all set to go ten rounds in the world wrestling championship title fight for women.

So I turned to her and tried to freeze her out of the conversation.

"I beg your pardon?" I said. "I was speaking to my mother."

She leaned over the nice old dears beside me and placed a drinks mat on my mother's drink holder. I could smell her perfume – a strong waft of Tommy. Of course . . . with hair like that, she had to be a Hilfiger girl.

"You're gonna quit?" She clicked her fingers sharply. "Just like that?"

Her eyes bored into me and I could feel my face beginning to burn up. I gave my mother a quick glance but she was still in full-on sorrowful mode. So I tried to give the airhostess what I hoped was an icy stare but there was a shake in my voice when I spoke.

"*Not* that it's really any of your business but I was trying to tell my mother that I'm reviewing my options regarding college."

That was a bit dishonest. What I had actually said was that I wasn't going back to college. End of discussion.

"Are you *crazy*?" The airhostess was leaning right across the old couple. She hadn't taken her eyes off me. I tried to give her another of my withering looks but they seemed to bounce off her like ping-pong balls off a table.

"Are you out of your *mind*?" The words sprang from her blood-red lips, a short burst of gunfire from a semi-automatic. *Pow, pow, pow!*

She looked up to the other end of the aisle, probably to check where her boss was. Then she leaned in, so the elderly couple had to pull their heads right back into their headrests. They didn't seem to mind though. They seemed downright pleased with the interruption. I suppose long-haul flights can be very boring if you don't watch the in-flight movie. They didn't strike me as the kind of people who would shell out extra just so they wouldn't be bored. I bet they were saving every cent. I bet they were frugal as anything. Old people get like that. I wish it didn't happen. There you are at the end of your days and you can't even go mad and pay for the movie in case you need the money for the bus into the city or something.

"Do you know what I was doing with my life four years ago?" she asked.

I found myself looking straight into her neck, a mottled shade of pink. We all waited. Me, my poor mother and Derby and Joan. The suave cool-looking man, sitting next to my mother, just kept on reading *The New Yorker*. It must have been a good article because he didn't even look up. But the rest of us were in the clutches of the airhostess now for sure.

"I was studying drama at New York State University."

Joan gasped and grabbed Derby's hand. He looked pretty shook too. What was so amazingly awful about doing a drama course, for Christ's sake? The old lady's head started to shake from side to side.

"Our Billy studied drama. Before . . . before . . ."

The old fellow looked across at my mother. His skin hung in two deep pouches on either side of his nose. Even if he were in a good mood he probably would have looked sad.

"Our son is not that well."

133

My mother's face was all sort of crumpled looking, too. Oh my God. I had gone and ruined *everything*! All I wanted to do right then and there was to pick up the pieces – tell her I'd changed my mind again. It would be OK. I'd go back. Just let this holiday not be ruined, OK?

The old lady leaned across her husband and, looking straight past me, spoke to my mother.

"He's in a coma."

Her lips were quivering and when I looked at my mother she was gaping, her mouth halfway open. The old guy perched up on the edge of his seat, so that his hands gripped the tabletop in front of him.

"He's not in a *coma*, Marjorie." He announced this with the authority of a leading physician.

Marjorie ignored him. Her head bobbed up and down like a turkey. "Been in it for ten years now."

She looked as if she had Parkinson's disease. I knew all about that. My grandfather eventually died from it – the start of all our woes.

The old guy was having none of it.

"He's got some form of viral infection. Makes him *seem* like he's sort of comatose. Does nothing all day long. Nothing. Just sits in his chair at the window. It's not like he's actually sick or anything." He was looking at my mother but you could tell he was really someplace else. I suppose he was thinking about Billy sitting in a room staring out of the window.

The airhostess leaned in way over the couple so that I could see the sharp outline of her lip-liner. Her hand must have shook a bit when she was applying it because it veered off course a little on one side. Her breast with the nametag on brushed past Marjorie's face. It said *Lorene*.

"Drama at New York State University." Lorene separated out all the words again and said them really slowly, as if Irish people couldn't understand her damn New Jersey accent. I was watching her big hair and started smirking on the inside. But I was careful to maintain my interested look. She handed my mother her gin. There was no sign of the tonic. "Have you any *idea* how hard that course is to get into?"

She was staring at me, accusation written large on her face. Mascara had caked and creased on her lower lids, making her seem even more dramatic than she already was. I shook my head. Her eyes narrowed and I could see her nostrils moving slightly in and out.

"Way the hell hard. Straight As.'

I tried to look impressed. My mother was still holding the gin in her hand and looking sort of lost. I had ruined everything. An hour before, we were laughing, picking the out-of-town shopping malls to visit from the tour guide. Damn it, I was almost happy before they showed that film. I could have predicted that this was not a good idea. Not a film about reference points in your life and big tough decisions. I was way too fragile for that kind of thing.

Lorene was studying my face closely, like she'd just discovered an amazing map she was desperate to decipher. I readjusted my features in what I hoped was an expression of interest and admiration. Straight As.

Imagine! Without looking round she grabbed a tonic from the trolley and put it in front of my mother. It was slimline, which my mother always said tasted too sweet, but this wasn't the time to have a hissy fit. Lorene didn't miss a beat. "I was always that kind of person. Had to give everything my best shot."

The old lady was looking at my mother and me, her eyes fluttering between us like she was watching a highly competitive tennis match.

"Billy was the very same. Just that sort of attitude. Only the best always. The way he studied for exams. I used to say to him, I'd say, 'Billy, you gotta take a break here. You'll get sick.' I used to tell him that. 'Slow down,' I'd say. 'There's more to life than exams.'" Her head started to bob again. "I used to say all that."

Lorene ignored this interruption and continued to address me in a low voice, her eyes narrowed into tiny slits. "Then I started to hang with the wrong crowd."

She had abandoned all pretence at doing her job. She was just kind of leaning on the headrest of the person in the seat ahead. Like we were all old buddies here. Just chewing the fat.

"You know how it is." She looked at my mother and George, who were both giving her the kind of reverent attention she'd get if she was telling them the plane was going down and here's how you use the oxygen mask. She examined her nails – long, bright red and perfectly filed. "I started to skip classes. Only a few at first but I got out of my depth with the work in no time. Not handing in assignments."

136

Marjorie nudged George. "The very same."

George took her hand and gently patted it.

Lorene dropped her voice to a quiet, intense whisper and we all sort of huddled in to get the next words to drip from her lips. You could tell she was enjoying herself. Any fool could tell she was born to be an actress.

"It got pretty bad. By the next semester I was in trouble. Couldn't tell my folks. It would *totally* cut them up." She shot me a meaningful look. I lowered my eyes. "I quit school by the end of the year. All I'd ever dreamed about – opening my own drama school one day for all the little kids in my neighbourhood – entering Miss New Jersey – everything gone down the tube."

We were all staring at her now, even the guy with the magazine. Well, Marjorie wasn't. She was dabbing her eyes with a tissue. The airhostess took one last look around her audience, peering into each face to make sure we'd got the message, resting a little longer than was strictly necessary on me. Then she straightened up and flashed a smile, the sort that doesn't go all the way to the eyes, the kind you get when someone says: "Welcome on board!"

"So . . . here I am. Working the transatlantic route with Delta. Trying to turn a buck."

None of us smiled back. It suddenly seemed like a sad thing to be doing. She pulled her shirtsleeves down where they'd got crumpled leaning on the headrest.

"Anyways, got to get my sorry ass back up that aisle or my days on this airline will be over. Have yourselves a good day now."

And she was gone. I was really sorry to see her go. Now I had to face the music with my mother. I put my hand on top of her hand where it was resting on the armrest between us and opened my mouth to speak. But I'd forgotten about Marjorie.

"It's so hard at our time of life. What will become of him? I keep asking George what's going to happen when we're gone."

Her pale eyes were fixed on my mother, as if she were some kind of learned sphinx who would summon up the perfect pronouncement any second now.

George coughed out a harsh, bitter laugh. "You can bet your bottom dollar he'll shake a leg when he has to." He rested his head on his hand and looked at my mother. "Do you know what he does all day?" He didn't wait for a reply. "Watches *Simpsons* reruns. Nothing else but the goddamn *Simpsons*. I mean if it was National Geographic . . ."

My mother poured the tonic and drained half the glass in one gulp.

I swallowed hard and leaned in towards her. My hand rested on the sleeve of her jacket.

"Mum, I didn't mean to say that. I don't know what came over me. I really don't."

My mother put her head back and whispered in my ear, "If you didn't mean it, then why did you say it?"

My mother was like that. Always in with a logical question. She never quite abandoned her wig and gown even when she was at home.

"I don't know. Look, let's forget about it, OK? Let's

forget all about it and have ourselves a good holiday and when we come back –"

The prosecution pounced again. "So, in other words there *is* something you want to tell me about quitting college but you just want to put it on the back burner for a while."

Any minute now she'd jump from her seat and start strolling up and down the aisle, establish an emergency court session here on Flight 272 bound for New Jersey. Time for an early guilty plea. Yes, mother dear. That's about the size of it. I have in fact definitely decided to get the hell out of college but I just hadn't planned to tell you about it. Not here. Not now.

Instead I headed for the undergrowth.

"Well, let's just say I'm a bit confused about things. That's all."

My mother slurped back the last of her drink. I took the opportunity to elaborate on the confusion theory.

"You know I never liked psychology, Ma. I've been trying to tell you that for years. I'm just not into all that mind stuff.'

My mother's face crumpled up some more as if I was always wearing her out with this sort of thing. Which wasn't actually true. I never hassled her about my life. She looked at her empty glass.

"Well, even if you don't like psychology, surely it makes sense to finish. I know plenty of people who don't like law but who did the degree and then did something else."

"But there's all this pressure once you've got it. Don't

you see that? Once you've got your degree, then it's the post grad. And on and on. I really want to take a break. Get my head straight. I deserve a break, don't I . . . after everything?"

This was below the belt but I didn't care. My parents' marital bust-up had taken its toll. To tell the truth, it had broken my heart and I wanted a bit of time to just reappraise things. "Fallow time" was what the therapist had called it. I'd gone to see her after my father finally left home. She talked about having time just come to terms with things. She said that everyone needed some time in their lives in which nothing much happened, the way fields lie fallow to enrich the soil again. She said that it was good for the soul.

"Pardon me."

My mother and I both turned in the direction of the suave *New Yorker* reader. We had both forgotten all about him. It came as a bit of a shock to hear his voice, which was every bit as silvery smooth as he looked.

"I'm sorry to intrude like this but I just couldn't help overhearing you mention something about careers in psychology."

We must have been staring at him and not saying anything so he just stretched out his hand to my mother.

"How rude of me not to introduce myself first. I'm Hamilton Skinner. How do you do? Please don't think I was earwigging on your conversation. In fact, I hadn't been doing that at all but when you mentioned psychology my ears sort of automatically pricked up. You see, I'm a behavioural psychotherapist. As a matter of fact, I've just spent a delightful three weeks on the lecture circuit in your beautiful country." He smiled at us – a kind, twinkly sort of smile.

I don't know what my mother did but I started to smile back. There was something warm and friendly about him that made you want to do that.

"Anyway, this whole thing of doing psychology . . . well, you might just say it interests me when I hear young people just starting out on their careers wondering what they should do, which turn in the road they should take . . ." He glanced at us both. "Perhaps I've said too much. Please forgive the intrusion. It really was most inappropriate."

My mother put her hand on his sleeve, just a very quick, light sort of touch, the kind you almost wouldn't even see.

"No, you mustn't think that. How interesting – I mean about you being in the same field."

Hamilton nodded. "Well, we happen to be a growing and diverse breed, us shrinks."

He started to take up *The New Yorker* again but my mother was having none of it.

"Please, do tell us a little about your background. I'm sure we'd both like to hear all about it, wouldn't we, Alison?"

I nodded slowly. Why not? Everyone else on this plane had an opinion on my life, why not old silver-tongued Hamilton here?

Hamilton signalled to the airhostess on his aisle, not the drama queen from New York State University, and smoothly ordered us another round of drinks. I noticed that this was my mother's third gin in a row.

Then he turned to us both and raised his glass.

"To new beginnings, whatever they may bring!"

My mother looked a little doubtful but she seemed to shrug it off pretty quickly.

Hamilton settled himself and so did we.

"Well, let me tell you a little about myself. I've been a therapist now for, let's see, it must be going on thirty years. And I don't mind telling you that I'm good at what I do. Yes, there are even days when I can be quite brilliant."

Why did I get the feeling that there might be a "but" coming?

"The money is good. I have a place in the Hamptons and my children and I go there on weekends."

Was it my imagination or did I see a tiny tightening of my mother's mouth at the mention of children?

"It's ten years now since I lost my wife . . ."

I didn't dare look at my mother.

"And I get a lot of time to do things like I've just been doing. Touring around various colleges, giving lectures. It can be interesting, stimulating . . ."

He stopped talking and he was just sitting there, in a daze. He didn't look to me like he found it all that interesting. He looked sort of tired. Hamilton seemed to remember his audience.

"Anyway, Alison, tell me what branch of psychology you're thinking of going into?"

I shifted a little and glanced at my mother. "Well, that's just it really. I mmm . . . I dunno really."

Hamilton smiled, a sort of wry smile. "I was a bit like that when I started out. Not really knowing whether I was picking the right subjects. You know how it is."

My mother and I nodded, though privately I was thinking that I probably understood Hamilton's dilemma a lot more than my mother ever could. From the first moment my mother smelt a law book, she was hooked.

Hamilton smiled. "I remember one of the first lectures I ever attended, there was this guy talking about monkey experiments. I think it was developmental psychology. And he was just so boring. I couldn't see the connection to human behaviour and, even if there was one, I couldn't see that it would be all that interesting. And then I thought to myself, 'I don't want to know a single bit more about this subject.'"

I nodded. Maybe I had the same guy. Maybe he just travelled around the world torturing each new wave of bright young psychology students.

Hamilton caught the nod. "You got him too, right?"

My mother put down her drink. "But even though you had your doubts back then, you persisted and it all came good for you. I mean, for heaven's sake, look at you now!"

Hamilton nodded. "Sure. I guess you could say it came good for me. I've done all right."

He was looking thoughtful again and we both just waited.

"But you know something?" He paused.

He was good at making speeches, I could see that. Yeah, I bet when Hamilton stood before a hall full of students he had them eating out of his hand.

"I've been in this game for all that time and I still get that same feeling of wanting to . . . who knows? . . . just do something else for a while."

He looked at us both.

"I don't know why I'm even telling you both all this. It's a bit late for me compared to you, Alison. But there are days, I have to admit . . ."

Maybe I imagined it but it seemed to me that for all of his suavity, he looked a little shy.

My mother looked at him nervously. "Admit what?"

"Well, admit that maybe I'd be better off growing peach trees in some quiet out-of-the-way sort of place. Always did hanker after things like that." He swirled the last ice cube in his glass. "Yes, sir. If it's a contest between reading a groundbreaking piece of research on neurochemical brain functioning and a new seed catalogue . . ." He smiled. "Well, let's just say I know what would win hands down."

There was a silence during which we listened to the pilot telling us where we were – mid-Atlantic, if you're interested – and then Hamilton smiled a brighter sort of smile, directed at my mother.

"Anyway, we've heard quite enough of all that midlife crisis stuff for now. Tell me, what do you do to turn an honest buck, as they say on my side of the world?"

My mother smiled back. She was looking pretty relaxed compared to when I dropped my bombshell, so I was grateful to old Hamilton. She didn't need any more grief in her life. It was eighteen months since my father walked out on her. My granddad had just popped his clogs, hardly cold in the grave, when my father headed for the hills. The thing about it was there wasn't even another woman involved. He said he needed "space". At fifty-three years of age, my father was going on about needing space! He just kept on and on about it to whoever would listen. About how he'd been stressed out all his life in work and now it was time for him to stand back a little and think about *his* needs for a change.

My mother bore the whole thing with amazing dignity. She just kept on working, never missed one day. Tried to be normal with me, never slagged off my father in front of me. He got himself an apartment and took up white-water rafting. So now he goes off to some place up in Scotland. He says he loves the smell of danger on the water. I don't understand it myself. Before all this, my father did the odd round of pitch and putt at the weekend and that was about it.

Hamilton and my mother were deep in conversation so I started to read the in-flight magazine. I noticed the old couple had drifted off to sleep. Marjorie's head was resting on George's shoulder. They looked peaceful but in her hand the old lady still held the crumpled tissue from when she had been crying.

I used not to believe in life-changing events. You know, the kind of stupid film that begins with "On that fateful day, Flight 272 was to change all our lives." But now I do. I really do. I don't know what it is about planes. People get on a plane and just start to talk to each other. They're liable to say anything. Anyway, that Delta flight to New Jersey really did change everything. As my mother and Hamilton began talking, I closed my eyes and promised myself that I would quit college after all and maybe in the end I'd find something as dear to me as Hamilton's seed catalogues were to him. I must have drifted off because when I woke up, Mr Peach Tree and my mother were exchanging business cards and Hamilton was gently persuading her of the benefits of a weekend in the Hamptons. Maybe it's that thin air you get in airplanes. My mother was practically fluttering her eyelashes.

As we queued to disembark, I saw Lorene waiting at the door. A cold fear gripped me but the queue of tired passengers behind me propelled me relentlessly towards my fate. Sure enough, when I got up close to her she grabbed me by the arm.

"Look –" I said.

"No!" She had this smile on her face, like she'd seen the Second Coming or something. "I'm sorry I gave you a hard time." She spoke in a loud voice and I could feel the other passengers behind me shuffling in close to hear more. "Ya know what I said back there about me quitting college and all?" She squeezed my arm and leaned in and whispered in my ear. "I'm gonna go back. When I listened to myself talking I said to myself in the galley, 'Lorene, honey, nobody is going to get you what you want. You gotta get that for yourself.' So – thanks, huh?"

I nodded slowly.

She let go of my arm and flashed a set of straight, shiny white teeth. "You have yourself a good one."

Later that evening in our room, which looked over

Central Park – my mother said that if we were going to take a holiday then we were going to go in style – I had a lot of time on my hands. Maybe it was all those gins but as soon as we hit the room my mother wrapped herself in a cosy rug and went to sleep. But I was wide awake. I sat on the window seat and watched the old cypress trees swaying. It was a wonderful summer's evening, the kind that makes you feel sad but glad to be alive all at the same time. The air outside was warm and a gentle breeze fanned my face. The faint clip-clop of horses' hooves drifted up from the park. Gradually the sun faded behind a bank of drifting cloud and a carpet of twinkling lights took its place. The whole of New York City was showing off, swaggering its towers of light-filled windows. The world was muffled, quiet. In the room behind me, my mother's breathing grew slow and deep. I closed my eyes. And I found myself thinking about Billy. On the far side of the River Hudson, he too might be looking out his window, doing nothing much at all. While George and Marjorie lay sleeping, was he there now . . . alone, adrift? Somehow I knew he was.

So I whispered to him, sending my words into that summer night breeze: "Hang in there, Billy. Because it might just all work out."

෨෧

Ellen McCarthy was born near the Comeragh Mountains of West Waterford. With a degree in Literature and Sociology from DCU, she pursued her dream of writing professionally. This dream was realised with the publication of her short story "Family Life" and completion of her first novel. Ellen lives in Waterford City.

Winner

Family Life

Ellen McCarthy

Family Life

The snort took her totally by surprise. It was like an eruption in the back of her throat. Her palpitations had reached such a crescendo she could now see the rhythmic drumming of her heart as she looked at the tears running down her carefully tanned bosoms. That was the only word you could conceivably use when you described heaving breasts encased in satin, encrusted in Swarovski crystals and seed pearls. They were heaving partly because of her crying and partly because her lungs were so crushed in a bodice that was two sizes too small they had to fight gallantly to take in a new breath.

As her mind cleared briefly, she heard the knocking on the door start again.

"Please. Lucy, darling. Let me in."

"No." She heard a hard, cold voice coming from her own mouth. A voice devoid of feeling and emotion, despite the onslaught of pity-filled tears. Those were silent, for her only. The voice was how she wanted the world to hear her.

"Lucy!"

"Go away or I won't be responsible for my actions!"

"Lucy, if we talk face to face we can clear this whole thing up."

"Really, Mother? Years of lies and betrayal can be cleared up in a civilised moment of conversation? What magazine did you read that rubbish in?"

"Lucy, there's no need to be cruel!"

Lucy tried to whirl around and burst through the door but she was a victim of her own lack of forethought. Her voluminous skirts were wedged in tightly between the sanitary bin and the toilet-roll holder and she really couldn't move without a ripping disaster. Her beautiful veil, which she had waited on tenterhooks for her bridesmaids to pin on her head just a couple of hours ago, was draped precariously around the cubicle. A portion of it lay on the shelf behind the toilet, which normally held someone's handbag. The rest of it was stretched across the toilet roll and around the hook on the back of the door. She was effectively a prisoner inside a sheath of ridiculously expensive satin and lace while her mother pounded on the door in front of her red nose. How had her wonderful morning come to this?

She really had been the model bride. Money hadn't been an obstacle to anything she'd suggested and she'd had a fantastic wedding co-ordinator. There had been no disappointments, no tantrums and no major stress. She hadn't had to worry about a thing as she'd been, as always, surrounded by people she trusted implicitly. Mark was a wonderful man. He was kind, faithful and sexy and she couldn't wait to be married to him. Lucy knew she was such a lucky girl. She had fantastic friends, she'd never had a financial problem in her life and all her dreams had come true since the day she was born.

When she was ten years old she and her friend Miriam started the Wedding Book. They planned in detail when they'd marry, who they'd marry (in outline – Mark hadn't arrived on the scene yet) and, of course, all the minute details of the fabulous day. She had sketches of the dress and her veil, colour swatches for the bridesmaids' dresses, everything for a perfect day and it actually went according to her plan. Miriam, of course, had to be her maid of honour. She'd had to stick to that too though Miriam had been between two minds.

Poor Miriam! Nothing had gone according to her plan. Miriam had been the beauty when they were kids, with the best personality. She discovered boys, booze and, consequently, matrimonial bliss long before Lucy and well ahead of the plan. Now two pregnancies later and six months after her divorce, it took a lot of persuading to get her to stick to Lucy's plan and be her bridesmaid. "Why should I?" had been her response. Why stick to Lucy's plan when the heavens had intervened and made a mess of her own?

A new wave of tears flooded Lucy. Maybe that was

where they both went wrong. That stupid plan! How cruel was God? At least as far as Miriam was concerned He stopped the plan at the outset. She got used to real life fairly quickly but in Lucy's case He had let her go to the end. She had a lot that she wished to say to Him when she had the time. Right now she suddenly needed to pee and, considering how tightly she was wedged on top of the loo, she could see no way of actually raising the seat and using the thing.

Last night she'd slept in the penthouse suite of a beautiful castle. When she opened her eyes this morning, through the posts of her four-poster bed she saw purple heather bathed in an early morning mist that seemed to roll off the hills. Her excitement was so great that, despite a fairly late night the night before, she was wide awake before room service arrived with her tray. She ate her obligatory breakfast dressed in a terry-cloth robe watching the sun shaking that pale mist off the face of the mountain. The next hours rushed by in a blur of make-up, hair-care products and women rushing around her room in their underwear. By two fifteen they were all ready and poised for action. Lucy sat amongst them, the only one calm and serene, confident that nothing could possibly go wrong. Nothing ever had before. Why on earth would life start unravelling now?

At two thirty her father arrived at the hotel, looking so handsome. He was a young father and he always kept himself fit. Ever since she was a little girl he took her breath away. There was never a time in her memory when he wasn't available to her when she needed him. He talked to her when they were alone. Not like her friends' dads asking a never-ending barrage of questions. No, he talked because he had something to say and she listened, hung on his every word and looked up into his animated face as he told stories and explained about nature and, when she was older, discussed world affairs and politics. He was her best friend in the whole world and the most handsome man she knew.

Her heart skipped a beat when he walked into the room and just looked at her. She felt beautiful. He held out his arm and she linked it without speaking a word – there was no need. They walked arm in arm from the hotel to the waiting carriage.

The wedding was taking place in a small church in the grounds of the castle. The wind had whipped up slightly and gently blew a stray tendril of hair across her cheek as the horse trotted along the tree-lined drive.

Lucy was so happy.

The wedding was due to start at two but, of course, the bride wanted to be traditional and keep the groom waiting. The carriage trundled along the winding road through lines of green leafy branches that blocked the bright sun and replaced it with a green glow. Still they didn't speak; there was no need. They held hands, with both of them lost in their own thoughts.

Conor Gavigan thought of the day he first laid eyes on this beautiful woman sitting beside him. She was the tiniest little thing he'd ever seen, with huge blue eyes that followed him everywhere he went. He was there for each milestone in her life and always tried his best to be everything she needed because she was everything in life he ever wanted. He remembered the day Mark came and asked for her hand. It was such an old-fashioned thing to do but Mark was old school and that's what he liked about him. He'd always do the right thing by Lucy. When they had a child Conor knew he'd have another little person in his life to care for. He couldn't wait to be a granddad. He didn't tell Lucy that, in case it scared her. She was only twenty-three. Life had gone by so quickly.

Finally the carriage crunched to a halt on the gravel drive in front of the chapel. Conor jumped down and held his hand out for Lucy. She jumped lightly down beside him and felt tears threatening for the first time when he kissed her gently on the cheek. She smiled and they turned to walk into the church.

And there she was.

Lucy felt her father stiffen by her side when he saw her and for the first time in her life she saw actual fear on his face.

"Dad? What's the matter?"

But he seemed unable to speak as she walked towards them.

"Lucy," she said.

"Who are you?"

"I'm your grandmother."

"What! Dad? What's she talking about?"

"I'm your father's mother."

Lucy turned around again and gazed up at her dad. "Dad! Is she crazy? I remember Nana."

The woman spoke directly to her, cutting Conor out. "Not Conor's father, Lucy. Your real father. Stephen."

"You're crazy! This is my real father!"

"No, Lucy. My son was your father. He died shortly after you were born."

"No! You're lying!"

"No, Lucy. She's not." Conor's face was ashen.

Lucy turned horror-filled eyes to this man she'd called dad. There was a loud sound in her ears like the beating of wings and she could feel herself swaying but she steadied herself against the wheel of the carriage. Her dad couldn't look at her. That strong, confident expression she'd always depended on had melted into the gravel.

Without raising his eyes he continued speaking. "He was my best friend and your mother's childhood sweetheart."

"But that was you. *You* were her childhood sweetheart!"

"No, baby. You were two years old when we got married. She was still little more than a child. She was sixteen when she had you. She never married your dad."

"How did he die?"

"Lucy, this isn't the place." There was a break in Conor's voice as he spoke.

"*How?*" The scream that erupted from her surprised everyone, including herself.

"He shot himself."

Lucy turned to her grandmother and looked deeply into her dark, hooded eyes. "Why didn't I ever meet you before?"

"Your mother thought it would be better if we went our separate ways and pretended it never happened."

"And you, Dad, how did you feel?"

"I loved her. Eventually I fell in love with her. I'd do anything to help her get over the pain. It was difficult for us to be together considering the circumstances, so we made a clean break from Stevie's family."

"I didn't have a say." The woman's voice held a note of self-pity.

"You pushed everyone away. Long before we got together."

"*Lucy!*" The panic-stricken shriek from her mother caused them all to turn.

Lucy grabbed her father's arm and gestured to her bridesmaids, who were standing back at a respectful distance, unsure what they were expected to do in the face of such revelations.

"Girls. Get my veil. Mark will be waiting."

With as much dignity as she could muster she grabbed her father's arm and, sidestepping her mother's outstretched arms, headed towards the gaping door of the church. The beating wings continued their onslaught on her ears until they were finally drowned out by the organist playing "Here Comes the Bride".

Slowly the little group walked down the aisle with all

eyes turned in her direction. They smiled and gasped at her beauty until they finally started to notice the frozen smile etched into her face. It was such a contrast from the usually radiant smile she had for the world. Mark had a little frown-line between his eyebrows; she knew by that look he was nervous and she wasn't helping, so against her will she roused her smile out of its pity zone and turned it on him with as much heat as she could manage. It worked.

The little line disappeared and he whispered: "You're so beautiful. I love you." It's only nerves, he thought. For an ugly moment he'd thought she'd changed her mind.

The priest droned on in the background and miraculously Lucy answered in all the right places. Her head was swimming and she couldn't wait to get outside for some air. She had no idea where her new grandmother had planted herself. Why on earth had she chosen today to get to know her? There had been years when she could have done that but she chose to invade her wedding day. How could her mother lie to her all these years and how could someone pretend to be her dad? Tears were starting to well up inside her as she said, "I do," and finally kissed her groom, gluing a smile on tightly for his benefit. He had signed up for a wedding and a wedding he was going to get. Life after the wedding, at least in the immediate future, might be rocky. Gently, Mark guided her through the lighting of the candle and the signing of the register and finally they were descending the aisle and were heading back out into the brilliant sunshine.

Outside, people trooped from every corner to kiss her

cheek and congratulate the new couple but she couldn't take her eyes off the smartly dressed woman in the pinstriped trouser suit who stood confidently off to the side. Her grandmother was certainly a sharp dresser, she'd give her that much. Lucy wondered how old she was. Lucy's mother was forty now. Only sixteen when Lucy was born! Her father presumably had been the same age. Her father was dead. A suicide at sixteen! She had to keep saying it. Her cousin Kyle walked past just then. He had just celebrated his sixteenth birthday. Lucy watched his skinny body walk along, his blue eyes darting over the backs of every pair of tanned bare legs that passed them by. This was her dad. A post-pubescent child with raging hormones and the acne and enthusiastic shaving scars to prove it. To her, Kyle was a child. She couldn't imagine him as a dad now.

Eventually the buses arrived and left and the wedding party had taken the last of their photos in the garden of the church, which was manicured carefully to facilitate the many weddings that took place here. It had been so beautiful in the brochure, so full of promise. Her strength was ebbing quickly as the carriage carried her and Mark back to the castle. She couldn't wait now to get away by herself for a while and try to get her head around this. Her mother was going to have to delay the reception; it was the least she could do.

When they arrived at the castle steps Lucy was dismayed to see her mother and grandmother standing shouting at each other in front of the door. People were turning sideways to get quickly past them. "Lucy, what's going on?"

"Nothing!" she snapped at her new husband, more curtly than she'd intended.

"It doesn't seem like nothing. Who's that woman shouting at Claire?"

Lucy didn't answer. She jumped from the carriage before Mark had a chance to stop her and ran at the two women.

"Have you two got no respect? This is my wedding day!"

"Darling, she has no right to be here. I won't have her coming here ruining my life!"

"*Your* life, Mother? This is *my* wedding day!"

"Claire, you never could think of anyone else but yourself!"

"And you drove your own son to suicide!"

Before anyone could stop her, Lucy's grandmother clawed at Claire's hat and ripped it from her head, throwing it into a rosebush sitting pretty by the door in a china bowl. Lucy snapped it out to try and defuse the situation, heard the net lining rip and saw an extra splash of pink attached to the thorns.

"That's it! You two are ruining my day. Mum, you've lied to me my whole life. And you!" She turned to face her grandmother. "You chose the wrong day to get to know me. I'm sick of both of you. I can't take this!" She muttered the last words as finally tears gushed down her face and she ran to the bathroom to hide them and that's where she was now, stuck, until she could get someone to rescue her.

Minutes ticked by and the tears were dried into her cheeks. Lucy heard the bathroom door opening quietly and feet padded softly into the room.

"Lucy!"

Relief flooded when she heard Miriam's voice.

"Miriam! You've got to help me. I'm stuck – my dress and veil are tangled up in everything in here – and I need to pee."

Miriam started laughing and once again Lucy felt tears start.

"Don't laugh. Please!"

"I'm sorry, darling. Open the door and let me in. Stacy is here too."

Lucy stretched up as far as she could and the two girls gently manoeuvred the door back and eventually extricated their friend from the cubicle's confines.

"Someone will come in. I look a mess."

"No, they won't. We've locked the door and Rob is guarding the end of the corridor." Rob was Miriam's ex-husband. They had a complicated post-divorce life.

"I really need to pee!" Lucy could feel her lower lip quivering again.

"OK. Out of this dress!" Miriam was opening the hooks and buttons as she spoke. She tugged down the skirt until Lucy stood there in her very expensive Agent Provocateurs Miriam had picked up for her in LA. Miriam worked as cabin crew with Delta Airlines.

Relief-filled moments later, Lucy walked back out to her friends.

"Girls, what am I going to do? I haven't time to process all of this and I can't sit at the top table now, I'm too miserable. Look at my face!"

"Right, Miss, sit here." Stacy pulled out the stool at the vanity mirror. She had a large cosmetic bag with her. She owned her own beauty salon.

"I'm beyond even you now."

"Oooh! A challenge! I love that. Now keep still and put a cap on those tears."

It took a while and the complete removal and reapplication of Lucy's make-up before they'd restored her to her former glory. Stacy was a genius. The puffiness was reduced and the make-up flawless. Stacy couldn't stop the pain in her gut though. It throbbed and robbed her of every second breath. The thought of facing a room full of people was too much. Her head was full of a teenage father, leaving no room for cake and speeches.

There was a light knock on the door. Miriam shrugged off Lucy's restraining hand and opened the door slightly. It was Rob. He whispered something to Miriam and disappeared again.

"Lucy, come with us," said Miriam.

"I'm not leaving here. I can't."

"You are and you can," said Miriam sternly. "Come on!"

Lucy was shocked into submission and meekly followed her with Stacy bringing up the rear in case she

163

turned and did another runner. They walked down the length of the corridor and turned right onto another corridor that stretched off into the distance. They walked the length of that and again turned a corner.

"Miriam, are we just walking around in circles?"

"No." She said nothing more and gave no room for any response. Finally she stopped outside a set of double doors and walked in.

Stacy pushed Lucy in after her and before she could move the two girls left.

"We'll be outside." Miriam kissed her cheek as she brushed past.

Lucy was left in a small library with an open fireplace resplendent in painted tiles and a roaring wood fire. The reading table stood in the centre of the room and around this sat her mother, Claire Gavigan, her dad-that-was, Conor Gavigan, and this woman who called herself her grandmother.

Lucy turned to her first.

"What's your name?"

"Margaret Rice."

"My father's name was Stephen Rice?"

"Yes."

Conor pushed a photograph across the table to Lucy. The throbbing in her gut was getting stronger. Lucy looked at them, lingering on each nervous face before she finally picked up the picture.

These must be her parents. Her mother had black hair scraped back in a tight ponytail, emphasising the severe sweep of her plucked brows and liquid black eyeliner. She wore a long white tunic dress under a baggy black cardigan hanging loosely from her shoulders. Under the dress she wore Doc Martens. She was turned sideways towards a tall skinny boy in tight black jeans and a blue shirt. He wore a white tie tucked into the front of his shirt. His bright, happy smile was framed by blond hair spiked high with gel. His eyes crinkled around the edges as he looked over the top of her mother's head where he was planting a kiss on her brow. They were standing in front of a metallic blue car parked in a grove of trees. His smile shone out of the picture and his eyes seemed to gaze into his daughter's. Lucy tore her eyes away and turned it over. *Dance with me. I feel you bleed. Sing with me. Fill me.*

Claire started to gently weep. "He wrote that for me. He loved words. We used to rush into Power's newsagents every week on our lunch break to get *Smash Hits* and look up song lyrics. He wanted to be a songwriter. He was always writing little notes for me. I was so sad the day we took this photo. I was sick and worried. I knew I'd have to see a doctor soon but I was really scared."

"I took the photograph." Conor seemed about to cry too. "That was my dad's car. None of the three of us could drive but Stevie and myself loved that car. It was a metallic blue 1982 Ford Capri, 1600 cc, petrol engine."

"I'm sure we don't wish to hear about the car." Margaret Rice turned disdainful eyes on Conor.

"I do. Don't interrupt him." Lucy turned back to Conor.

"The three of us went everywhere together after Stevie and Claire started going out. Before that it was just the two of us."

"You were always jealous of him."

"Mrs Rice, I asked you not to interrupt him. I'm not interested in your side of it. If you can't shut up, please leave."

Margaret Rice pursed her thin lips together.

"Your mother was pregnant in that picture," Conor continued. "I knew but they hadn't told anyone else. When she did tell, she was six and a half months gone. There was uproar. Their parents freaked. Especially Stevie's family, as they never thought his choice in friends was good enough. They thought he'd outgrow me when he got to college but a girlfriend and baby was a bigger burden. Margaret had only three months to prepare for being a granny."

"I wasn't even forty yet."

"I wasn't even sixteen and I was going to be a mother!"

"Well! That was your own fault. What did you expect?"

"I didn't do it alone!"

Conor frowned at the two women and resumed. "War broke out from the moment they discovered the baby was coming. Margaret did everything she could to split them up. She insisted the baby probably wasn't his and even tried to convince him you were mine. After you were born it was worse. They fought day and night and Stevie couldn't take it. The Rice family decided to move and take Stevie. He said he wouldn't go so they threatened to cut him off. He'd never have been able to afford college or take care of you and your mother. Four months after you were born she found him in the garden shed, the shotgun by his feet."

For a few moments nobody spoke. Lucy tried to let it all sink in. Margaret's face was wooden and unemotional and she met Lucy's eyes with a defiant stare.

"Why did you want to find me now?"

"I read the piece in the paper about your upcoming wedding. Lucy Gavigan marries Mark Kennedy. I knew Stephen would be very proud. You finished college. It said with a Master's in Child Psychology."

"No. I'm still working on my Master's. Childhood relationships don't have to spoil your life, you know. You can still achieve your dreams and be in love."

"Well! You are a little older than your mother was at that time. Mark seems like a wonderful young man. I've heard of his family of course. Kennedy Estate Agents! We used to know his grandparents years ago." She paused. "I wrote a few months ago but obviously you didn't get my letter."

"Claire, did you get a letter?" Conor looked at his wife.

"Yes."

"Mum! You should have warned me!"

"I know. I had so much on my mind and I couldn't think straight. I decided to let things lie and hoped she'd stay in her own life and leave ours alone."

"Lucy – this is why I was so proud of how you turned out. With the start you had in life."

Lucy felt white-hot anger boiling inside her. She turned her flashing eyes on her grandmother.

"How dare you! I have never had anything but love and happiness in my life until today. These people brought me up and both of them went to college. Dad went first to start earning as quickly as possible and Mum went later when I was a bit older and they could afford childcare. Mum is a midwife and Dad is a secondary-school teacher. I turned out well, thanks to them. Your son is dead, thanks to you."

Lucy had never spoken like that to anyone and immediately felt guilty and went to apologise but again her eyes met the cold, calculating stare of her grandmother. There wasn't a tear in her eye and not even a flicker of emotion softening her steely mouth.

"Why are you here?" Lucy had to ask again. She couldn't understand this woman's motive.

"I only had one child."

"Any more would have ruined her waistline!" Claire snorted the words at her.

"I invested everything in him and she stole it from me. I wanted something of him for me."

"You wanted a return on your investment?" Lucy was incredulous. "Am I your dividend? What's the matter? Do all your friends have their successful children over to dinner on Sunday and do you meet during the week and discuss the potential of your grandchildren? You saw I'd been to college and found myself a husband – a rich one with a good family – were you hoping we'd all be around for Sunday lunch?"

"Yes. Is that too much to ask?"

"Yes, it is, too much to ask on my wedding day." Lucy lowered her head as she spoke. "You gave me nothing. Thanks to your efforts I could have grown up with nothing. You turned your back on all of us when things weren't going your way. You lost your son and still you couldn't make an effort with your grandchild, your only grandchild."

"I did what any mother would do. You'll see that yourself in a few years when you have your children. It's called tough love. I couldn't let him throw his life away."

"I could never do what you did," said Lucy. "He didn't throw his life away. You did. Your son wanted to face his responsibilities and take care of his girlfriend and baby. That was something to be proud of."

"He should never have been in that situation in the first place."

"But he was, Mrs Rice. I'm the situation he found himself in and luckily for me his best friend took over his responsibilities when he died. The only thing my dad did wrong was not having the strength to stand up to you!"

Claire and Conor reached across the table and held Lucy's hands. Suddenly Lucy felt a strength she'd never had to use before.

"I'd like you to leave now. We have a room full of guests we need to go see to."

"You're not inviting me to stay?"

169

"No."

Lucy turned and, holding her parents' hands, left the room and shut the door quietly behind her. She knew she'd left a lonely, bitter woman behind but Lucy also knew that sometimes you had to feel the nasty bite of your actions. Her grandmother was a woman in denial. You couldn't go out and purchase a granddaughter the way you did a thoroughbred.

Lucy raised a glass of champagne and toasted her parents as she finished her speech. The sound of clapping rang around the room and, looking about her, Lucy could feel nothing but love. Propped against the jug in front of her was the photograph of her dad. So much had happened today and she still needed to go away and process it when she had the time. That's what honeymoons were for. Mark was a good listener and she knew he'd always be there for her and their children. They would be able to face anything life threw at them, unexpected or otherwise. Her heart was soft and she could never hold anger inside. Already her feelings towards her grandmother were turning to ones of pity but she still couldn't see herself ever spending much time with her. You had to prepare the ground and sow the seeds if you wanted to harvest a crop and Margaret Rice was learning that tonight. Lucy had known nurturers who saw in her tiny, unexpected arrival a seed that they would all one day be proud of: for that she loved them dearly. She was lucky to have had their tender touch in her life and she wished her dad had the same. She had no doubt that if he had, the people surrounding her today would still be here. Conor would be her uncle, her mum would still be her mum and her dad, that skinny blond-haired boy who hadn't yet realised the strength of a man, would have walked her down the aisle.

Lucy picked up the picture and kissed it gently. Mark picked up her other hand and kissed that. He'd ask later. Right now they had a party to go to.

Maura McClean was brought up in Belfast and is the eldest of three children and the only daughter, which means she's well and truly spoilt! The person who most inspires her and is a constant source of comfort and support is her best friend, Josy, who, coincidentally, is also her mother.

Mothers, Daughters and Frogs' Legs

Maura McClean

Mothers, Daughters
and
Frogs' Legs

"You're not half piling the pounds on. Those trousers look far too snug on you! Oh, yes, definitely, no doubt about it. D'you know it's really noticeable on your bum when you turn around! Best pull that jumper down over it, try and disguise the size a little!"

Those were the words that greeted me at the exact moment I entered my mother's house. I had only just turned round to close the front door, but obviously my huge backside had already entered the room minutes earlier, confirming that her overweight daughter had arrived. I wouldn't mind so much but her next words were: "Have you eaten?"

Well, Mother, obviously I've done nothing but shovel food down my gob since you saw me yesterday, which explains this obese mass in front of you and the incredible weight gain in less than twenty-four hours!

But I wasn't brave enough to say that, so a simple "No, Mum, but I'm not hungry" sufficed.

It was hard not to say *"Actually I'm starving and would happily chew the arse off a low-flying duck!"* as I felt the presence of her eyes taking in every little bump on my body.

"There's no good will come of that," she began. "You can't starve yourself to lose weight. You need to eat sensibly, that's the only way."

I nodded in agreement. What else could I do? Why did I put myself through this constantly? And why, after these crushing remarks, did she spend the next few hours telling me what food she had and offering me different selections of biscuits, ice-cream, buns, sandwiches, takeaway curries, frozen pizza, chips and noodles?

Basically, everything that wasn't classed as sensible food.

Occasionally on my visits she would tell me about some lovely new clothes she had bought and beckon me to the bedroom to see them. Once there the doors closed and I'd be trapped. I knew so well what was coming.

"Isn't this skirt lovely? I got it in Dunnes! Half price! I just couldn't resist so I treated myself."

"Yes, Mum, it's really nice and I bet it looks great on," I would say.

"Well, slip it on there," she'd reply. "See what it's like on you."

Being the ever-obedient daughter I would dutifully strip as she closed the curtains, because God forbid the neighbours should catch a glimpse of the ogre in her bedroom. And once I'd put it on I would stand in front of the long, gold mirror and prepare myself for her next line.

"Oh, that looks lovely on you, Teresa, you may as well keep it. It's far too big for me, I'm swimming in it!"

I plonked my whale-sized body down on the armchair. I'm sure she was watching the feet to see if it tipped to one side. I'm not sure the furniture in her house was built for people like me. I mean, size fourteen is hitting that critical stage where you're no longer able to fit into an airplane seat, and I'm sure she spends nights in bed wondering how I squeeze myself in and out of my Nissan Micra, only a cream bun away from being trapped in it for all eternity. But for all that she still loves me, and I'm sure her reward will come in heaven, where she'll not be too slow to tell me, when we're reunited, that my wings are out of proportion with the rest of my angelic body.

I was dreading this visit. I tried to do it last night but in the end I decided my bruised ego had taken enough of a battering and the best thing I could do was leave her in blissful ignorance for another night. Maybe it was more a case of me burying my head in the sand and enjoying the normality of my mother rather than facing up to what had actually happened and what I needed to tell her.

What you need to understand about me is that my life tends to lunge from one disaster to another. To be perfectly honest, I get a feeling of unease when things run smoothly. I usually take this as a sign that something big is waiting to pounce and knock me for six. And I'm normally always right.

I have a theory, just to fill you in on the background, that all girls (especially me) are fairy princesses and all boys are frogs. It won't take a genius to figure out that Walt Disney has been one of the biggest influences in my life. So it follows that I believed when I grew up I'd have to take the rough with the smooth and kiss a few frogs before one turned into my Prince Charming. Which in turn would lead to a breathtaking romance, followed by a magical proposal, a big square diamond engagement ring, a lavish wedding and a happy-ever-after-ending.

I think the downfall for me is that Walt wasn't big on making sequels. He only ever tells the story as far as the wedding. He never gave an update on how Cinderella's life turned out. Did her glass slippers start to pinch after a while? Did her prince become a work-obsessed dragon-slayer, resulting in her chronic dependency on alcohol to suppress the feelings of loneliness? Did Snow White marry in haste (given that she'd only just recovered from a very serious coma) – then, once she'd had time to reflect on the situation, realise that her true love was really Dopey?

We never got to hear the "ah buts" or the "Poor Belle, did you hear that Beast started knocking her about?" But devoid of the "what really happened next?" information, I grew up loyal to my belief that one day my prince would come and I too would be the fairy princess who lived happily ever after.

I met more than a few frogs along the way, but

eventually I met Jack. He was everything I'd ever wanted: tall, dark, funny, caring, romantic, with a big black slinky BMW and money enough to spoil me with gifts, nice dinners and surprise weekends away. Finally I was living the dream, and I felt sorry for other girls who were still kissing the frogs they met, only ever getting warts for their trouble. Jack made me feel like I was the most beautiful woman in the world, and every time I gazed into his big brown eyes my heart melted. This was true love, and I had to pinch myself sometimes just to believe that a man as fantastic as he wanted to be with someone like me.

My mother adored him and felt comfortable sharing this with me when she said things like, "We're so blessed that he saw the beauty within you, Teresa, we really are. To have a man like Jack in our family, well, he's like the son I never had." I'm sure she was just dying to ask him why he wanted to waste his life on a girl like me. The only reason she didn't, I suspect, was the fear that it might put doubts in his head.

She'd be heartbroken if he left "us".

The wedding plans had been in full flow for the past year, and a week from today was to be the big day.

Nothing else could be done until a day or two beforehand when I just needed to collect the cake and drop it off to the hotel. Well, as it turned out, there was a lot more to do, this being the first and (I was under no illusion) the hardest.

Holby City was now on the television, my mother's favourite show. She loves the blood and guts. This wasn't a good time to tell her my news – not only would she be pissed at missing her favourite show but also the reason would break her heart.

I should let her watch this, I thought to myself. *I may need tips on CPR shortly.*

As the final credits rolled, I watched as she ran her hand through her fine greying hair. My mum's very pretty and has the greenest eyes I've ever seen. My dad says that's what first attracted him to her. She has perfect high cheekbones with a very healthy glow about them, and her skin is smooth and soft although there are a few wrinkles round the sides of her eyes and mouth. She's a very young-looking fifty-six. She blames the crow's feet on me and the stress I cause unnecessarily, through things like driving at night. I keep forgetting that cars are only to be used in daylight hours. Unless you're an adult you can't drive after sunset, and in her world thirty-three doesn't qualify as being an adult. On the up side, though, I don't have to visit as much in the winter.

My hands were sweating, so I gently rubbed them on my trousers, feeling the grain of my cords, and from the pit of my stomach I felt myself starting to overheat with that feeling of sickness coming upon me slowly, getting stronger with every second.

I had this planned so well, exactly what I was going to say and how I was going to say it, remaining calm, so as not to alarm her and try to encourage a more civilised response and mature discussion about what I'd done.

I was petrified, lonely and scared; no one could help me now. At the thought, my composure just crumbled and I let out a muffled cry. Her head turned toward me and she pulled her glasses down, so they now sat perched on the middle of her nose as she peered quizzically over the rims at me.

"What?" came her gruff response. Again, typical of my mother that she can pick up on an emotion instantly and find just the right retort.

I couldn't talk. I just broke down, crying inconsolably. Now I couldn't breathe. I was completely out of control. I tried to stand up and move towards her, but on the way I tripped over the strap of my new black Gucci handbag (that Jack had bought me for my birthday), fell on the floor and banged my head on the corner of the coffee table on the way down. I knew my head hurt but didn't for one second think there was any real physical damage.

"Ah, you're bleeding. I'll get a cloth," she said as she reluctantly roused herself from the corner of the sofa where she'd been curled up, legs tucked neatly under the settee cushion. She fixed the glasses back on top of her nose and said, "Well, that's gonna teach you not to leave things lying at your backside."

Yes, Mother, you're right – that's the thing I've learnt today, a lesson that was well and truly needed, especially now. This became translated into my actual reply of "I know. I'm sorry."

When I finally left the house that night I had a black eye from my close encounter with the coffee table, which thankfully, after close inspection by her, was deemed not to have sustained any damage. As for me, well, let's just say she'd quite happily have sent me home with a matching set.

The horrible thing is that for the first time ever none

of this is actually my fault. I know I say that a lot, like the time I lost the keys to our rental car in France and thought the obvious solution was to break the driver's side window to get in. Jack arrived back five minutes later with the car keys and a very distressed face when he saw what I'd done – especially as I'd done it to the wrong car. Innocent mistake and another lesson I learnt: make absolutely sure that when you think you've lost keys no one else has them and, more importantly, ensure that if you're to smash a window it's to gain access to the right car.

I can tell *you* what really happened, but it's a little different from the version I told my mother. Jack and I had planned not to spend the night together for the week before the wedding, just to add a bit of spice to the wedding night. Feeling a bit at a loose end one evening I went to bed early, as the TV was awful. So I lay in bed and just stared at the ceiling, thinking about my wedding and my dress and how great it was all going to be.

I got a little peckish so decided I'd alleviate the boredom by making something to eat. Once in the kitchen I decided pancakes, would suit the mood. Jack loved my pancakes especially when I served them with strawberries and cream.

Minutes later I was covered in flour (which matched the kitchen quite well) and thought to myself how romantic it would be to sneak down to Jack's with my comfort food and surprise him.

Excited by my plan, I quickly got changed and jumped in the car with my parcel of delights. The lights were all out in the house and I felt a pang of love when I realised he'd gone to bed early too, probably due to missing me so much and feeling a bit out of sorts without me. It just added to the brilliance of my plan. I went to the back door, put my key in the lock and very gently turned it.

Once inside the house I tiptoed to the kitchen, got out a plate and put the pancakes – which were still warm and smelled delicious – on it, unloaded the strawberries from the tub, decorating them with a big squirt of cream.

I made my way up each stair as quietly as I could, I'd even removed my shoes, and as I got closer to the bedroom door my heart was beating so fast and loud with excitement I thought he'd hear it. I vowed to myself then that I'd do this kind of thing when we were married – a husband should be spoilt and surprised from time to time so he knew he was valued and loved, and besides he'd do the same for me – *This is how to keep a marriage alive*, I thought.

I opened the door and candlelight flickered in the room. I could hear his gentle snores. OK, so he wasn't lying awake missing me, but I bet he was dreaming about me! I set the plate at the foot of the bed, put a strawberry in my mouth, then lifted the bottom of the quilt and ever so slowly started to slide myself up the middle of the queen-sized bed we'd bought a few weeks earlier.

The funny thing was something didn't feel right but I just couldn't put my finger on it. I felt the bedspread move slightly and wanted to laugh, but I couldn't or I'd risk choking on the strawberry. I looked up and could just make out the light peering through the top of the quilt. Nearly there! Slowly, slowly, I wriggled up the bed – *almost there, here I come, this is so much fun* – my head just about to pop through the top – *yes, I'm here* – I see him lying with his back to me and, isn't that sweet, we're so in tune he can sense my presence and he starts to rub my back, bless him . . .

Hold on, if he's lying with his back to me, and I'm looking at his back, then how can he be rubbing my . . .

Oops! There goes the strawberry! I can't breathe! I jump up, trying to dislodge it by coughing and choking and banging my back against the headboard. Obviously I was completely focused on liberating the strawberry so I didn't really have time to comprehend that I was on the verge of dying in between my soon-to-be husband and a girl from his workplace . . .

It was all a bit of a mess and more than a little awkward. In these situations who's meant to leave the bed first? The naked girl your fiancé has just spent the night with? The naked cheating fiancé? Or the poor shocked, hyperventilating girlfriend? A dilemma indeed.

The three of us just sat there stunned and all I could say, once I got my first breath, was: "I brought pancakes."

Idiot, sure why not go the whole hog and offer them a cup of tea to help with the shock! I would think later.

As it turned out no one really thought about the correct etiquette of the situation, as both she and Jack jumped out of the bed simultaneously, both fumbling for something to preserve their modesty. Although God knows why in his case – he had nothing I hadn't seen before. But I wanted to get a good gawp at her so I could pick out flaws, like cellulite or a disfiguring mole or, better still, abnormal hair growth. Alas, this wasn't to be, but I made a mental note to come back to this later. "Teresa? What the hell are – shit – I mean you're not meant to – how the –? Why? Shit!"

He actually used a lot of other profanities but best I stick to the ones more familiar to me.

"Yes, shit indeed! Who's this slag?" Not that I normally go around insulting fellow-sisters but on this occasion I had to improvise as we hadn't been formally introduced, and I felt she would best suit a short and snappy name, so "slag" just jumped right into my head.

She wasn't thrilled with my name choice and started to interject with "How dare you!" and "Who the hell are you calling a slag?"

Isn't it funny how people ask the most obvious questions sometimes? It's hardly like we needed to call in Miss Marple to help get to the bottom of my insinuation.

I didn't think it even warranted an answer, but I've always had compassion for people who couldn't quite keep up, so getting out of the bed and making my way towards her I tried to answer her question as simply as possible.

"You! You fat slag!"

I watched as she moved round me picking up her bits and pieces, and they were only bits and pieces, but I couldn't help but notice the pretty pink and black lacy bra and matching thong. This made me a little self-conscious, knowing that if it were me, I'd be picking up a pair of black cotton knickers and a sensible white bra (and not even a crisp white one, more an off-white greyish shade – I've never been very good at white).

She threw on a pretty pink top then hopped round the room pulling her jeans on. She was saying something to Jack, but I wasn't listening, all I could think about was how bloody co-ordinated this bitch was. She even had the cutest little pair of pink slip-on shoes with sequins round the toe – I'd kill for those – I could kill *her* for those – it would be a crime of passion – and it was a real crime that she had them and not me – the slag!

So that's how Jack and I broke up, and to be honest I'm fine with it, totally fine. It's just one of those things, really. Shit happens and we deal with it. Well, we try to deal with it, but I live by the motto *"If it's broken, unfixable and you can never see yourself recovering, then open a good bottle of wine, a big bar of chocolate, put on loads of sad music then wallow in self-pity"*. Which is exactly what I did when I got home from my mother's.

I'd told her that I'd called the wedding off because I wasn't sure if I really loved Jack. She thought I was crazy and was so angry at me for not being able to give her a proper reason. How could I tell her what had really happened? She'd probably have turned it round to being my fault! So I'd decided the best thing to do would be just take the grief for this and let it go, rather than be reminded forever that I couldn't keep my man happy. That I was a failure and I forced him into someone else's arms because I bought processed foods, couldn't bake, was undomesticated and didn't know how to look after him like a proper wife should. Oh, and how could I forget, he probably just wanted to see how it felt to put both arms round a woman without getting halfway before being stopped by an ass the size of Kilimanjaro.

So just for good measure, and to add to my misery, which I find is always a nice touch when you're wallowing, I went to my room, opened the wardrobe and took out my beautiful cream-satin wedding dress.

I laid it on the bed and looked at the exquisite detail in the bodice, the pearls shimmering from the lights above, the shine of the material. The freshness and cleanliness of it was just what I needed to fall deeper into my pit of despair. In the background "Endless Love" was playing and the tears just kept rolling down my cheeks.

I'd never really felt suffering in my life, but at that moment I knew nothing physical could ever feel as painful as the way I did inside. My whole life had crashed and burned in front of me, and I had no control over any of it. How could this have happened? The obvious solution to help me make sense of the situation and to calm myself down was . . .

Oh dear, first I had to sit down because my head suddenly felt a little faint.

Half an hour later, wearing my spectacular wedding dress, I re-entered the living room, red wine in one hand, ciggy in the other, looking like the most beautiful bride in the world.

I do *look pretty*, I told myself and I proceeded to perch upon the back of the settee, which meant I could get a good look at my pitiful reflection in the mirror as I continued to drink and sing my heart out to all those very depressing songs.

"*I've lost my frog!*" Sob, sob, hiccup, sob! "*I'm a princess without a frog!*" Large gulp of wine, long drag on fag.

The wedding dress was very much christened that night but, unlike its original intended fate, it was introduced to slurps of red wine and one or two burns from some encounters with my cigarette-tip as I threw out my arms to emphasise my pain (it adds to the dramatic effect, I feel, and drama is the only talent I think I was born with). In fact, my mother often said I was the best actress she'd ever seen, although, having said that, it was normally when I'd been caught doing something I shouldn't have been, and I can't have been that good because she never believed any of my performances.

But at that moment I didn't care about the stupid dress, it was only a prop in my one-woman heartbreaking show, not that I wouldn't care the next day when I sobered up and thought about how much I'd spent on it.

But that night it was trashed and all I wanted to do was keep on drinking, smoking and singing while watching myself in the mirror . . . the prettiest bride that the world would ever have seen . . .

This is the part when I think I passed out, as all I remember after that was waking up on the back of the settee with a very painful neck and a mouth that felt like a rat had climbed inside it and decomposed during the night.

What woke me was the front door slamming shut and when I finally got my eyes adjusted to the light beaming through a crack in the curtains I looked up and saw Jack and my mother standing with mouths open and sheer fear on their faces.

Great! As if this woman doesn't have enough on me already!

It seemed my mother had taken matters into her own hands, and my mother's hands must be huge because she seems to take a lot of matters into them. She'd phoned Jack and apologised for my irrational behaviour, explaining that it was only pre-wedding jitters. Knowing then he was off the hook as I hadn't told the whole story, Jack played along, convinced that I wanted to give things another go.

I'll never forget the disgust in my mother's eyes as she peered down on me, then still looking at me said, "Oh, Jack, I'm sorry you had to see this, it's pitiful. You should be ashamed of yourself, young lady. I know *I'm* ashamed of you. Get off that settee and get that dress off you at once!"

I rolled off the top of the settee, and not because I'm immensely overweight and it's the only way I can get around, but because I couldn't feel my legs. I ended up on all fours on the living-room floor, which again was great for the dress. Satin picks up even the tiniest particles of dirt, you know! I crawled past them as she tutted and sighed and made all sorts of other loud, wonderful noises to show how disapproving she was of my conduct.

I got into the hall and I heard her again apologise for

what a terrible time I must be putting him through and how I should be grateful to have met a man like him! How he treated me so well and how lucky I was that he was willing to give me a second chance.

Call it mind over matter, call it still being slightly drunk from the gallons of wine the night before, but somehow I found an inner strength to pull myself up – well, with a little help from the radiator beside me – and return to the room where judge and jury sat.

Well, you know what? It ain't over till the fat lady sings! and by her interpretation that, of course, was me.

I walked in to face them both.

Jack looked at me with a slight smile on his face, almost patronising, as my mother turned to see me in the door.

And just as she opened her mouth to throw out the next barrage of insults, I looked from one to the other and I started.

"Here's the thing, Jack. I'm not marrying you because I just don't love you. I thought I did, but I was just in love with the idea of being in love. I thought because you spoilt me it was a reflection of how much you loved me, but the truth of the matter is you don't know how to love. You use people and things, you've no respect for me or what I believed in and you've taken a relationship and my trust and, being the coward that you are, you abused both. It's easier for you to hurt and destroy than be honest and noble."

"Mother," I bravely continued, "I love you in more ways than you'll ever know. I've admired your strength

190

and determination over all the years I've known you. You've always been behind me, supporting me, although the methods you've used are sometimes more damaging than constructive . . ." I wavered. "But I know you love me and I thought that was all that mattered. But to stand here and listen to you apologise to him is unforgivable. You're my mother. You're meant to know when I'm hurting, be on my side, listen to my story. Instead you assume that I'm the one at fault. Pre-wedding nerves, Mother? Is that what they call it now when you find your fiancé in bed a week before your wedding with some slapper from his office?"

Silence.

I never really understood the expression "deafening silence" but it all made so much sense now.

Jack stood like a lost schoolchild with his head hung down as my mother staggered slightly and made her way towards the couch before easing herself down to sit. No one spoke – there wasn't too much to say. I felt I needed to finish this, or rant a bit more to be more honest . . .

I walked towards Jack and I put my hand on his face, looked into his big brown eyes and said, "You know, I always believed I'd grow up, find a frog who turned into my prince and live happily ever after. Well, I still do, but Jack, you're just a frog, well, more a toad actually."

The realisation had hit me. I had created this fairy-tale romance with Jack in my own head, and I didn't stop to see the flaws we had as a couple. I was so consumed by living my perfectly wonderful Walt Disney life that I ignored the voices within that told me it was all wrong.

"I don't hate you, Jack. I'm hurt by your betrayal, but truth be told it really was only a matter of time. We weren't meant to be together. We're too different. It's just a love that was never meant to be."

I'd remembered that line from one of the songs I'd listened to last night, and I really had to fight the urge to start singing it. I made a mental note – *this is a serious matter and not a televised musical*. Although the fact that I could catch my reflection in the mirror didn't help.

Jack and I talked for a while about cancelling the wedding. Who would do what, and of course what we'd tell people, but he never fought my decision. It was like he knew I was right and we parted that night knowing that there would be no rekindling of flames.

My mother was still sitting silent on the settee. She had a few little tears running down her face, which moved me more than what had happened between Jack and me, as I couldn't remember a time when I'd ever seen my mother cry.

I sat beside her and I took her hand. It was the first physical contact she and I had shared in a long time. She wasn't the overly emotional kind and rarely displayed acts of affection, but at that moment I felt closer to her than I ever had in my life as she squeezed my hand. She wiped away the tears from her own face, then leant across and brushed mine away too. She looked at me and she smiled, a beautiful, loving smile that only a mother can give. A smile that said a thousand words, telling me that everything was going to be OK. We sat for a while just holding hands. We stopped looking at each other as that, I think, was making us both feel a little uncomfortable.

Then she said, "You know, I think the French are on to something!"

"Sorry?" I knew she could jump from one conversation to another, but even for her this was a new departure.

"Well," she said, "in France frog's legs are a delicacy."

"Yes, Mum – and?"

"I'm just thinking it's not a bad idea. Maybe some frogs deserve to have their legs slashed off, deep-fried and served on a bed of garlic mash!"

A joke? My mother made a joke! After all this time and in this situation. She was on my side, at last, helping cheer me up, giving me a reason to love her and more importantly to smile.

"Why don't you go and pack a few things? Come home with me for a few nights? Just for the company. Let us look after you for a while."

I could think of nothing I'd like more. I reached over and gave her the tightest hug. "Thanks, Mum," I said. "I would really like that right now!"

"Good, because Ann and I are joining Weight Watchers tomorrow night, and it'd do you no harm to come with us."

Mothers. They always get the last word . . .

∽

Antoinette Mangan, originally from Ennis, Co. Clare, has spent most of her adult life working and living in Dublin. She is married with two young children. An accountant for almost twenty years, she is currently a stay-at-home mum. A voracious reader, this is her first foray into writing.

Runner up 1

Poles Apart

Antoinette Mangan

Poles Apart

The journey was punctuated by the constant sound of the siren. Quite loud from the inside of the paddywagon, really much louder than I thought it would be. Though I never had seriously considered the matter in great detail. First of all, I was not expecting to be examining one or its sounds from close quarters. Here I was, Arleen Mc Reddy, in her fortieth year, in the back of a garda van. Yes, me: mother of two young children, wife of Ritchie, eldest daughter, the rock of sense and an accountant.

I lifted my face from my hands and looked at the other occupants. Six in all – well, seven if you counted the female garda accompanying us: only one as really we were not putting up much of a fight. Mind you, not a particularly approachable garda either. I had tried to explain but she was having none of it and stated we could speak to the booking sergeant at the station.

Maveen had her head in her hands. Yvette and Rocca

looked quite terrified. God, perhaps there was a chance they would be deported! Beverly seemed calm. Anna looked serene, almost relaxed. She must have been in this situation or similar before. She leaned forward from the opposite side of the van and patted my knees, saying in her heavily accented Eastern European voice, "Arleen, you need no worry. All will be good for you."

The garda looked up and said, "Ladies, no talking. Remain in your places."

The other thing about these vans is there are no windows, only one on the back door, but you would have to be standing to see out. As we sped across the city I had no idea where we were heading.

I sighed and worried about how I could ever explain my way out of this one. What would people think? My friends, my family, the neighbours? Then I figured, who cares about them? The only person I really should be worried about is Ritchie. Would he believe me?

"And so in conclusion, my Lord, it is patently clear that whatever doubts there were before the incident culminating in this woman's arrest, the said arrest and reason for it leave no doubt that she is unfit to be mother to these children and we recommend that Mr McReddy be granted full custody."

My heart pounded loudly, almost outdoing the siren. My two babies, I could not bear to be parted from them. The madness of it all hit me and I cried silently to myself, trying to pinpoint exactly when my judgement and any shred of common sense, which I once had in abundance, had departed.

Of course, it was the caterpillar.

To be more precise, it was the caterpillar jigsaw. Yep, a puzzle for thirty-six months plus. That very bright, cheery jigsaw made me realise the wide chasm that had developed between Ritchie and me. We had grown apart little by little over the months. I know two small children bring stresses, sleep deprivation, snappy moods and then some disharmony thrown in for good measure. I had been using this to brush aside a number of unpleasant and heretofore uncharacteristic exchanges between us. But that one scene clearly sent up red flags to some part of my self-conscious. How else could I have got into this mess?

Ritchie was playing with Rina, turned three, and had been doing the puzzle with her. I was sitting on the couch holding twelve-month-old Maude.

"That one in your hand goes just below the purple one," I said.

"No, it couldn't, the numbers are not in sequence."

The puzzle is made up of large colourful pieces with numbers.

"Well, it doesn't go in exact numerical order."

Ritchie raised his eyebrows in response.

I was fuming. I couldn't believe it but my own husband, who had witnessed me do the damn thing a thousand times with Rina, actually believed I was not capable of doing it correctly. A lump caught in my throat.

That was what the caterpillar represented. Zero

respect. Being the stay-at-home slave meant I had no brain, I suppose.

Then, of course, he had volunteered to coach a local under-ten's soccer team. He had simply announced it, not put it up for discussion. Between that and his overtime in work it felt like he was spending less and less time at home. I suppose our various rows would not have encouraged that. Not that they were fierce, just constant low-grade snipping.

The day after the caterpillar incident, I was dashing around getting organised as I had a dental appointment at three thirty. Ritchie was due home to baby-sit.

It was two forty-five when I picked up the phone and left a message. "Ritchie, hiya, ring me when you get this. Are you on the way home?"

Shortly afterwards, standing in the kitchen, I picked up the receiver on the third ring.

"Shit, I forgot and I'm just going into a meeting. Sorry – can't you make another appointment?"

"Ritchie, I've waited weeks for this one and the dentist will go mad at my late cancellation."

"Look, I'm sorry but what can I do?"

"Ohhh, honestly, Ritchie – aah, nothing! What time will you be home?"

"Late, probably eight. This meeting will be a long one."

Half an hour later I was closing the door of our small period residence in Glasnevin and heading to the park with the girls. Soon Rina was up and down the slide while

Maude was dozing in her buggy. Sitting on the bench, I nodded as Anna, a tall dark-haired nanny, approached. We had chatted on many occasions in the park while Rina and the eldest of her care played together. Anna sat down beside me on the bench.

"How are you, Arleen?"

"Fine," I lied.

"You not look too good." She gently touched my arm.

I started to cry. Christ, I could not believe it! What was wrong with me? I just responded to the kindness in her voice and was feeling so low. I pulled a tissue out, trying to disguise my distress but in vain.

"Arleen, what is so bad for you?"

"Anna, oh, just feeling sorry for myself. A bad row with my husband."

"But you will make up good later." She smiled.

"I'm not so sure – things are not good for us right now." I ended up telling her my woes. It was a relief just to be able to talk to someone, a stranger really, removed from our lives.

"I have answer – works always to make things better."

"It's not that simple."

"Always this works."

"What does?"

"The pole dance."

"What, Anna? Send him to a club with strippers? How will that help?"

"No, not him go to club. You bring club to him."

I was looking at her in complete bewilderment.

She continued, "You will be pole dancer."

I laughed at the thought.

"But no, with help, you could do the dancing. I show you."

The look of shock and horror must have been written all over my face.

"It is not like you maybe think so. It would be like gym, exercise, no? Keeps figure good, no?" She patted her flat tummy as if to emphasis the point.

It transpired that Anna was a nanny by day but a few nights a week she was a pole dancer in a club in a side street just off Parnell Square. She was running a class on a Wednesday afternoon, her day off from nannying.

I didn't think about it again until the following Monday. Well, thoughts did drift across my mind from time to time. I pushed them away. For almost the last four years I had been consumed with pregnancy, new babies and motherhood. Freedom – God, I missed those single days! The ability to walk out the door with no one to think about except myself. Now it was buggies, bags, nappies, mugs, bottles. Sleepless nights, no lunch or coffee breaks, on duty twenty-four seven. Friends had fallen by the wayside. Single ones with no understanding of what my life was now like. Ones with children just the same as me, too bloody exhausted to go out at night. Colleagues at work were busy commuting. Sometimes it felt like I was the only adult on our road. Days would go by with no adult conversation, except the sharp exchanges with Ritchie. I really wanted some sense of adventure and to feel alive again. I needed to have fun. Anything other than this harried, wrecked and cranky forty-year-old woman I had become.

I organised baby-sitting, Ritchie's mum mainly. I told Ritchie I was taking up yoga. Well, it was practically yoga, wasn't it? All that twisting and turning. Ritchie seemed pleased that I was organising something to do for myself.

"Rina, baby, Mummy is going out but Granny is minding you. Come here – give me a hug."

"Where you going? I want to come!"

"No, baby. Granny needs you to help mind Maude. She'll read you a story."

I rubbed her head and she ran into the playroom. I kissed Maude. "Thanks, Marie."

"You just go out and relax and enjoy yourself, dear. You need a bit of a break. Go for a coffee after. We will be fine."

"Thanks."

And so there I was, standing outside a clean and polished basement door of the Balamorry Hotel, on Setanta Street. A large brass plate said "GIANNO DANCE CLUB". I had parked the car on Parnell Square and walked the three minutes to this spot. I tapped demurely and Anna opened up the door.

"Arleen, come in! Good you arrive, no?"

"Yes." I laughed nervously.

Stepping inside, I could see it was plusher and a lot less seedy than I expected. The stage was a good size with four poles at various points on it. There were crushed red-velvet drapes tied back with gold tasselled ropes. Tables and chairs were set out in a horseshoe arrangement around the stage. At the opposite end to the performance area was a bar, not unlike one in any hostelry in the city. The whole club was lit up and bright. In fact, a total modern and upmarket venue.

There were four other women there, two Irish and two of other nationalities.

Maveen was a few years younger than I, similar to myself and presumably in a situation like me. At least, I assumed so, as we did not exchange details regarding the reason we were there or where we lived or any other personal matters. Beverly was from Sean McDermott Street and was quite happy to share her life story with us.

"Hope to go to Turkey, you know. Mate of mine earns a packet out there dancin', like. They love the blondes and white skin. Good chance to work in an upmarket club. Need to do it while the bod is in good shape. Me ma would kill me if she knew I was doing this, like." She seemed to be at most in her mid-twenties.

Rocca and Yvette spoke hardly any English so it was difficult to ascertain why they were there. Perhaps they were the real deal and would have to earn a living here or like Anna were supplementing another income to send money back home.

Looking at us all gathered together in tracksuits and runners, we had the appearance of a group about to do a serious workout in the gym. My palms were wet with sweat. I had to remind myself I was not doing anything illegal – a bit subversive maybe, but definitely not illegal.

That first class Anna did a demonstration for us to Bon Jovi's "Livin on a Prayer". To be honest it reminded me of belly-dancing. Sensual and not sleazy in any way. Perhaps that was because there were no scantily clad women or no lecherous half-jarred male customers present. One thing was certain: Anna was a great dancer. She explained that after eight classes we would be able to do a simple routine. She showed us that it was how you did the moves that mattered. You always had to be elegant and smooth in moving from one position to the next. At least, with her not-perfect English, that was my interpretation. We went nowhere near a pole that first class. Just did some moves on the floor in a space she had cleared in the middle of the club. Finally she gave us some exercises to do before the next class.

Between classes, life continued as normal. Me running around all day with my two babies and doing housework and errands. Ritchie arriving home and the two of us not really talking except to function as a household.

"Can you drop this suit to the dry cleaners tomorrow?"

"Ritchie, can you get home early tomorrow, I've a doctor's appointment?"

"Any chance you could get Rina ready for bed for me?"

Conducting an affair must be something like this, I

thought. Sneaking around, telling lies and then feeling a bit guilty and even a bit, well, weird. Me a pole dancer! Imagine my mother ringing.

"Hello, dear, how are my little pets?"

"Great, Mum. How are you and Dad?"

"Fine, and you?"

"Have I told you I am pole-dancing on Wednesday afternoons?"

"That's nice, dear, good to hear you're getting out of the house."

What would Catherine, my best friend from school, make of it? She lived in Galway. I imagined the giggle we would have about it.

"Arleen, are you for real?"

"Yes, I am."

"Well, you'll have to show me some useful moves!"

Mainly I thought of Ritchie. His face and reaction as I would perform my dance for him. I mean, what occasion would I find to do this jigging around? I couldn't remember the last time we had a kiss or a hug not to even mention sex. When would I get a chance with the children, who between them had me up four nights out of seven? Jesus, who was I kidding? Did I honestly believe pole-dancing would save us?

Ritchie and I had been so happy. We had met fifteen years before, when I was twenty-five and he was twenty-eight, working together in the bank though not in the same department. I used to go from my finance department to his, following up on items in my reconciliations. As he was the assistant manager in the dealing room, over the team doing the transactions, he would help me resolve my queries. We got on really well and used to have a good laugh. He left for another job two years later. I was sorry to see him go but did not think too much about it.

Ritchie was gone from the bank about a year when I met him out one night on the town in the Palace bar on Fleet Street. He was well jarred and we got talking. I was with some friends and we were all chatting to the group with him. After a while we were alone together.

"Arleen, I always fancied you."

"How very subtle of you!" I quipped.

"No, Honest Injun, I did – well, I still do," he admitted somewhat sheepishly. "I just never had the courage to ask you out."

"Well, what's stopping you now?"

"Perhaps you won't take me seriously and I'll spoil a good friendship."

"Well, fine, Ritchie, but you might never get this opportunity again. A good-looking girl like me won't always be available, you know."

"Hmmm, you're right, better not let this chance go." Gently he placed his arm around my waist.

Later he walked me to a taxi and kissed me tenderly on the lips. We had agreed to meet the following week. I could not believe it. Little old me at five foot four with an almost-six-footer. He had lovely wavy light-brown hair and green eyes which just sparkled when he smiled. They were his best feature.

Soon we were very serious about each other. My family was mad about Ritchie despite the fact he was a Dub. My father and him were always ribbing each other about the Dubs versus Kerry in football. His family was warm and welcoming to me and in no time I felt like I'd known them all my life. We moved in together about twelve months later. Bought a house four years after that and moved to our current one after we married. Marriage happened when I was thirty-three and Ritchie thirty-five. We were in no rush to populate the planet. There was so much to do, study to complete, careers to progress, super holidays to go on. Ah, the holidays! Thailand, China, the States three times and Mexico. We really enjoyed ourselves. Course we had our rows, just like everyone else.

I remember the night I discovered I was expecting Rina. We had been out with some friends in a café in town. It was a balmy August Thursday night. We were sitting out on the pavement on chairs sipping wine – that is, everyone except me. For some reason I had driven my car into town. I felt that pre-period sensation with real tender breasts. In fact, I had been feeling like this for over ten days. My period was overdue. I wondered if I could be pregnant. I made my excuses and went to a pharmacy I spotted across the road and bought a test kit, popping it into my handbag for later. Finally, I got Ritchie home after a pint in Grogan's to round off the evening. Dashing in the door, I ran upstairs to the loo. My hand was shaking when I saw the clear blue line indicating the good news.

"Ritchie, a present for you!" I waved the wand in his face.

"What's that, love? Jaysus, is it what I think it is?"

"Yep. It sure is!"

"Wow! Arleen, that's just, just . . ." There were tears welling up in his eyes. "Let's keep it quiet until we're certain."

"Ritchie, I am certain, but yeah – until we get through the first trimester."

He hugged me joyfully.

The excitement. It nearly killed me to keep it to myself for those first twelve weeks. I could hardly pass a shop with baby gear in it without dashing in to buy those tiny little newborn vests. I think everyone knew long before I told them – well, in work where they saw me every day. Perhaps it had something to do with the way I kept patting my tummy. In the later months of my pregnancy a colleague used to laugh at the way I held my hands under the bump. She said it looked like I was afraid it would just drop out. I was so proud of that bump. Luckily, despite our late start at a family, I had a healthy and fit pregnancy with no complications. Equally the labour was short but goddamn painful.

When that scrap of humanity was placed for the first time on my tummy, I wept like never before. Unadulterated joy. Counting her toes and fingers and kissing the tip of her nose. Rina was such a perfect pink doll. Ritchie was speechless. Holding her tiny little hand and just staring in amazement at it. We were so proud of our little bundle and so delighted to show her off. Twenty-five months later Maude arrived. Another day of excitement to treasure.

After Maude I felt I could not continue to work at the pace I had done up to that point. Over the years I had been promoted in the bank and was head of a large department. The hours were cruel at certain busy periods and I felt I needed time out to spend with the girls. We decided that I should take a career break for two years and then reassess the situation. Like any other job, I had good days and bad ones. The bright warm days in the park made up for some of the not-so-good ones: the days when exhaustion made it difficult to remain calm and loving all day. I never regretted my decision for one moment, though I wondered if my husband would have appreciated me better if I was out earning a crust.

Ritchie was fantastic with them both. Adored his girls and they him. It was wonderful to see them at play. His head and Rina's buried in a book. Both had the same hair colouring and same aqua-green eyes. Maude had my colouring – dark-brown hair and brown eyes.

By week five Anna progressed us to the stage and dancing, or rather moving, around the pole. She also had us in high shoes and some costumes she had put together. Well, the tracksuit and runners were too cumbersome. These outfits were more like belly-dancing gear. We could wear as little or as much of it as we liked. I opted for the complete outfit. I wasn't altogether comfortable with dancing around in tiny thongs. Put everyone off childbirth. That is, those present that hadn't ravaged their bodies with it.

Anna showed us how to put a special powdery substance on our hands to stop slipping on the pole. The powder had shiny silver scattered through it so that it was more silver than white. "That is so no messy on clothing or customers. Not looking like baker-woman, eh? These men not want to see like woman of house." We all laughed.

The funny thing was that I was really enjoying my "yoga" class – well, certainly when I was there, and it was a laugh with the other women. I loved the freedom of just letting my body go and dancing. But I still was racked with guilt every time I left the house. My mother-in-law must have thought I was the most dedicated mother who reluctantly tore herself away from her babies for two and a half hours weekly. Christ, if only she knew! I suppose I was nervous of being found out but somehow that added an edge to my Wednesday-afternoon activity.

At last the paddywagon arrived at whatever station was dealing with us. It was in the Phoenix Park. The place was heaving with gardaí and some obvious-looking suspects, while others in suits were running around with files talking rather excitedly about their clients.

Immediately we were directed to a room down a long corridor. We were informed we would have to wait, as personnel were taken up with a very serious arrest. I turned to the female garda who had accompanied us in the van.

"Can I ring home? My kids are being looked after by my mother-in-law and I am expected home about now."

"I'm afraid you'll have to wait until you're processed."

"But surely I cannot be detained like this without contacting my solicitor?"

The rest of the women started to grumble and growl in support of my request.

"Jaysus, officer, you got to let her. What about her kids?" Beverly asked.

"Sorry, ladies, you'll be dealt with soon."

Two hours later we were processed. I was going up the walls and really upset. My bag with my mobile phone and clothes had been left behind, or at least I had not been allowed to lift anything during the chaotic departure from the club. I was wearing loose see-through red pantaloons and a bra top to match with gold metal discs decorating the neckline, and six-inch heels.

The sergeant in charge of our case was unapologetic. He took Maveen, Beverly and me to another room and explained that we were free to go. We had been arrested as part of a suspected racket of illegal-immigrant trafficking. The other three were left behind. We were then taken to another smaller room nearer the front of the building and allowed to make our calls. I phoned Ritchie and asked him to pick me up. In fairness, he did not ask for any details and said very curtly that he was on the way.

I heard Ritchie long before I saw him. That was unusual for him.

"Officer, there has to be a perfectly rational explanation. My wife was at a yoga class, for Christ's sake! I don't know how she ended up in a, in a . . . club," I heard him mumble.

"Well, sir, all I can tell you is that the club was where she was picked up. As you say, there is no doubt an explanation."

When Ritchie entered the room I walked meekly over to him. I was shocked at how worried and distressed he looked.

"Jesus, Arleen, are you OK? When you didn't turn up at home we were so worried. We thought an accident. Christ, I even thought you'd gone and done something stupid like . . ." he trailed off.

"Well, I have done something stupid."

"You mean you tried to . . . you know . . ."

"Harm myself? God, no! Nothing like that."

"Just, you haven't been like yourself. I mean, we haven't been. That is, I really have been neglectful and not helping at home as much as . . . I've been a selfish prick. If anything had happened to you!"

I touched his face. "Ritchie, honestly, I am fine physically and mentally. The kids?"

"Fine, fine, really."

"Look, I'm sorry, I can explain."

"Arleen, shush, let's just get you out of here." Ritchie gently placed his arm around my shoulder and led me out of the room.

"Wait a sec." I turned to Maveen and Beverly. "Are you OK?"

Both smiled, and I hugged each one of them.

"Best of luck then. Ritchie, let's go."

We walked to the front desk and the officer went through the bags they had lifted until I pointed out the one that was mine. Ritchie picked it up and carried it. We walked through the doors and into our car.

Sitting in the car, Ritchie hugged me. "Listen, I've organised for the kids to stay overnight with Ashling." Ashling was his sister. "We need time and space to talk."

All I could do in response was cry. The tears came with big rasping gulps. I felt so overwhelmed and could not control my physical response to his softly spoken words. Ritchie hugged me even tighter.

I smiled and said through the tears, "I'll need to get out of this gear before I get arrest – ed," I stuttered and mumbled, "Sorry."

We both started to laugh.

"Arleen, I do want to know what in Christ's name you were up to, but later when you can talk about it." He tenderly kissed my nose.

As we drove off I began to relax and knew that somehow or other we would weather this episode of madness. We would be all right. Our family would remain intact.

"Begging your pardon, My Lord, I know this is unusual but it appears that Mr McReddy has withdrawn his petition for divorce and apologises to the court for wasting their time."

❧

Vanessa O'Loughlin is thirty-seven, the busy mother of Sophie, seven, and Sam, two. Writing everything from detective fiction to children's stories, Vanessa runs INKwell Writers' Workshops, bringing bestselling authors to inspire and guide writers at intensive one-day workshops. Vanessa also won second place in the RTÉ Radio 1 Today with Pat Kenny Show, the RTÉ Guide and Mills & Boon Writing Competition this year.

Runner up 2

An Elaborate Deception

Vanessa O'Loughlin

An Elaborate
Deception

Can I tell you something in confidence? It's always difficult to know if you can trust someone, trust them absolutely I mean, not just trust them to water the plants while you're away or to collect your newspaper. So I need to know that you can be trusted. Particularly as the subject's a little delicate.

Delicate. Perhaps that's an understatement.

Would you describe having an affair with someone else's husband *and* getting yourself stalked into the bargain as delicate? That's how Nicole put it, pushing her straggly blonde hair anxiously from her face.

"It's a bit delicate, Emmie," she said, "I don't know where to begin . . ."

I knew something was bothering her. She's my oldest friend; we were in college together, used to be inseparable, although we've drifted a bit in the years since I married Adam. We were both terribly young but it was all so perfect: the ring, the fabulous wedding, exotic honeymoon. After college he went into the family diamond business and his parents gave us this beautiful house overlooking Killiney Bay, and then the kids came along. Nicole and I lost touch a bit – things were so different for her. But she had her career, all those media parties, rubbing shoulders with the in-crowd. She was always in the glossy magazines looking fabulous with a glass of champagne in her hand, laughing with some celebrity – she didn't want to be stuck at home with two-year-old twin boys with chickenpox.

So there we were, sitting in the conservatory on a Sunday morning. Adam was away and the boys were over with friends, and really it was the first time we'd sat down together for such a long time. Nicole had dropped in with the twins' birthday presents – she never forgot birthdays and Christmas – and she was rushing, but she looked so miserable I just had to ask her in.

We made small talk as I put the kettle on, the morning sun slanting in through the kitchen window, dust particles fairy-dancing along its length. Chatted about the family, about a holiday she was thinking of booking in the Maldives. Then as I poured the tea there was one of those uncomfortable silences. It's funny how people change; we really are so different now. So I asked how work was going.

"Same as usual." She had been perching on the edge of a wicker armchair, as if she didn't really have time to stay, but relaxed back into the seat as she answered. "There's always some panic on in PR. It doesn't matter what the project is, something always goes wrong. It's just a case of how bad it is and how fast you can fix it."

"Are you still working for that awful woman?"

"Sally? No, she left. I run the show now. They made me a partner a couple of months ago."

"Really? That must be terribly stressful."

Nicole smiled. "It's not too bad . . ."

"So why the long face? Had another disaster on the man front?"

She blushed slightly. "Not exactly. Love life's fine actually, but," she hesitated for a moment, moving back to the edge of the chair, "I seem to have acquired a stalker."

"Good God, what on earth's happened?"

"It's a bit delicate, Emmie, I don't know where to begin . . ."

I sat forward in my own chair as I poured more tea. I couldn't help feeling enthralled. "I thought you had to be famous to get stalked. Are you sure?"

Nicole nodded, sighing again, staring blindly out of the window. "The guards seem to think so."

"The guards? It must be serious."

"It's getting that way. Someone left two blackbirds outside my front door. Dead. Horrible. Apart from a pool of blood under their heads they were perfect. Male and female, one brown, one black. At first I thought it was a cat but they'd been sort of positioned, their breasts together, heads facing the house." She shivered involuntarily.

"But that could have just been a teenage prank. My

221

boys get up to some awful tricks – you could write a book about them."

"I thought so too, but then there's the silent phone calls and these wretched flowers that keep arriving. Ugly great orange things. Positively phallic. Parrot flowers, I think they're called."

"But why didn't you call and tell me? When did all this start?"

Nicole stood up, and although it was warm in the conservatory, the air heavy with the scent of hyacinths on the windowsill, she pulled her coat around her, folding her arms tightly as she looked out into the garden.

"A couple of months ago. When my briefcase was stolen from my car."

"Why on earth did you leave your briefcase in the car?"

"I didn't do it on purpose. I was at the petrol station and the phone rang just as I was putting the petrol cap back on. I had my handbag so I didn't even think of the briefcase. And of course I forgot to lock the car because I was on the phone."

"But who took the briefcase? The guards must have some idea. Surely there are fingerprints or something?"

"Nope. He had gloves on apparently. And the CCTV footage is terrible. It's that place in Sandymount – you can see from the monitor inside it's very poor quality. He was wearing a fleece jacket and baseball cap and dark glasses and it's all so blurry that his own mother wouldn't recognise him."

"But surely it isn't a real stalker? It couldn't be – have

you upset anyone who could be playing an awful joke?"

Nicole paused. It was a long pause. "We really can't think of anything. Except, well, this man I'm seeing. It could be something to do with him I suppose. He's . . ." she paused again, her face blazing red, "married."

"Well, there you go then. Must be his wife – she's hired someone to follow you. Problem solved. Why don't you just get the guards to go and have a chat with her?"

"It's not her. We're absolutely certain. She doesn't suspect a thing."

"How can you be so sure? If this chap's lying to his wife, he could be lying to you as well. He could have let something slip."

Nicole shook her head emphatically. "No. There's no way she knows. He's tested her just to make sure."

"But she must know – she's trying to frighten you off."

Nicole shrugged. "I doubt it. It just wouldn't add up. No, the guards think it's some bloke I've bumped into who was following me when I stopped to get the petrol. Problem is they can't do anything until they find out who it is. And I'm not sleeping." She put her head in her hands. "I'm just so scared. You read about these things. What if he comes after me in the middle of the night, breaks in . . . I just don't feel safe any more."

I went and hugged her. Her face was streaked with silent tears as, wrestling a tissue from her pocket, she blew her nose noisily.

"I just don't know what I'm going to do. I've got to get my act together in work. They've been great, but their patience can't last forever. I just feel that if I could get some sleep I could get on top of it."

"You poor thing. All that worry. What about this man, is he supporting you?"

"He's trying his best, but he can't exactly move in, can he?"

"Could he leave his wife?"

She shook her head vigorously. "God, no. And I wouldn't want him to. He's talked about it, but I couldn't live with myself. There are children involved."

"I see." I paused, thinking. "Look, Adam's away for a few days, but I'm sure he'll think it's a good idea. Why don't you move in here for a while? We've tons of space and the security system's excellent. Your stalker couldn't possibly get in. We regularly use a security firm to patrol the place if Adam has to bring stock home. I'll call them. If your stalker turns up he won't be expecting an ex-SAS man with an Alsatian, that's for sure! They might even be able to catch him for you."

"Oh, Emmie, you're so kind, but I couldn't do that!"

I ignored her protests. "Of course you could. You certainly aren't giving in to this maniac by staying with an old friend if that's what's worrying you, and you'll be completely safe here. The twins would love to see you, you won't believe how they've grown, and I know Adam wouldn't hear of you staying in that house all on your own. It's decided. Pop home and get a bag. I won't take no for an answer!"

Ten minutes later I watched the gates gently closing on the fiery red tail-lights of her car. She really was a complete wreck, had almost jumped into the air when her mobile rang. I'd had to be firm about her staying, but it was the perfect solution.

As soon as the gates closed behind her, Nicole glanced into her rear-view and wing mirrors, checking behind her, trying to be sure she was leaving the mansion alone. It was becoming a habit. Sometimes she was sure someone was following her, catching the flash of light on a windscreen out of the corner of her eye, a woman in a grey raincoat on the pavement, a man with a hood pulled down over his face running for the bus.

Pulling up outside her own pristine townhouse, pinpricks of sweat stung Nicole's back. The complex was gated, exclusive, but this was the part she hated most. Unfastening her safety belt, pulling her handbag onto her knee and flicking off the central locking, she looked around anxiously, trying to see through the low walls separating the front gardens, peering behind the manicured shrubs. She could lock herself into the house, into the car, but she was totally exposed as she approached her front door. *What if someone ran up with a knife, tried to bundle her into a van?*

With the door key in her hand, she felt a sharp blast of icy sea air as she sprang from her enviable red convertible and sprinted up the steep flight of granite steps. Waves crashed on the other side of the Dart line, the early morning blue sky now replaced by a monotone grey, as sea and sky merged into one. Her heart slowed marginally as she slammed the front door behind her, hammering at the alarm pad with a manicured nail, double-checking the perimeter was still secure.

Oh God, Nicole thought, *Emmie was so sweet, so concerned.* Sinking onto her haunches, her back to the comforting strength of the door, Nicole buried her head in her hands. *It was all such a mess.* Her whole life was a bloody mess. Worry began to claw at her gut as she thought of her best friend. What the hell should she do? What was the right thing? Should she tell her the truth? Nicole had considered every conceivable method of communication over the years, of writing a letter even, perhaps sending an email. A message in a bottle would be the right way, dropped into an ocean from an island a million miles away. *But writing just wasn't the right thing.*

The letter reappeared before her eyes, the hand neat, sloping, confident, the ink blue. *Dear Mum . . .*

After all the years, after all the nights of lying awake staring at the ceiling wondering what if? What if things had been different? What if she had told Emmie the truth at the beginning when they had first become friends? What if she'd had someone to share her grief with, to help her get on with her life? And Emmie was right: her love life had been a disaster. Nicole couldn't help wondering if it was because part of her was missing that she was drawn to totally unsuitable men who would never commit, never come close enough for her to share her secret, bare her soul. Tears began to prick her eyes again as a sob escaped from her lips.

Dear Mum . . .

Lisa she was called now, she was eighteen, doing well

in school, looking forward to university. What else? What else? Nicole ran her hand through her untidy curls, already escaping from her ponytail, clutching at the roots in despair.

The rest was in the letter.

And the letter was in her briefcase.

But she'd been late for work, realised before she'd read the first few lines, her key in the ignition, that she'd forgotten to fill the car with petrol – her mind had been so preoccupied with the bloody pitch for that contract. So she'd glanced at the postmark and torn herself from it, thrusting the letter into her briefcase, her bloody briefcase, promising herself a full half an hour to read it locked in her office after the meeting.

Oh God, everything was a total mess. Had Lisa wanted to meet her? Had she given her phone number, suggested a date? Now she'd never know, and Lisa probably thought that she, Nicole, didn't care, that she didn't want any contact with her baby. And as if that wasn't enough, now she had some lunatic after her. Someone who had Lisa's letter, someone who knew her darkest secret. A sob catching in her throat, before the dam burst Nicole picked herself up off the mat. At least she'd be safe at Emmie's – she could get a couple of nights' sleep and be back here on Friday ready and refreshed for the board meeting. There had to be some way of finding Lisa now she'd made contact. If she only she could get some sleep, Nicole was sure she'd come up with a plan.

I checked my watch as I went back into the house,

closing the front door firmly behind me. It would take
Nicole about twenty minutes to get home and another half
an hour to pack. Plenty of time to get ready. She was going
to ring work and tell them she needed a few days off, was
taking a break. And the twins wouldn't be home until
tomorrow so I knew we'd have plenty of time to talk.

What could I do? She obviously needed a friend, was
quite at her wits' end.

As I passed the hall table, I picked up our wedding
photograph. Two beautiful people smiled back at me,
apparently blissfully happy. I had done my absolute best,
but somehow the truth had always bobbed around me
like a marker buoy, hidden by the everyday waves of life
but rearing itself in my mind every time we had an
argument, whenever he went away. Adam's mother's
voice came back to me as I looked into his hypnotic blue
eyes and I died all over again.

"Emma, darling, just sit down beside me, will you? I
know this will be a shock, but it's for the best that you
know. I need you to help me."

It was only a week until our wedding. She had sent
Adam off on some errand, had called me over to the
house "for a chat". My stomach had flipped as she spoke
– what on earth could she be going to say to me?

"It's about Nicole." She said her name as if it left a
bad taste in her mouth. Immediately defensive of my
best friend, my bridesmaid, I opened my mouth to speak
but, expecting it, Adam's mother held up her finger,

"I know how close you two are, my dear, and that
might make this more difficult, but I have to tell you a

story. I'm sure you know that Adam and Nicole were at school together, that they both ended up going to the same university where they met you. But I'm not sure whether you know that they were more than good friends."

I interrupted her. "They went out together when they were sixteen, Nicole told me."

Again the finger. "She did, but did she tell you that she was Adam's first love and that they were inseparable for six months?"

I shrugged. *It was young love, of course they were inseparable.*

Adam's mother continued, the rings on her fingers catching and refracting the morning sunlight like flashes of lightning.

"And did Nicole tell you that during that spring she became pregnant?"

My mouth opened involuntarily in surprise. "No, she's never mentioned it . . . and Adam never said . . . ."

Adam's mother arched her heavily plucked eyebrows and pursed her lips. Her lipstick was brown, her thin lips outlined in a darker shade that bled slightly into the fine cracks which were appearing under her heavy make-up. She always wore her dark hair dragged back from her face, giving her a perpetually surprised expression.

"Adam didn't, doesn't, know."

"What?" I almost shrieked. "How on earth could he *not know?*"

His mother put her arm firmly around me and patted my shoulder, her pearls jangling and clanking against the numerous gold chains she always wore.

"Don't worry, my dear, it was our secret, mine and Nicole's, and now it must be yours and mine."

"But I don't understand . . ."

She held up her hand serenely. "It was all a long time ago. Nicole and Adam had been going out together for quite a while, but that night she called over and seemed a little upset. Adam's bike had had a puncture or something and he was late coming home from his scout meeting, so I sat and chatted to her. I could see something was wrong and eventually it all came out."

"But how can Adam not know about it?"

"Well, we decided it would be for the best if as few people as possible knew. You know Nicole's parents were terribly strict and she was terrified what might happen if they found out, so I arranged for her to go and stay with a friend of mine in France. It was a sort of placement to improve her language skills, a chance of a lifetime scholarship. She went for six months."

I nodded slowly. "Her parents were delighted – she told me she came home virtually bilingual, sailed through her exams."

"Exactly."

"But what happened to the baby?"

"I arranged for it to be adopted by an American couple. It was all very neat. No loose ends, no need for anyone to fret. Adam was a bit upset about her going away, but of course he met someone else over the summer, and then I decided he'd do well to board for his last two years of school, so he didn't really see her again, which was probably just as well. It was quite a surprise when I found out they were at the same university, but by then, of course, Adam had met you, and you're so good for him, my dear, that I really couldn't allow anything to come between you."

"But –"

"There's no need for buts, my dear. You love Adam and he loves you and you will build a family together. I just didn't want this thing suddenly appearing at you out of nowhere in perhaps twenty years' time and ruining everything. I might not be around to explain to Adam, so I just felt that it was important you knew but that we kept it between ourselves."

The gate buzzer interrupted my thoughts.

"You were quick, darling, was everything all right at home?" I opened the front door wide, embraced Nicole on the doorstep. She had been crying, her make-up scored below her thick lashes. She kissed me, held me tight for a moment before we parted. Dropping a small overnight bag in the hall, she nodded. "No more flowers, thank goodness, and I've set the alarm, so I only hope there won't be any problems. I wondered if I should have left my car there to make it look like I'm in?"

I smiled reassuringly. "I don't think it would make much difference, honestly."

"Oh Emmie, thanks so much for this! You really don't know how much it means."

I patted her on the arm. "Come and have a cup of tea, tell me all about it."

"Emmie? Emmie, where the hell are you? The traffic

was mental – it's taken me two bloody hours to get here from the airport."

We were in the drawing room, Nicole curled up like a cat on the sofa. I'd lit the fire, opened a bottle of wine after lunch. She froze as the front door slammed shut.

"Emmie?" Louder this time, then the door opened. "Emmie?"

Adam's voice trailed off as he marched into the drawing room, his grey pinstripe jacket half off, tie loose. "Nicole?"

I put my glass down on the mantelpiece – I'd hardly touched it as I listened to Nicole talk about her career, about the things that had been happening to her over the past few weeks.

"Darling, I wasn't expecting you so soon – I thought your flight was later."

Staring fixedly at Nicole, he replied, trance-like, "I took an earlier flight. Meeting finished early. Tiffany's want everything we can give them."

"That's wonderful news, darling. I'll get you a G & T. Nicole's staying with us for a few days. " I reached up to kiss him, whispering in his ear. "She's having a tough time."

"How are you, Adam? Haven't seen you in a while." Nicole forced herself to speak, her tone wooden.

I turned, smiling. "You two chat while I get some ice. Sit down, darling, take the weight off your feet, you've had a long day."

His eyes locked to Nicole's, Adam nodded.

Slipping from the room, I pulled the door behind me

but hovered for a moment in the hall, my hand on the polished brass knob.

What would they say? I could just hear Adam. He sounded like he was hissing.

"Nicole, what the feck are you doing here?"

Nicole's voice was a loud whisper. She sounded affronted, wounded. "Emmie's my friend, Adam. I came over earlier with the stuff for the twins. She saw I looked wrecked, asked how I was. I had to tell her about the stalker. I got more of those awful flowers yesterday. I'm scared, Adam. Really scared. I can't sleep. She suggested I come over for a few days. I thought you were in London until Thursday – she said you were away."

It was Adam's turn to sound confused. "We have a dinner party on Tuesday night, clients. Emmie's organised everything, caterers, some girl who sings . . . but what the hell were you thinking? You can't stay here."

"It wasn't my idea!"

"What do you mean? Do you think she knows?" His voice had risen slightly, had lost its normal confident edge. The sofa creaked as he collapsed into the soft leather. I didn't need to hear any more. I left them to chat, humming as I went into the kitchen. They had a lot to discuss – we were bonded in more ways than one.

"How are we getting on?"

I closed the door firmly behind me and handed Adam his drink. Cork dry gin with Schweppes and a slice of lime. Just how he liked it. He gulped it down like it was a lifesaving elixir.

"Emmie, darling, I'm getting a bit of a headache – would you mind if I skipped dinner and got an early night?"

"Oh Nicole, darling, don't leave us yet! Adam's only just come home and he hasn't seen you for ages."

Nicole uncurled her long legs and started to get up. "Really, Emmie . . ."

Before she could move any further I picked up a silver-framed photo from the bureau and handed it to her wordlessly. It was heavier than she expected and she nearly dropped it.

"What's this? Oh, how could I forget? Weren't the Botanic Gardens the perfect place for a wedding reception? Do you remember the butterflies?"

As she spoke, she smiled and looked more closely at the photograph.

Her smile faded as she took it in. Suddenly she paled, two bright red patches flaring on her cheeks. She really didn't look well.

"Emmie – the flowers!"

"South African, just like my diamond . . ." I raised my hand, the huge lozenge-shaped rock on my finger catching the light thrown from the fire. It was beginning to die, the last embers glowing at its heart.

Nicole stared at me, her eyes beseeching, disbelieving.

"Adam, darling, do you have something to tell me?" I looked from my husband to Nicole. I knew for certain that the last time she had seen him she had been lying breathless and sweating in his arms, their souls joined as they had been when they were sixteen.

Adam didn't respond but contemplated the ice cracking in his glass as Nicole's mouth fell open.

I looked from one of them to the other and cleared my throat.

"I'd like to hear it from you, Adam, if you don't mind. Have the decency to do the right thing and tell me honestly."

In the soft light from the side lamps his face looked older, creases etched by laughter and salt air running like a road map from the corners of his eyes. His sandy hair was thinning, strands of grey glittering at his temples. I sighed inwardly. He was getting better looking as he got older, his face maturing like a Hollywood star's. Unlike a Hollywood star, he didn't seem to have anything to say.

I filled the lengthening silence myself. "Well, perhaps we'll move on. You never were very good at telling the truth, my darling. Now I think Nicole has something very important to tell you, Adam. I'm sure it would have been simpler to put it all on the back of a postcard, but I think it's high time we got a few things out in the open, don't you, Nicole?"

"I, Emmie, I don't know what you mean, I don't understand . . ."

"Oh, I think you do, Nicole. I know there's rather a lot going on here, but the flowers rather give the game away, don't they? I thought you'd remember, realise immediately. Parrot flowers, darling. South African parrot flowers. The Botanic Gardens. Our wedding reception?"

Her eyes darted from me to Adam, her face paralysed like an animal trapped in a corner.

"But why? Why, Emmie?"

I paused, considering my words. "I would have thought that was obvious even to you, Nicole, with your rather peculiar interpretation of friendship. You've been sleeping with my husband. For quite a while actually, but I don't have to tell you that, do I? And to be perfectly honest, it really has gone far enough. There's only so much even I can take. So now it's time for us all to do the right thing and face a few home truths."

"But those birds . . . they were horrible!" Her lips were contorted, the pain written across her face like a headline.

"I know. They were meant to be."

It sounded blunt, but it was the truth. It had been pretty horrible finding out my husband was spending half his business trips with my best friend. It had ripped me to the core. But tonight I was determined to stay in control, determined to win one last battle.

"So, Nicole, I think you have something important to tell Adam."

She was shell-shocked, was looking at me in total disbelief, her head to one side.

I sighed impatiently. "That summer, when you went to France. It's time Adam found out the truth."

Nicole's skin turned to alabaster as I spoke, as she realised what I meant, her mouth hanging open. She didn't seem able to make a sound.

I helped her along. "It was in your briefcase, Nicole, darling. Would you like me to get it – to get the letter? I don't think it's my job to spell it out, do you?"

The gate buzzed as I spoke. I looked at my watch – this had gone on longer than I'd planned. After all the years of deceit on both their parts, of the furtive glances, the stolen moments, I suppose I should have expected it to take a few minutes for them to face the truth. Perhaps there were just too many secrets.

The gate buzzed again.

Picking up my glass, I knocked back the rest of my wine before I spoke.

"There's really no need to maintain the charade any more. I have someone I'd like you both to meet."

The foot of my glass cracked on the marble mantel as I replaced it, splitting a silence that was heavy, suffocating, the room thick with emotion.

"I'll let her in."

So do you think I did the right thing? I did honestly think about leaving them both a note, of spilling it all out on paper, of telling them everything I felt, but somehow it wasn't enough. I needed to see their faces, needed to have *my* moment, and somehow the write thing just wasn't enough.

☙

Photograph by Garrett Byrne

Ita Roche On having to put this biographical note together, Ita asked a friend in the Arklow Camera Club for guidance. Sir Andrew (His Lordship!) replied: "Why use fifty words when one would do!" Whereupon she fell around laughing!

So who is Ita Roche? She'd like you to read this story and her upcoming books and then tell her!

The Locket: Coincidence or Divine Intervention?

Ita Roche

The Locket: Coincidence or Divine Intervention?

It is the 19th of August 1996 and a scorching hot summer's evening, 4.30 p.m. to be precise. There is hardly a cloud in the sky. Family and friends have gathered around me. Just close family and friends, I might add. We wanted this to be a private affair, not something open to the public and the hypocrites (coffin chasers, my friend calls them) who thrive on the intensity of other people's pain. You know, the ones that come to give you their condolences and yet are really there so they can say, "Oh, yes, I was there, and it was so awful!" They are more interested in the story they can tell afterwards than how you are really doing. I have very little time for hypocrisy at the best of times, but I sure as hell had no tolerance whatsoever for it at that stage of my life, and that's basically why it was just family and close friends, and to be honest too, it was enough. I was in no fit state to deal with crowds.

I am sitting. Someone – I don't to this day even know who – brought out a chair for me, which I really appreciate, as I am not well enough to stand with the pain radiating down my legs from sciatica, something I have suffered with now for years but has been exasperated by the trauma of a difficult birth.

So many emotions run through my mind, my heart and my soul, that it's almost impossible to even try to capture it here in words, as I reflect back to that heartbreaking day. A day engraved so deeply on my entire being that it literally changed the course of my life.

First of all, it seems all wrong that it is such a beautiful evening. How can it be so beautiful, so bright, so wonderful, when I am in the midst of my darkest hours?

The heart is being totally ripped out of me; the pain is far beyond anything I thought possible for one to endure. I never in my wildest imaginings thought that this kind of emotional pain would engulf me at this stage of my life, or at any other stage for that matter. I never fully comprehended the true meaning of the dark night of the soul until now, even though I am no stranger to death, tragedy and hard times in my life.

This, however, is different to anything else I have ever endured before. It is at such a personal and deep level that I know I am staring into a black abyss of pain and horror, and darkness completely engulfs me. There is no sight of any light at the end of the tunnel. There is no end to the tunnel, period! There is pain and nothing but cruel, intense heart-wrenching pain.

This is not right. It just could not be right. It is against the grain. This is *not* supposed to happen. It is just not the way it was meant to be, but I can't, no matter how I scream with the pain, change a single thing. I am out of control. I have no control over this at all. None! I have never been out of control like this, not to this extent at any rate! What am I supposed to do? How am I supposed to sit here on this chair and watch this and do nothing? I can't do this, but I have no choice, no choice! Oh, I want to die, I want to go with him, I want to be with him, I can't leave him here all alone, I can't do that. No, don't ask me to do that, not my baby, not my little son, I can't leave him, I can't. How can I do that? I'm his mammy, you can't ask me to do that, you can't ask me to leave my little son here! That is too much to ask me to endure.

No one should have to endure this; no one should outlive their children. We are just not supposed to bury our children before us, and yet here I am sitting on a chair in the graveyard looking at my little son, my little Martin, being lowered into the ground!

Stop, *stop*, I scream inside from the very depths of my soul, stop, please stop, don't put my baby in the ground! I want to bring him home, home to his little room that I have prepared for him. Don't put him in there – I'll never see him again.

Don't do that to me. Don't do that to him. He will get cold, oh God, he will get so cold, I don't want him to get cold. I'll never see him again, he needs his mammy, I need him, he's my baby. Please stop! What did I ever do to deserve this? Why is God punishing me? What have I done? I did not smoke a lot during the pregnancy! I had but two glasses of Guinness, each half-full of black-currant I might add, and that was only the other night, just last Thursday for my mother-in-law's seventieth birthday.

I was delighted when the pains started as I sat at the table that night during the meal, and I was timing them. Then it all stopped, and he started kicking me. It really hurt too! I remember thinking, "Well, you're not coming out of there tonight if you're back kicking again!"

Even though the pains had stopped, just the odd kick, I went home anyway, as soon as the meal was over and we'd had a chat, just in case the contractions might start again. I left alone and drove home, but then the kicking stopped too. Thank God I went home though. I'm so glad now that I did that at least. I lay on the bed and waited but nothing much happened. Little did I realise as I lay there and he moved once more that it was to be the last time I would ever feel my son alive inside of me again. It was, in fact, possibly even the last move the poor little mite ever made! It surely can't have been the two glasses of Guinness and blackcurrant I had? Surely that would not kill my baby. I did not touch a drink during the early developing months. I only had the two glasses the whole nine months. That can't have harmed him, surely to God? I took no medication for the sciatica either. What did I do wrong? Why did this happen?

Again and again I silently scream, *stop*, don't put my baby in there, please, don't do this to me! Please, please don't do this . . . *but they did* . . . Nobody was listening, for no one could hear the screaming that was going on inside me.

My heart was being ripped open this was shaking me to the very foundations of my being. A mother's primal instinct is to protect her young, but here I am, I am just bloody sitting here, *doing nothing, saying nothing*, letting them put my baby in the ground. Oh God, I cannot save my son. I can't save my little boy . . . *I am so sorry, son* . . . I did not give you life, I gave you *death*! I am sorry, Mammy is so sorry for hurting you! *Did* I hurt you, *did* I do this to you, son? I am sorry for not taking care of you, for not knowing what was wrong . . . I fell asleep.

Oh my God, I fell asleep!

I fell asleep as you were dying!

How could I have slept when you needed me? How could I sleep while you were dying inside of me? I was supposed to take care of you. How could I not know what was wrong? Why did I not make someone listen last week, when I felt you were in trouble? Oh God, how can I ever sleep again? How can I ever sleep now without you? So, so many things, going round and round in my mind, I can't cope with this, I feel I am going to go insane! Am I being punished because I did not want the pregnancy in the beginning?

My heart is bursting with emotions and my soul is dying with my son.

I know in this moment that part of me will never be

the same again. How can life ever be right after this? It can't ever be, as part of me is going into the grave, part of me has died. Nobody knew him, but I did. Oh how well I knew him, and how wrong all this is. I honestly believe that to bury a little one that nobody knows is not an obvious wound for all the world to see, but far more a silent internal bleeding of the heart and the soul. If I were sitting here with my two legs broken from an accident, people would understand, but because there is no outer wound to see, plus the added cruel fact that no one even knew my son, how on earth can they possibly understand the intensity of my pain? Oh God, stop this, please stop this! If I've said that once during that burial, I've screamed it silently a hundred times. I've begged God. I've pleaded, but all the pleading in the world is not going to change anything this awful summer's evening!

I do not, in all honesty, hear one word that our beloved parish priest says, as I sit there staring at my son's tiny white coffin being lowered into the ground.

How am I supposed to hear him? What does it matter if I can't listen to what he is saying? Everyone else can do the praying right now. I can't say prayers now. My mind could not hold the one line of thought that long. It's all just words right now. I don't know whether to talk to God, scream at Him or just never recognise that there is a God in heaven any more. God is supposed to be good. No, now I know better than that. God did not do this, *it's my fault!* I should have made the doctors listen last week when I was up at the hospital. I told them that I felt I could not carry him any longer, that he was clawing at me, that his movements were hurting me, that he needed to be born, but did they listen? Oh no, I mean what would I know, I'm only the mother, the one carrying him! I've no medical degree! All I had was my gut feeling *screaming* at me! Why did I listen when they told me I was just in pain and that it was best for me and the baby if I waited. "Come back Monday," they said, "if you have not had him before then."

Well, it certainly was not best for me or my son. Here is Monday and he is being buried. Why didn't I make them listen? They told me I was *depressed* because I was in so much back pain and taking nothing for it. *Depressed! In pain and depressed, I thank you!* I got a little pat on the back and a condescending reassurance that everything was absolutely fine and told quite frankly that they were the experts after all and that it was best for both baby and me to wait until the following week! (Boy, that turned out to be great advice!) They wrote out a prescription for strong medication and said it wouldn't do any harm at this stage. I didn't take it, so it was not the medication that harmed my little Martin.

What happened to my son? Why did he die on me? Why could I not make anyone listen? Why? Why? Why?

It's done . . . they've covered the grave with some board and then placed the flowers on top of that. They are praying again. Now silence . . . *now what?*

Nobody seems to know what to do now.

People start hugging me – I can't even see who they are . . . *now nothing* . . .

Am I supposed to go now? *Oh, God, no*, how am I supposed to get up and walk away and leave my son here? They're waiting for me to make the move, to walk away.

Oh God, give me strength!

I'm in the car! How did I get here? I look across and there are still people around the grave! Can I go back? Yes, I'm going to go back ... but then the car door opens ... It's my mother! My poor mum – oh, this must be awful for her too! Martin is her little grandson after all. She wraps her arms around me and tells me to go home *and get some rest*! Ah, God love her, how the hell am I supposed to rest?

Her voice is so low, so soft. It's awful to see the pain in her eyes too!

I don't want to rest – I can rest any time. Right now I want my son back!

I just want him back!

Pat, Patrick and Edel get into the car, and Pat informs me we are going to his sister's for some tea, while our longstanding friends and neighbours fill in the grave.

That's it! That's the final blow!

I can't take hearing those words. Those awful words "fill in the grave" rip straight through me to my core as I sit in the car. I sob and beg Pat not to go, I don't want to leave, and he promises me we can come back later, if I want, when they are done. Fill in the grave. They are going to put all that soil back in on top of his little white coffin, on top of my baby. Oh God, what if the little coffin breaks underneath the weight? No, no please, this is too much pain. I can't take this. I want my baby back. I don't want him put in there and left under all that clay! Somebody tell me this is not happening!

You know if Isa, Pat's sister, had not been so thoughtful as to cover the clay surrounding the sides of the grave with blue rhododendrons, I honestly believe I would have had a complete mental breakdown at the sight of that tiny grave!

Chatter, just idle chatter, everyone trying to talk and no one really knowing what to say. Someone hands me tea and I drink it. I'm thirsty, so thirsty, and I don't even know why. I have more tea and more tea. I can't face food but I drink tea, cup after cup, and I inhale a cigarette to what seems like my toes. I pull on that cigarette as though my life depended on it. I can't inhale the smoke deep enough. I somehow hope that the cigarette will help to ease the horrendous pain and emotional hell I am going through. It doesn't, of course, but I keep on having cigarette after cigarette in the hope that I can numb some of the pain. I can't possibly be expected to live with this, to cope with this kind of pain on my own!

You know, I can honestly say, if anyone handed me heroin, at this precise moment, and said, "Here, this will ease the pain," I would take hand and all off them! I would literally take anything to stop the pain, but thankfully no one has anything like that on them, or if they do, I do not get to know about it. So instead I just have more tea, and even though I can hardly breathe from the cigarettes I have inhaled, I have yet another one.

Look, you must appreciate something here! Nature is *so* cruel at times!

You see, I had Martin at one thirty Saturday morning, and it's now Monday evening, sixty-three hours later! My breasts are now full, and so sore, and ready to feed my baby. Oh yes, one's body continues as normal, but there is nothing normal about this evening, and I have no baby to feed. All of this adds to the enormity of conflicting torturous emotions racing through me.

I have no idea who is here. There are faces, and they are all talking and I know they are family, but exactly who is here and what they are saying goes way over my head. It's almost like you are there, but you are not really there, you feel as though you are watching a horrendous event, but you have no control over the proceedings. Circumstances are all outside of your control. You're just sitting there like a zombie, but a zombie in an indescribable state of pain, I might add.

Someone hands me a little book about the size of a cigarette box that has *Baby's First Visitors* written on the cover and proceeds to explain that it was part of a present my sister-in-law had bought for me, before everything went so horribly wrong. She then brought the book to the funeral, and everyone there had signed it and wrote little messages in it for Martin. One of the many messages that stands out clearly is written by my twenty-year-old nephew Garret. It reads: *"As he fell before he flew, he swept to heights no others knew."* Such wisdom, and from a lad so young! Another by Audrey my niece: *"Peace without*

Peace, where is Happiness?" Amazing the wisdom of youth! And how right she was: Martin was at peace, but I have no peace!

I know I will treasure the book in the following weeks and months. Little things can mean so much. I am really touched by it. I grip it tightly in my hand, along with a blanket. A little blanket. Martin's little blanket. It was wrapped around him when we were in the hospital.

I never left that blanket out of my arms since he was taken from me. I couldn't – it was all I had left of him now! I held on to it like my life depended on it, as close to my heart as I could get it. I could still smell him from the blanket. It comforted one tiny piece of my soul to smell his little scent from his blanket and to hold it to my heart. I felt in some small way I was still hugging him. I had lots of clothes that he had not worn, and now never would wear, but this was the only thing I had that he had on him, even if only wrapped around him. The hospital managed to lose his clothes after changing him.

Finally we are back at the grave, and as I stand here now, with just Pat and our two older children, Patrick and Edel, the enormity of the pain, and the finality of it all, rips through me, and I go weak at the knees. Pat wraps his arm around me and holds me up, and my heart breaks as I cry for my little son, alone now in the cold earth. I know his little soul is in heaven, my faith is strong enough to assure me of that, but his little body is underneath all that clay! I start to shake with the cold. I feel so empty, so lost, so alone! I know Pat, Patrick and Edel are there for me, but I have never in my entire life felt so alone. They too are all in shock, in pain and hurting, and for the first time in my life, I have absolutely nothing to give to them. I cannot help them. I have nothing in me, nothing but pain, this horrid wrenching pain. There is a physical, heavy dragging pain in my chest from the intensity of the grief that engulfs me. I try some deep breaths to clear it, but every breath hurts.

I look at the flowers to try to ease my pain and somehow soothe the horror of what is becoming far too much for me to bear any longer. The flowers are beautiful, I can see that. Then for reasons I do not at this stage understand, something makes me look up, and there in front of me is the most magnificent blood-red sunset I have ever witnessed. It strikes me instantly how beautiful life can be and how horrid in the same moment. Yes, even though life is cruel, nature in this moment is very, very beautiful. The paradox of pain and suffering, with peace, tranquillity and sheer beauty, all wrapped up in this one moment. It is breathtaking, humbling actually!

To each its own season, its own moment of beauty! I will never forget it.

I know this may sound crazy to you, but it somehow brings just a breath of ease to my soul. It touches me somehow deep within. It is the peace of it, the sheer beauty and peace of that magnificent sunset. It is such a massive, blood-red August sunset, and I feel, in a way, it understands and represents my bleeding, grieving heart. It touches me at a level that only God could have reached this evening. It is almost like it is the first little bit of soothing balm being wrapped around my burning broken heart.

So I have shared with you my feelings on that terrible day.

Now, look, let me take you back a bit here.

At the time Martin died I was married nineteen years. I had married very young, the tender age of fifteen to be precise, way back in 1977. Seems like a lifetime ago now.

I had two children within the first four years of marriage. Patrick born in November of 1977 and Edel born 1st January 1981. At that stage we lived in a very cold and damp council house. Pat worked in a fish farm twenty-odd miles away. We did not for years even have a car. All four of us, in fact, travelled on the motorbike! Not many guards around where we lived, thank God! I mean, can you picture this?

There is Pat on the front of the motorbike, with Patrick facing him, his little arms wrapped around his dad, Edel in the middle with her arms around me, and me, at the back, with my arms around Edel and Pat, trying to hold on to Patrick as well, by whatever I could grip. Edel never got a breeze in the middle. If you take into account the fact that there were already three on the bike, it's a wonder there was any room for my rather large "means of sitting", as Pat's dad always called my oversized butt. To be totally honest here, I had very little seat at the back, but in fairness what could you expect? Well, until we could afford a car, it was travel that way or stay at home, and I did my share of staying at home too, I can tell you.

As for school in those days, you walked the kids and then walked home, and repeated that in the evening. When I think of it, I don't know how I had such a good "means of sitting" with all the walking I did back then. In the early eighties we got our first car and by 1987 I got totally focused on buying our first home.

Things were still very hard and money was tight, to say the least of it. Luxuries, of any sort, were non-existent, and we did whatever we had to to get by, but that is all we did, get by from one pay cheque to the next. When we finally bought our first home we really had our backs to the wall, but thankfully I got an evening job which helped pay the bills and ease things a little. You see, we had taken on paying for our home in a ridiculously short number of years. It was tough going but worth it in the long run.

Needless to say, considering how tough things were financially, I never even considered having another child. We were hard set to make ends meet at times, let alone think of another child. Anyway, I had my two, one boy and one girl. What more could I possibly ask for? Before I knew what was happening I had severe back pain and a back operation for slipped disc. I also had arthritic scarring and other lower lumbar complications. The operation was successful, but a year later I had horrendous sciatica again – serious now, as the surgeon would not operate on me again so soon, and to be honest I don't think I could have handled another back operation either. To be totally honest here, I'd never let anyone near my back again!

Then shock! I was pregnant. I said nothing to anyone, as I really did not know for sure what way I was feeling about it, and before I could really get my head around being pregnant, I miscarried. I had only a couple of babygros bought, but I have to say it hit me far harder than I ever expected it to.

With time I pulled myself together and decided that was it for me as regards having babies. Never going there again. I had my two and that's the way it would stay. Part of me thrashed out the logic that with my back the way it was, the last thing I needed was to be pregnant, as I certainly did not have small babies, so that was an end to it. With being in and out of hospital several times more over the next few years with my back, I finally came to the decision that it was best if I got sterilised. I was finished with my family and no longer wanted the worry of pregnancy or the effects pregnancy would have on my back, let alone the rest of my life. So decision made, no more children for me.

Things had improved financially and Patrick and Edel were both young teenagers and life was good. We could take small breaks now, and I even had my own little car at this stage. Wasn't so little actually, it was a VW Jetta. A black one, and I loved it. I really did. I was very proud of my lovely black car.

Well, guess what? Murphy's Law strikes, and

Christmas week I am feeling so unwell, and very teary-eyed, and I realise to my horror that it's quite a few weeks since my last period. Now please remember, I have done all the counselling and preparation work necessary for my upcoming sterilisation, and my bed is booked for the middle of January, only four weeks away. I can't be pregnant! I am being paranoid surely, just because the operation is getting close. No doubts in my head about getting it done, none whatsoever. I decided to take a sample to the doctor to test, just to put my mind at ease for the Xmas. He said it was negative. Oh God, what a relief! I went home happy. I really was delighted to be honest. Pregnancy with my back really was not an option, especially as I carry such huge babies.

I was only in the door and having my tea when the phone rang. It was the doctor and he asked me to go back in to him and would not discuss it further on the phone. I remember thinking, Jesus, I did pay him, didn't I? I'd be so lucky that that was all that was wrong!

Oh no, now comes the shock!

He explained that when he went back to the shelf, where he had left down the test, to throw it out, it was showing a definite positive. I cried and cried. I just kept asking, what was going to happen to my back? He agreed that it was "seriously bad timing, to say the least"! I'll be totally honest here: I cried the whole way home and told Pat. He did not know what to say either. We really were both in shock. God love him, my little baby, he shocked us in the beginning and at the end of his little short life!

I warned Pat not to give me any of the "It's God's will" stuff, but you know, God really does work in strange ways, because over the next couple of days on the final run up to Xmas, I kept thinking: it would be nice to have Santy in the house again though, and I am only coming up thirty-four now in January!

Anyway Christmas morning we decided to tell Patrick and Edel, and they were shocked but OK about it. We told the rest of the family too. They thought it was great! Of course they did! They did not have to carry him, or give birth, or rear him. Please understand here, that is where my mindset was at that stage!

As the months rolled on, the pregnancy got really tough because of my back, and I ended up using a Tens machine for pain relief and needed a walking stick to get around, but other than that, I actually loved being pregnant. I knew from a very early scan that I was carrying a boy and named him Martin after Pat's dad. I had great fun buying all the things I couldn't afford when I was carrying Patrick and Edel. I was older now, and I was, I reckon, emotionally and mentally ready for a child. I was far too young having the other two to really appreciate what a blessing children are in our lives, and life back then was all about trying to make ends meet and putting a home together, and to be honest here, trying not to kill one another in the process! We were both far more mature now, and we realised we were both looking forward to a baby in our lives again. I was also really looking forward to Pat being with me for this birth.

In the seventies and eighties you had your children alone, I can tell you! The whole pregnancy and birthing experience was a totally different ball game back then! (Here's to us women who remember the rather large enamel jug of soapy water, eh?)

I loved doing up the bedroom for him, and I had everything ever needed for a baby by the time he was due. I even had the Calpol for when he started teething. Toys, clothes, teddies, rattlers, musical mobile over the cot, changing tables, Moses' basket, pram, *everything!* Patrick and Edel even put some of them together with me, and I enjoyed it so much. I was prepared for this baby, I was prepared for everything, everything, that is, except a funeral.

I was so prepared for him that I had actually collected over sixty pounds in change for the hospital phones, so Pat could ring everyone with the good news, and had all the names and numbers written out too. Lucky really, because with the shock of what happened, neither of us was in any state to try and remember phone numbers.

Neither of us had mobile phones at that stage in our lives.

During the pregnancy I really connected with Martin. I loved rubbing my tummy and talking to him about absolutely everything. I played a daily game with him too! I would press my finger against my tummy and say, "Come on, kick me here!" and he would! Then I'd move to a lower part of my tummy on the opposite side and ask him to do it there, and without fail he would give me a little kick or move there. I did that every morning, after rubbing my tummy and talking to him first. I loved knowing he was there, growing inside of me, listening to me, responding to my voice and touch. I felt such a strong connection with him, and I loved that too. I really did.

That awful morning the 16th of August 1996 when I awoke, I did what I had done for months! I placed my hand on my tummy to say good morning to him, but this time shock! And I really mean shock! I can tell you honestly here, *I knew instantly* that he was gone. A cold sweat of fear and knowing ran through my body, and I really knew instantly that my son was no longer alive inside me. There is nothing I can say to describe what I felt. I tried to convince myself I was wrong!

I got up and tried to calm myself with tea and tried again, and again, to get a response from him, but nothing! The doctor's was not open until nine.

I finally got the appointment to see him, and he confirmed the horror.

He could not find a heartbeat!

How I drove that car home that day, I will never know. I honestly believe God got me home safe, for I could not see the road in front of me for tears. Pat was in bed, as he was out working during the night, and I realised as I got home that I was going to have to tell him! I dreaded it, for I had no idea how he would react, and I knew he was going to have to drive to the hospital. I decided not to really explain. I actually didn't tell him that Martin was dead! I just said through tears that the doctor could not find a heartbeat, and I needed to go to the hospital straight away. I felt it was best to leave him with some hope that his son might still be alive. He said absolutely nothing. He just got up and dressed. Then we had the hour and a half drive. I prayed over and over again for a miracle as Pat drove and, you know something, neither of us spoke really at all during that journey. We were both just so deep in our own thoughts. Now and then Pat just reached out and touched my hand as I cried and prayed silently. To say it was a long journey would be a serious understatement!

And when we got there, they finally confirmed the nightmare by scan. They just said, "I'm sorry."

I screamed out! I literally screamed out at the top of my voice: *No, not my baby!*

I guess even I, though I knew he was gone, was still holding out hope, praying for that miracle or that maybe both the doctor at home and I were somehow wrong! I guess I just did not want to really face the fact that he was really dead on me.

The birth was horrendous to put it mildly, partly because of my back and because of complications, and partly because I, on one hand, wanted him born to hold him and see him, and on the other hand, I wanted him to stay inside of me, because I knew the minute he was born that it was the beginning of the end! My hours with him, I knew, would be numbered the minute he arrived in this world!

They were. Only sixty-three hours later, I was sitting at his grave side!

The months, and years, passed painfully, and I got through. Mind you, looking back, I realise only through the grace of God and a good Doctor! But I got through with anti-depressants and feeling totally suicidal.

I spent many an hour sitting on a bridge below our home, staring at the lorries, knowing that if I took only one step it would be all over. I can tell you now that I really did want it over, and I did not care by what means I ended it either. The intensity of the grief was far more than I could handle.

I went through a very serious depression. I wanted out; I couldn't endure the pain.

I wanted to be with Martin and to end the pain and suffering I was in. I couldn't sleep. I wouldn't sleep. When I did, the nightmares were horrendous. I wanted to die, I really did. I was totally consumed with the magnitude of grief. I did not think of what suicide would do to anyone else in the family. I was not capable of reason at that stage. In grief one's mind is not in any state of reason to decipher right from wrong!

The days dragged into weeks and months. The nights were so long and lonely, they were soul-destroying!

I knew that eventually I was going to have to part with Martin's things. I would have to clear out his bedroom, the little room that he was in for half an hour, as Pat and I got dressed for the funeral that Monday evening.

But it had to be done, and somehow, through anger and tears, a year later I did clear it all away. To ease the pain of having to part with his things, Pat gave me money to buy a locket to wear, to keep Martin's photo with me. That gave me a lift.

I liked the idea of being able to have his photo with me at all times. I found that soothing. So I set off to get the right locket for my little son's photo.

It was a beautiful locket. I bought a big locket and had a picture of him and one of Pat put inside it. I had his name and date of birth engraved on the back of it.

I treasured it. I felt close to him as I wore it. Needless to say I thought hard of even taking it off when in the shower. I had a long chain on it so it was close to my heart. I still talked to Martin all the time, just as I did when I was pregnant with him, but now I either looked up to heaven or held the locket, or both, as we talked.

It is not out of the ordinary for me to hold conversations with someone who is not there, as I would talk to the walls if they would answer me! Actually I would, if I were to be honest here, answer for the walls too, holding the conversation between the walls and myself alone, no problem – yes and I would enjoy it too, what's more. Well, I mean, the poor walls, what did they ever do to harm anyone?

Anyway to continue . . .

It was the August weekend, a few short years later. I was mixing paint for Rose, Pat's mum. I had none of my jewellery on, needless to say, not even the locket, as there was no way I was going to risk getting paint on something so precious to me! I had left it at home.

When we arrived home that day, the house was in a mess. To our horror, when I finished blaming our daughter, who had just come back from her holidays, I realised we had been burgled! *Yes, you guessed it!* All my jewellery but, more importantly, *my locket* was gone! The one and only time I had left the house without wearing it. They had taken the one thing I had left of him, that brought me the most comfort. The locket that helped me feel close to him.

Now when I say I fell apart I really mean I fell apart! I guess it was the straw that broke the camel's back, so to speak. Look, to the casual observer, it was just a locket, a piece of jewellery! But not to me! My God, not to me! It was far more than that to me! I did not really care what else was gone, but I wanted my locket back. That was precious to me, and no one could do that to me. Anyone could see it was precious, as I even had his name on the back of it. What use was it to anyone else when it was engraved? It was all of Martin I had left. That is how I felt at least.

Dear God, don't take that now! Martin, give me back my locket! I cried and I cried!

I begged God and Martin to just give me back my little locket.

The guards were with us and they repeated what Pat and everyone else kept saying:

"You're not going to get that locket back – you may as well accept that and buy another!"

Oh, how could they not realise that another locket would never be the one that I bought when Martin died and I had to clear his room! Nothing could replace that for me!

No, I'm putting my foot down on this one, God! I want my locket back, and I don't care how you do it, but just give it back to me. "Martin, you see to it that God listens to me this time. I can never have you back, but I want my locket back, with you in it!

Do that for Mammy, please, son. I want it back."

I was totally emotionally wiped over it!

Look, if you're sitting there still thinking it was only a locket, then I say to you, "Walk one mile in my shoes before you make that judgement!"

We had so few photos of him, so little of him, period. No, I wanted it back! End of story as far as I am concerned, I would accept no other outcome!

The next foty-eight hours passed in a daze of tears, and pleads, and demands to heaven to give me back the locket. I did not sleep and kept bombarding God and Martin to please return it. My foot had gone down to the centre of the earth on this one!

Sunday we had made plans to go to Wexford to visit a lovely old couple, Kevin and Kathy, relations of Pat's, and it was a day out that, up to this, I always loved. But that morning I could not even bring myself to go to Mass, let alone anywhere else.

Pat went to eleven Mass even though I had preached at him to go to the early Mass, simply so he could have a long day in Wexford. He was going anyway, with his mother and Auntie Joan, but Pat being Pat, he decided it had to be eleven Mass.

He is such a creature of habit! He always goes to the same Mass, same time, goes in the one door, sits in the one section of the chapel!

But something happened that Sunday morning that changed everything!

Pat approached the door on the right, having passed the left-hand door, and for reasons he did not understand, just as he was about to go through, he stopped and turned back. As he crossed the yard going towards the left door, he even remarked to himself that it was a stupid thing to do, as that side of the chapel was always packed, and chances were he would not even get into the body of the chapel for Mass. He had made that mistake once before and vowed he would never repeat it. You see, quite a few looking for a quick exit gather at the doors and back of the chapel. I'm being totally honest here – it's not, unfortunately, because the chapel was not able to hold the crowds gathering for Mass! Along with this is the fact that he was on the last minute and did not have the time to play around with. Even knowing this, he continued and entered through the first set of doors, and lo and behold he was right! The doorway was packed and Mass was just beginning.

At that a man from inside the glass doors turned and put his finger up to salute him, and Pat wondered what that was in aid of, as it was only a split second and then the man turned back towards the altar. The priest started

265

Mass and within minutes, as the crowd were kneeling to pray, the man turned again and, with his hands in outward movement, he parted the crowd, pulled open the door with his right hand, then using his left hand he grabbed Pat by the arm and led him through to the body of the chapel, until he had a clear space for them both. He then put his right hand into his pocket and pulled out something and while still holding Pat by the arm he placed it into the palm of Pat's hand and closed his hand over it. He then whispered to Pat, "I think that belongs to your wife," and he just turned at that, back towards the altar and continued praying.

Now you must realise something here: Pat did not know this man. He had seen him in the distance before, but that was all. This all happened in the space of a couple of seconds. As Pat was praying, he could feel the shape of something in the palm of his hand and he just glanced down. A wave of emotion swept over him, and tears started to just pour from his eyes, as he instantly knew, for him, that something Very Divine had just taken place, and in the midst of Mass, which was so precious to Pat as he has a very strong faith. The man never turned again and Mass continued as normal. But it was far from normal for Pat that day, and it was a Mass he will remember in detail to the day he dies!

Needless to say, when Mass ended, Pat spoke briefly to the man, got his name – Mr Kelly – thanked him and told him we would be in touch later in the week.

In the meantime I was at home, still refusing to go to

Wexford or anywhere else that day, as I was really down over the whole thing.

I was sitting on the sofa when Pat came in. He walked straight over to put on the kettle, and he did not even look at me as he asked, "Are you going to Wexford?"

To which I rapidly replied, "No!"

He then asked, "What would make you happy today, Ita?" never dreaming I would answer as I did!

I got up and walked over to him, put my arms around him for comfort and replied, "You would have to hand me back my locket!"

At that he turned, took something out of his hand and dropped it into the pocket of the shirt I was wearing.

I gasped, "Oh, it couldn't be!" and at that I looked up at him, and the tears were streaming down his face.

In that instant, I knew that I had Martin's little locket back! It was back, I had my locket back! I kissed the face off Pat and the locket. I could hardly believe my eyes. Again I cried and cried and cried! But this time with *joy*!

Pat recounted, through tears, what had happened in Mass and how Mr Kelly had spotted something on the ground as he went for a walk on the Friday morning. He looked inside and saw Pat's photo along with the baby's and remembered seeing him in second Mass one time before. He did not know us or that our child had died. He decided to go to second Mass again (not his usual Mass) and bring the locket with him in case he saw Pat again. Had Pat gone to his usual side of the chapel, Mr Kelly would not have seen him from where he sits.

The locket was battered and bruised, as was my little son's face in it, and the chain was gone. Obvious from the state of it that it had been thrown from a moving car. I did not care about the condition it was in or the fact that the very expensive chain was gone. I had my little locket back and that was all I asked God and Martin for.

I have thanked God and my little son a thousand times for returning the locket to me. I learned that day that, when the desire is big enough, the facts simply don't count! You see, to all and sundry, there was no way I was getting that locket back! But God spoke before them all, as my mother would say!

To this day, I carry my precious locket everywhere with me.

Many other unbelievable things happened during the course of the following week, and Martin's little life with us helped awaken us to the fact that there are greater forces at play in our lives than we sometimes realise!

But, alas, that belongs in a book I am writing and not in this short story.

As for the locket?

There is no doubt in my mind what took place that wonderful Sunday morning,

But having read it now for yourself, you tell me!

᭪᭪

The Locket: Coincidence or Divine Intervention?

Coincidence or Divine Intervention?
Now that you have read the story,
I will tell you that this is
Serious Fiction: i.e.
Inspired by actual events.

And I dedicate this story to
God and my Little Son,
Martin Joseph Roche.
Until next our paths cross
I leave you in God's care!
                    Ita

Jackie Walsh was born in Dublin where she lives with her husband Paul. She likes to spend time reading and dreaming up characters and storylines. This is her first attempt at writing, which she thoroughly enjoyed and hopes to continue.

The Black Wallet

Jackie Walsh

The Black Wallet

Tricia Glynn stood in line at the checkout of her local Tesco, happy in the knowledge that her least favourite chore of the week was nearing an end. Shopping for groceries was not Tricia's idea of fun. It was the most mundane task she was left with. She had already managed to delegate most other tasks to the thriving home-help economy, which had blossomed since the arrival of Europe's enthusiastic, desperate-to-work immigrants. Tricia once again promised herself she would check out Tesco's online shopping service as she placed her goods on the conveyer belt.

There wasn't too much of a wait as the guy in front wasn't purchasing much and then it was her turn.

"Have you got a Tesco card?" said the robotic checkout girl.

"No," said Tricia.

"Do you need bags?"

"Yes, give me four please." She was determined to shove her whole week's shopping into four weak plastic bags rather than pay the extra money. Tricia never remembered to bring bags.

She laughed at how the fussiness once adopted by her while packing her food was now gone. Caution was thrown to the wind as the checkout girl tumbled goods after goods in struggling Tricia's direction, like it was a race. Raw meat was packed with fresh, apples were thrown in on top of washing powder and unpackaged bread was squeezed in beside the bleach.

A week's shopping, all put at risk over the cost of an extra couple of bags. It wasn't meanness: Tricia wasn't mean. It was that feeling of not getting ripped off that can cloud so many normally intelligent people's judgement.

Tricia paid and left with her toilet rolls under her arm and four overpacked plastic bags, which were trying desperately to amputate her fingers.

She went to the car, put the shopping into the boot and then got into the driver's seat, where she stretched out and lit up a cigarette, patting herself on the back, delighted with the job done.

What Tricia didn't know was that, in the rush, she had just packed into her bags the first big mistake of the day.

Oliver Owens arrived back to work after lunch flustered. He had always taken time out of his day to enjoy a proper lunch, but today he had some running around to do. Oliver loved his new position as manager of the sales department as it gave him more power and respect. His tall, strong frame and dark complexion complemented his tailored suits, and he felt very proud to still be referred to as dark-haired at forty-five. "Just good genes," Oliver would say when people asked him his secret for staying so young-looking.

This position which he now held suited Oliver. He felt it was time to reap the rewards for eleven hard years on the road, yielding the highest sales for the company year after year. Oliver had been given his own office, which for BABI insurances was a sign of respect and achievement. Separate offices were almost a thing of the past, as partitions and plants provided most of the boundaries between the two hundred work force. Oliver entered his office.

His agitation did not go unnoticed by Elaine, his secretary. "Are you feeling OK, Mr Owens?"

"I'm fine, just a bit tired. I had to do some shopping for Tina and I missed lunch."

"Can I get you anything?"

"A cup of coffee would be lovely, thanks, Elaine."

Elaine returned with the coffee to find Oliver staring blankly at some weekly sales figures.

"How is Tina?" she asked. "Is she feeling any better?"

Oliver took the coffee, saying, "She has some good days and some bad, but I think overall the medication is working. The doctors are happy with her – they say it will just take some time."

He drank his coffee, his mind slipping back to the days when Tina was first diagnosed with depression.

Tina Owens thought she had landed the man of her dreams when she married Oliver Owens ten years previously. He was everything she had wanted, good looking, funny, sociable and with a good job, and he had treated her like she was everything he had dreamed of. Oliver was away a lot with his job, but he never failed to call her every day and night to tell her how much he missed her, and he would always return with gifts and flowers. This continued into the first few years of marriage, but slowly this marriage made in heaven seemed doomed to be demoted to hell. At first Tina put his lack of interest in her down to the stress of making his sales targets. They were like a vicious circle. The more he sold the higher his targets were set. Failing to reach them was just not in Oliver's vocabulary – he was driven by the success he was having and bragged about the enormous targets he had to achieve. Once Oliver achieved one thing he had to move onto the next. Soon Tina realised that she too had just been a onetime achievement of Oliver's. More and more he would go on the road for days without contacting her, returning without even trying to conceal the signs of other women. Lipstick stains, perfume smells and once she even found a false nail in his suitcase. Some bitch had actually helped him pack. Tina got no satisfaction from confronting Oliver, as he would just ignore her cries and continue on as if she didn't matter, which clearly she didn't. Oliver was high on figures and could not come down.

Tina, slowly allowing reality to creep into her mind, got more and more depressed. Her outside interests were minimal now, as Oliver had insisted she leave work when they got married. She hated leaving her job at the solicitors but saw sense in Oliver's argument that they had enough money, and someone needed to organise the renovation on the old Victorian house they had bought.

The years fell into one another, with no children arriving and no interest on Oliver's part to have the problem investigated. Tina just became numb. Her occasional visit back home to her ageing parents down the country was the only necessary cover-up needed to maintain her painful life. Tina would tell them how everything was great and how wonderful Oliver was. Her few friends which she seldom saw were full of advice for her, but her heart was broken and she found her only relief in drink. Tina would sit in nightly, drinking her red wine, wondering how she had let her life slip into such non-existence.

Oliver arrived home one night to find Tina unconscious on the floor in the hallway. He rang an ambulance and Tina was eventually admitted to hospital with severe depression.

It was the start of a long and bitter battle with herself. Six years of therapy, drugs and huge efforts to change seemed to have no long-lasting effect on Tina. She questioned daily whether she had embraced the depression or the depression had embraced her.

When Tricia Glynn arrived home after her shopping trip to Tesco, she placed her bags on the counter and went straight to the takeaway menus in the drawer. She had not planned to shop and cook on the same day. Tricia was not normally lazy, but during her two-month summer vacation from being a teacher, she treated herself like royalty.

She decided on an Indian takeaway and reached into the bag to ensure she had safely transported home the bottle of wine which would accompany it. She had begun to unload the bags onto the counter when she suddenly found in her hand a black folded wallet.

"How the hell did that get in there?" she said to herself out loud, which had become a habit since moving into her own apartment two years previously. Before that she had always lived with other people, and while she enjoyed her own space now it sometimes felt lonely.

Tricia looked in puzzlement at the wallet as she opened it up. *Oliver Owens, 1 Darkwood Place,* read the gym membership card. Tricia studied the picture. "How do I know that face?" she said and suddenly realised it was guy who had been in front of her at Tesco. "He must have left his wallet in the packing area on the conveyer and with me trying to keep up with Little Miss Speedy, I guess I just shoved it in with the rest." Tricia looked through all its contents, Visa, Laser, driver's licence, some other personal cards and some cash. "Wow, four hundred euro!" That would come in nicely, she thought. I'd better not, though. God would probably have my ironing lady drop dead just to punish me. I guess I'll bring it back to Tesco or, better still, Darkwood Place isn't far from here. I'll drop it over there. After all, he isn't bad looking and stranger things have happened."

Tricia was about to make her second mistake of the day. For stranger things were about to happen.

The house was easy to find, standing on its own at the top of the road. Quite dreary looking, thought Tricia as she parked her car. There were some trees surrounding it that offered some life to this otherwise rundown picture.

Tricia decided to ring her friend Sue to tell her of her adventure.

"Why couldn't you just leave it in Tesco?" said Sue when she heard the news. "I hope you're not walking into the hands of a weirdo." Sue had become very cautious of strangers after a near miss with one some years earlier.

"Are you joking?" said Tricia. "How often am I likely to meet a wealthy, single good-looking bloke?"

"How do you know he's single?"

"I don't, but there's no evidence from his wallet that there's a woman and no glorious picture of a beautiful wife or kids in there either."

"Maybe he's gay."

"No, he does have a florist's card in there, proving he buys flowers for his dates."

"But," said Sue, "he could buy his boyfriend flowers."

"Don't be ridiculous, Sue! No man wants flowers – most women don't either, they just like to see their husbands put out by having to buy them. Anyway I've got to go, my battery is running out. I'll call you later with the wedding arrangements."

They both laughed as Tricia hung up and got out of the car.

Tricia walked up the driveway, feeling a little nervous. She had put on some make-up and what she thought was her best casual look: tight denim jeans with a white low-cut T-shirt and sparkling flat sandals. Her long black hair was loosely tied to the back and she felt quite confident that she looked good.

Taking the wallet out of her bag, she rang the doorbell once, twice, but there was no answer. Should she just drop it in the letterbox?

She walked around the side of the house just to be sure he wasn't out there and found herself in a large overgrown garden. Tall trees surrounded the garden walls and the shrubs and rockeries had clearly not been seen to in a long time.

Suddenly there was a loud bang from inside the house and, as Tricia swung around, she could see through dirty patio doors and down the hall to someone rushing out the front door.

"Well, there's a welcome!" said Tricia aloud.

She walked back around to the front to leave, when she noticed the wide-open front door. Although nervous, her nosiness was stronger and she decided to enter the house.

There were three doors all opening off the hallway and a large wooden staircase to her left. Not quite as dilapidated as the outside, thought Tricia. She slowly entered the front room, peering round the door, when suddenly her body froze.

There, lying on the floor in the middle of the room about three feet away from her, lay a woman's body covered in blood, her eyes wide open but with no obvious signs of life.

Tricia nearly got sick with fright, her legs started to wobble and her body felt numb. She just turned on her heels and ran out the door to her car.

And she didn't notice that she had dropped the black wallet right there in the room with the body.

Tricia picked up her phone to ring the police and cursed at it as the battery had gone flat. She struggled through her shock but managed to get the car and herself home in one piece. She plugged her phone in quickly and then stopped.

What am I doing? she thought. I can't be involved in what could be murder. Jesus Christ, what will I do? How could I explain being in the house? Would anyone believe me about the wallet? God, where's the fucking wallet anyway? Oh God, what if the woman was still alive? No, she wasn't . . . but . . . oh Christ!

Tricia took her ID off the phone and made an anonymous call to the police.

Oliver Owens was just about to leave his office when two policemen walked in.

"Are you Mr Oliver Owens of 1 Darkwood Place?"

"Yes. Can I help you?"

"We have some bad news, Oliver. You may need to sit down."

"No, just tell me," said Oliver.

"Oliver, your wife Tina has been found dead at your home."

"Oh Jesus, what are you saying?"

"The circumstances are not clear yet but we have people looking into it. We'll take you there now."

Oliver fell back in the chair, rubbing his face with his hands, trying to bring the blood back into it. "Yes, just give me a minute."

He didn't know how he was going to get back out of

the chair. He couldn't move. He didn't know what to ask.

"Tina," he said, "Tina, what have you done?"

The police station's call centre was always very busy, some calls requesting information, others requiring action, but when an anonymous call came in reporting a dead body it was taken very seriously. Detective Jack Cunningham decided to investigate it himself. His day had started quite slowly, having recently solved a major murder case involving a gangland killing. He expected things to be quiet for a while, which would give him a chance to catch up with his paperwork. However, it was not the kind of job which could be planned out. He had to go where and when he was needed.

Jack called on Charlie to accompany him to the address given over the phone. Charlie Getham, a lot younger in years than Jack, had become his right-hand man. It started when the age of technology began to impose on the daily work at the station. Jack, having ignored its possibilities in the past, now found himself struggling with the daily impact it had on his work. Charlie liked Jack although he often felt like his secretary. He was very grateful for Jack's fairness, appreciation and his investigating skills, which after thirty years at the top of his game were second to none.

"We'd better get to the scene quickly, Charlie, before someone else does and messes up things for us."

"OK," said Charlie as he grabbed his jacket.

Charlie, a tall, neatly dressed man, looked the complete

opposite to Jack, who, with his baggy trousers and jacket pulling to the sides displaying his large beer belly, always looked like he'd dressed in someone else's clothes. His grey hair, windswept no matter what the weather, was a distinct feature of his, unlike Charlie who could never last a month without having his dark crew cut trimmed.

When the two men arrived at the house they saw the open door.

"Is there anyone there?" shouted Jack, but there was no answer.

They slowly walked in, paying attention to every detail. Charlie entered the front room first.

"In here, Jack."

They saw Tina Owens lying dead in the middle of the room, her bare legs sticking out from under her tightly tied pink dressing-gown. Her two arms lay outstretched and large pools of blood surrounded the body on both sides.

"This appears to be suicide, Jack," said Charlie. "Both her arms are cut deeply above the wrists and there's no sign of a struggle."

"Sure, Charlie, it would appear that way, except for the phone call. The lady certainly did not ring in her own death."

"But what if she rang before she did it, like it was a cry for help?"

"Possible. We'll need the coroner's report on the time of death and the phone call."

"What's this?" said Charlie, as he leaned down to pick up a black wallet, which lay in the blood.

"Don't touch it!" shouted Jack.

Jack approached the wallet and looked at it.

"OK, Charlie, it's like this. The wallet was either here before or after the blood. If it was here before the blood when we lift it there will be a dry patch, no matter how small, in the centre of the space, possibly with blood travelling towards it. However, if it landed after the blood, there will be no dry space and the wallet will be completely covered in blood on the downside."

As Jack suspected, the wallet had arrived after the blood.

"So now we know that someone was definitely here," said Charlie.

"OK, let's see who this belongs to."

Jack was searching the front garden, while awaiting the arrival of the forensic team, when Oliver arrived with the two policemen.

Expecting an outburst of sympathy, Oliver was shocked when Jack Cunningham and Charlie Getham said they wanted to see him down at the station as soon as he was ready.

"What is this about, officer?" said Oliver. "Can't you see my wife has committed suicide? I need time to arrange things and contact people and – and –"

"There are suspicious circumstances surrounding your wife's death, Mr Owens, and we want to talk to you as soon as possible," said Jack.

"What suspicious circumstances?"

"This, for a start," said Jack, holding up a plastic bag containing the black wallet.

"What, how, where did you get that?" said Oliver.

"Just meet me down at the station at eight and we'll talk then," said Jack.

The apartment was cold when Tricia awoke, having nodded off. It was after eight.

I must have slept for hours, thought Tricia as she went to switch on the heating. Then it hit her.

"Oh my God, the body!"

She went to her phone and noticed she had three missed calls, each from Sue.

"Shite, she'll be wanting to know how I got on at the house!"

She rang Sue back and asked her to call over. Then she went straight to the wine and opened it. Puffing hard on her cigarette, she waited for her friend to arrive.

"Well, how did it go?" said Sue as she entered the hallway. "Did he propose yet?"

"Not exactly," said Tricia.

"What's wrong? You look crap – are you OK?"

"Not really," said Tricia as she broke into tears.

When Tricia had finally managed to get the story out, Sue was dumbfounded.

"What am I to do?" said Tricia. "Say something!"

"Well, I could say 'I told you so' but I won't," said Sue. "Let me have a look at the wallet. Where is it?"

"I don't know."

"In your bag? In the car?"

"No, I think I lost it at the house. I couldn't find it when I got back."

"What! Lost it! Look, Tricia, you check the apartment, I'll check the car."

The two women searched for twenty minutes but could not find the wallet.

They then sat back on the sofa and poured more wine.

"Look," said Sue, "you did the right thing. You rang the police – I don't know how much more you could have done, and with the wallet gone now I think you should just try to forget the whole thing."

This was just the advice Tricia wanted to hear but knew it would be some time before she would get the picture of the dead lady out of her head.

Sue got up and switched on the TV. "There's a great movie on after the news – it'll take your mind off it."

"A man is being questioned by police after his wife's body was found today at Darkwood Place under suspicious circumstances. Initial findings of what appeared to be suicide were put in doubt after an anonymous phone call was made to the police. A wallet was also found at the scene leading the police to suspect foul play."

Tricia's heart began to beat fast and she felt herself getting weak. "Oh fuck!" she cried. "What the hell is going on?"

Sue grabbed Tricia's hand. "You'll be all right – take a deep breath!"

Tricia sat up straight and took several deep breaths.

But the panic would not leave her. "What am I to do? Some poor fucker is being questioned for murder because of me! What if they arrest him? What if he's sent to jail? Oh, Jesus, what have I done?"

"Don't panic, Tricia, please, slow down."

The two women sat in shock looking at the TV as the interviewer standing outside the house at Darkwood Place listened as neighbours told how shocked they were and how Tina Owens was a very quiet person who always kept to herself.

"There's only one thing for it," said Tricia. "I'll have to go down there and tell them what happened."

"I'll go with you, Tricia, just let me give Gary a call to tell him I'll be home late. Or, if you like, I could stay with you tonight."

"Please, do you mind?"

"No, I'll ring him now."

When Oliver Owens arrived at the station, he had with him the company solicitor, John Sharpe. Sharpe was not experienced in criminal law, but Oliver had no one else to call.

They were brought down to a room near the back of the station where Jack and Charlie were waiting. The room was small with no window. The only evidence of its use hung in the shape of a six-inch camera, mounted high on the corner of the wall. There was one table in the centre of the room with two seats on either side. Jack and Charlie sat on one side and indicated to Oliver and John to sit at the other.

When introductions were over Jack came straight out and said, "Mr Owens, we have evidence which places you at the scene of the crime."

"But how?" said Oliver. "I was nowhere near the place today."

Jack held up the wallet in its plastic bag.

"What? But I used that at Tesco at lunchtime today – I must have left it there!"

"Well, yes, we know from checking your cards that you used your credit card there at one thirty-two."

"Yes, and then I went back to my office, not home, so I cannot for the life of me figure out how you found my wallet there!"

"Well," said Jack "let's propose that when you left Tesco, you went to your home, where you slit your wife's wrists to make it look like suicide, and then returned to your office – not knowing you had dropped your wallet."

Sharpe interrupted. "My client is saying he does not know how his wallet was at the scene and that he did not commit murder. It would appear there has to be another explanation for the wallet being there. Could it be that he's been framed and what about the anonymous phone call – have you any leads on that?"

"Not as yet," said Jack "but we're working on it. But what reason would there be for a set-up? Mr Owens, do you have many enemies?"

"No," said Oliver.

Sharpe spoke again. "Are you aware, detective, that Mrs Owens had already tried to commit suicide twice but was saved by her husband's interventions? She was being treated for severe depression for over six years and was on heavy medication, which of late she does not appear to have been taking regularly."

"I am now. But may I remind you, Mr Sharpe, that my job is to look at the evidence – and the evidence clearly points at Mr Owens being at the scene, yet he denies it."

After some routine questions and answers, Jack decided to take a break. "We'll continue in fifteen," he said.

Jack and Charlie poured two strong coffees in Jack's office.

"It doesn't seem to add up," said Charlie. "Why would he save her life twice, just to kill her then?"

"Firstly, he may have only recently felt the want to be rid of her. We need to find out what has changed in his life over the past year. Is he seeing someone else? Is he in any financial difficulty? And how much his wife is worth dead? Also, check to see if we got any more on the anonymous call – that part really baffles me."

Just as they were about to leave the office the phone rang.

"You're wanted at the front desk, Jack," said the clerk

"Not now, I'm in the middle of an interrogation."

"I know but this lady says she's the anonymous caller."

When Jack interviewed Tricia Glynn, she was so nervous he couldn't help but feel sorry for her. She explained the whole event to him through tears and apologies. He took her statement and details and asked her to be available for furthering questioning if necessary.

Tricia, while clearing up one situation, had introduced another problem.

"She says she's in no doubt that someone ran out the front door when she went round the back, but she was too far away and it happened too quickly for her to get any decent picture in her head – just tallish and dark, she thought."

"Well, we can't hold Oliver Owens, Jack – we have nothing to place him at the scene now."

Two months later, Jack and Charlie opened the file *Tina Owens*.

"Nothing new on this one then, Charlie," said Jack.

"No, I guess the idea that a burglar broke into the house just after the suicide is still the most probable assumption."

"I guess so, but that case bothered me for some reason. I would have liked to have been able to investigate the husband more. Ah well, I guess we can't always be right."

Tricia Glynn sat at her computer ordering her groceries from Tesco online when she noticed a small card sticking out from under her keyboard.

Oliver Owens, 1 Darkwood Place.

"Christ, I don't believe this! I still have his gym membership card."

Tricia realised she'd never replaced it in the black wallet.

She rang Sue. "You'll never believe what I have in my hand."

"What?"

"Oliver Owens' gym card."

"Jesus, Tricia, are you stalking the guy now?"

"No, I just found it under my keyboard. I must not have put it back in the wallet."

"Good, well, just fuck it in the bin now, Tricia – don't keep it and don't dare return it."

"As if I would!"

Tricia Glynn put on her make-up, grabbed her coat and headed out the door. She arrived at 1 Darkwood Place. The house seemed a little less drab this time, like some effort was being put into its appearance.

Tricia rang the doorbell.

Oliver Owens came to the door holding a bottle of wine he was opening. "Hi! You're the girl who found my wallet."

"Yes," said Tricia.

From the distance came a woman's voice. "Who is it, Oliver?"

"Nobody, Elaine, I'll be with you in a minute. Go ahead and serve the dinner."

Didn't take him long, thought Tricia.

"I just called by to return your gym card. It must have fallen out of your wallet."

"Oh, thank you!" He pocketed the card, smiling at her. "It's very important to stay fit." Then, bending down towards her ear, he said, "You'd never know when someone might disturb you and you'd have to make a quick exit out the front door."

Katie Ward Originally from Devon, Katie moved to Dublin in 2004 with only €900 in her pocket, no job, high expectations and not a lot else . . . However, having made the city her home, she has worked hard and managed to attain many of the aspirations she set before leaving the UK.

Defying Gravity

Katie Ward

Defying Gravity

I t's raining in my mind again, a little worse than before now that my fears have been confirmed, the autumn shower that has been hanging above me turned like lightning to biting winter rain, numbing my body from within.

On the contrary, to my mind it is sunny outside, not warm but sunny and if I had been able to have a day off work just for the hell of it, I would have spent it outside, maybe gone to the beach, but instead I am sat in a stuffy waiting room with the sun streaming into the window making pretty patterns on the carpeted floor. The warmth of storage heaters and the heat from the warm winter sun mix into a thick humidity that starts to make me feel sick, although nervousness could also be a cause.

"Miss Sanderson to Dr Finnegan's office."

I knock sheepishly on the door. Even though they are expecting me I always feel that I am intruding.

"Come in!" calls a broad male voice

I open the door and see Dr Finnegan sitting behind his desk; he is wearing a suit, although it is a casual suit. He is a youngish man of around thirty and is new to the locality. He is tall with broad shoulders and big brown eyes, his hair is short with tight curls and he has a very infectious smile. All in all I find this doctor quite attractive.

"Miss Sanderson, is it? Please take a seat. So, Liberty – do you mind if I call you Liberty?"

"No, not at all."

"Right, well, you're here for your test results?"

"Yes, that's right," I shakily confirm in a breathless tone.

I feel the blood start to rush to my face and I feel the wetness of tears prick at the back of my eyes as I anticipate the results before he speaks them.

"I'll get to the point." There is a slight pause as he looks down at his desk. He could have been looking at his notes but I could see it was bad news. "Liberty, I'm sorry but you have Hodgkin's Lymphoma. This is a cancer of the lymph glands and this is what has caused the swelling under your arm. Now we hope we have caught it in its early stages but this is an aggressive cancer and you will need to undergo a PET scan to determine how advanced it is and most likely chemotherapy."

I sit there in silence; I heard what he said but the only words resounding through my head are "cancer, cancer, cancer" again and again but despite this my brain still finds it hard to comprehend what I am being told.

I thought that I would cry but I'm numb. I look

blankly at his face but do not see him. I am brought out of my reverie when he says, "Now, I know you are here on your own today but have you told your family about the lump?"

"Well, I didn't want to needlessly worry them. I thought it would be nothing really."

He looks at me for what feels like an eternity; I know he is trying to read my thoughts so I look down, suddenly finding a curious interest in the wood grain of his desk.

"Do you know what I find?" He pauses as if expecting me to enquire exactly what it is he finds. I don't and so he moves on and answers his own question. "I find that sometimes people cope with news like this by pretending it's not happening and they don't tell their families because if they did it would mean they would have to face the truth. I cannot stress enough how important it is to have your family behind you in a time like this – you really do need their support."

Again tears sting the back of my eyes and I feel the first one fall down my cheek and I know there is no way I can hold them back now.

He hands me a tissue and comes around the desk to comfort me. I don't know exactly what he was saying but I look up through my tears and see his broad smile and before I know it I am promising to tell my family tonight.

I remember reading stories in magazines about women who had overcome cancer and some of them saying that they didn't feel sorry for themselves. But I do and in truth I want everyone else to feel sorry for me too. You spend a whole lifetime being told that you have no reason to complain as there are people far worse off than you and then when you do have something to complain about you're told to be strong but I don't want to be. Yesterday I had a whole future ahead of me, but now it feels as if a fog has come and I can't see past today.

My twin sister Callie is the first of my family to return home. I want to wait until everyone's home to tell them; I only want to say it once.

"Hi, Libby, good day today?"

"Yep."

"Are you OK, Lib?"

"Yeah, I'm fine, why?"

"You sound a bit distracted, like you have something on your mind."

"No, I'm just really tired, not feeling a hundred per cent."

"You do look very pale, Lib. Sit down and I'll make you a cup of tea. Just rest up."

Callie has always been the protective one. She is older than me by a few minutes and ever since I remember she has been the one I turned to for everything, even more than my mother.

I remember when we were about six, we went for a bike ride, and I didn't want to ride mine as I always got too tired so I rode on the back of Callie's. We were down near a farm, most likely where we shouldn't be, and were surrounded by a swarm of geese; I was scared and ended up falling off the bike in the middle of them. Callie was so brave, she came back, got rid of the geese and took me home to patch up my knee. I remember it was at that point that I knew she would always be my protector, but I have always wondered what I am to her, if I have a role in her life like she has in mine.

"Here you go, Lib, that'll make you feel better. I think you've been working too hard – you should take some time out and look after yourself."

"You're probably right. I'll make sure I look after myself before it's too late."

"It's never too late, Lib – you taught me that, remember?"

"I thought it seemed a bit too much sense for you."

"Exactly, I have never been sensible, Lib – that's you."

"Callie, do you believe in destiny?"

"To a certain extent. I mean, I think it is also down to the individual because it doesn't matter how many chances life gives you – if you don't take them what will change?"

"Do you think everything happens for a reason?"

"Absolutely, even when you don't see it, everything has a reason for happening."

I always thought I was in charge of my own destiny but now I feel as if I am part of some grotesque human lottery, just waiting for my number to be called. My thoughts, usually a haven in times of trouble, have now become a dungeon where I relive the day's events over and over as the rain continues to fall all around.

My parents are the next to arrive home. I thought I could wait till after dinner to tell them but I can't. I have to tell them now or I never will.

"Right, well, I have some news for you. Firstly, I don't

want you to get upset and please let me finish before you ask any questions."

Everyone agrees but the mood changes and I see my parents look at each other with a worried expression.

"I can't remember when it was, but I noticed a lump under my arm and went to the doctor about it because you never can be too sure. I went back today for the –"

"You've got cancer!" said Callie.

"Er, well, yes, I have Hodgkin's Lymphoma, which is cancer of the lymph nodes. We have hopefully caught it in the early stages and that's half the battle apparently."

I try to sound optimistic but I see the devastation on everyone's face; I see the realisation sink in that this won't just go away and there is nothing any of them can do to change it. I feel like I am to blame, like I am the biggest burden in the world, and for the first time wish I had never been born. At least then my family would never have had to feel this pain.

"So what happens now?" my mum ventures, trying to stop herself from crying but unable to stop her voice cracking halfway through.

My heart bleeds to know that this is all my fault. Why don't I have the answers that they need?

"Now I have to undergo intensive treatment starting with a PET scan to ascertain how far developed the cancer is and whether it has spread to any of the other lymph nodes – which will determine what course of treatment I need."

I am surprised at how robotic I sound, like the doctor has programmed me. My body goes numb with each tear my mother cries, as if I am leaving my body to watch this scene from a safe place, away from the pain.

"Please don't cry. I'm going to fight this. I'm too young to die."

I feel the lump start in the back of my throat as I say this. I am too young to die and I can't accept that my life will end here.

"The doctor is scheduling an appointment for my scan on Friday. Callie, will you come with me?"

"Absolutely."

I see the tears well up in her eyes and know her pain. I wouldn't know what to do without her. They say you're born alone and you die alone in this life. I may die alone but until that day comes I have never been alone. Callie has always been right by my side.

I know this is in some ways harder for her than it is for me, as she is the one that would be left behind.

The tears and questions eventually stop. Nobody talks about the cancer any more after that unless they have to. Every cough, sneeze or headache I have brings a concerned look from my family. They try to hide it but each is petrified that the sickness will start to show itself in me in a way that is undeniable.

I lie in bed the night before the scan and play out every scenario in my head and I mean every scenario. I think about if I die and if I don't, if I am ill for years and if it goes as quick as it came. I am determined to stay completely positive about my chances but I decide to cover all angles and make a will. Then I begin to find it hilarious that I'm making a will. I mean, I have nothing of any real value; I have about two hundred quid left in my bank until payday and the usual electrical suspects but nothing to give that is worthy of remembering me by. I decide to think about it all later but again the thought of making a will makes me chuckle. I always thought making a will was synonymous with being old, something that you knew you would do but not anytime soon.

The day of the PET scan arrives and I'm not as nervous as I thought I would be. Maybe it is because Callie is with me and she always makes me feel safe.

I'm finally called to the doctor's room with Callie in tow. The doctor greets us both but a confused expression stretches across his features as he timidly asks, "Er, which one of you is Liberty?"

"That would be me." I smile warmly at him. I forget that we are identical and always wonder why people give us strange looks.

"Please take a seat." He ushers us both to a seat opposite him in a very cheery manner. I wonder how he can be so cheery when he deals with so many sick people every day.

"Right, today we are going to be conducting a PET scan. Now this is a procedure we do to try and find the malignant tumour cells in the body. What we'll do is inject you with a solution called 'radionuclide glucose'." He looks up at me with a smile before saying, "That's sugar to you and me. So we do that to show where glucose is being used in the body. You see, malignant tumours show up brighter on the scan because they are active and therefore use more glucose. This then in turn allows us to see where the tumours are and if they have spread to other parts of your body. Do you have any questions about the procedure at all?"

I nod that I don't and am taken to the scan area and given my sugar injection. I soon find myself wishing I could have eaten them instead; I always loved sugar cubes as a child and would have eaten them all day if I could.

The whole thing didn't take as long as I thought it would and before I know it I am sitting with the doctor again talking about the scans.

"Well, it's actually good news: it's as we thought. We have caught it in the early stages and as yet the tumour has not spread. So it's really important that we act quickly and aggressively to stop it having the chance to take hold. We are going to put you on combination chemotherapy with radiation therapy to kill the existing cancer and stop it spreading further. Do you have any questions at all?"

"Does that mean I'm going to lose my hair?"

"Yes, I am afraid you will and the treatment will make you very poorly. We will also have to put you on a course of tablets that will help your immune system because that will be severely affected by the treatment and you will be prone to a lot more illnesses and a cold could easily develop into pneumonia, which would be an extremely bad situation for you. You have to be as good to your body as possible now."

After the consultation I feel as though I have been given a second chance. I see a look of relief on Callie's face. However, I can't get complacent: the battle has just begun. But to know that the cancer hasn't spread to other parts of my body makes me feel as good as if he had given me the all clear. This surely is the best news I could expect under the circumstances.

So tomorrow is the start of my treatment. I have to go home, pack up my things and go back to the hospital as an inpatient. It's all happening so quickly I feel as though I am lost in a dream that I cannot wake up from, but then I feel the lump and I know that this is not a dream; it's a living nightmare.

I remember as a child always wanting to be in hospital, to have all the lovely flowers and chocolates. To have everyone come and visit you while you lie in bed. I suppose at that age I wouldn't have realised exactly why people are in hospital and how sick they are.

"So how do you feel?" asks Callie.

"A little relieved, to be honest."

"I know my heart skipped a beat when he told you. I swear I could not hear better news in my whole life other than that you'll make a full recovery."

"And I will, we just have to believe it."

"I know but it's hard when you just don't know."

"It's more exciting that way."

"I'd rather not have that excitement if your life is at risk."

"I know it's hard but a positive attitude is half the battle. I can't spend every day thinking I could die because I would just waste what time I have left."

I go home and have the last family meal I'll have in a while. Again we hardly talk about the cancer, we just talk about what's on the TV, but I don't mind because in a way I feel closer to them now than I ever did before. Not since we were children have I really appreciated what my family means to me.

We all go together to the hospital and all the way in the car I am freezing cold; my toes feel like ice and I can't distinguish if this is caused by the weather or my own fear.

As we arrive and make our way to the correct department it kind of feels like I am starting school all over again. The feeling is surreal and I don't fully realise how isolated and alone I will feel when my family leave. There I am in a cold and clinical room, bordered by sick people and the faint din of muffled talking caused by the various bodies watching television with headphones on.

I lie on my bed and read a book, hoping that I can beat this and that my positive attitude will remain in even the most trying time of my treatment.

"Miss Sanderson, it's time for breakfast."

I awake and for a second I forget where I am and for a moment it is like nothing is wrong. Then I remember and the dread is like a lead balloon stuck in the pit of my stomach weighing down my soul to the ground.

I try to eat but I can't; I find it hard to swallow and after a few feeble attempts I give up completely.

The first treatment makes me so sick I feel like I have been stuck in a very warm room too long. My head feels thick and my body starts to tingle painfully all over. I just want to sleep but I can't because I feel so sick.

"Hi, darling, how are you feeling?"

I open my heavy eyelids and see my mum, dad and Callie by my bedside.

"I don't feel so good at the moment but that may just be because I'm not used to the treatment." My voice feels very shaky and comes out almost as a whisper.

"Oh love, I don't think you will get used to it but it will probably get better."

I smile weakly and feel the familiar urging in my stomach and before I know it I am being sick as a dog. I know I was told that the treatment would make me poorly but you could never realise to what extent.

The rest of the treatment makes me feel worse and after a month of therapy I am convinced that I am about to die at any moment.

My hair has started to fall out; even my eyebrows and eyelashes succumb to the chemotherapy. I have tried to stay strong but now after all this I am beginning to break and in my pain I take it out on the people closest to me.

The more I see myself deteriorating the more I cannot bear to look at Callie; all I see when I look at her is how I used to be. We are identical and when I look at her I am reminded how awful I look now and how ill I am. I just can't take it any more.

"Mum, hi, it's Libby."

"Hi, love, we're just about to come see you. How are you feeling?"

"I'm not too bad today. The rest of my hair has fallen out now so I'm wearing a head scarf."

"Oh love, I'm sorry."

"I was just calling because . . . well . . . do you mind if I just see you and Dad tonight?"

I feel awful but I just can't bear to see my sister; I

can't bear to see how I was before and how I might never look again. I know it's selfish and I hate myself for it but I just can't bear it, I can't bear to see her, not when I am like this and she is like that, how I used to be.

"Well, if that's what you want, dear, but . . ." She moves into a place where she can't be heard and lowers her voice. "Callie will be devastated. She would be there all day every day if you let her. Can't you reconsider?"

"No, I can't." I start to get angry because I know how much I will hurt her, but she doesn't know how much it hurts me every time I see her. If she had any idea how much it hurts me I'm sure she wouldn't want to come anyway.

"OK, dear, it's your decision but I want you to tell her. She would never believe it from me."

Before I know it I am on the phone to my sister telling her the awful truth.

"Hi, Callie."

"Hi, how are you feeling? We were just leaving to come and see you."

"I know – that's what I was calling about."

"Why? Are you trying to hurry us along? We'll be there really soon, so don't worry, but you know how Mum and Dad faff around."

I smile at this because I do know – whenever we went on holiday we were always still at home two hours after we were supposed to leave because Mum had to check something again "just in case".

"No, that's not why, Callie. I hope you understand but I don't want you to come tonight."

There is silence on the phone and I feel the tears start to prick my eyes. I know this is the right thing to do but it is just so hard.

"What! Lib, why would you say that?"

"I just want to spend time alone with Mum and Dad, that's all."

"Stop lying! Don't think I haven't noticed how you have been acting lately!"

"What do you mean?"

"Well, the last few times I've been there you have hardly spoken to me and wouldn't even look at me. I know it must be hard for you but it's hard for me too, you know."

"Hard for you? Why? You're not the one dying here."

"Neither are you – positive thinking, remember?"

"Yeah, well, it's hard to be positive when you look in the mirror and don't recognise your own face any more."

"I know it's hard but it'll be better and you'll be back to your gorgeous self soon enough."

"Callie, just leave it. Just leave me alone. I don't want to speak to you and I don't want to see you again, is that clear?"

"Perfectly."

As I put down the phone and make my way back to my bed, I know for the first time what it feels like to be alone in this life. They say blood is thicker than water but I don't know – sometimes family blood can get very diluted.

My parents arrive to see me but they are quiet, I am quiet and we hardly say a word. I think that they must hate me and wish I were dead. I mean, if I were dead it wouldn't be like losing a daughter, would it, because they would still have the other healthy one who looks exactly like me. No, I am convinced I would soon be forgotten and nobody would even care.

Days and days pass and I lose track of them. I continue to go through my therapy but I just feel lost, like I am just going through the motions. My will to live is waning.

The nurses start to lose patience with me. My parents come to see me everyday but I refuse to let them talk about Callie. I know she is hurting but so am I. Why can't they understand how hard it is for me?

"Liberty, it's time for your walk." The nurse motions for me to stand up.

"I don't want to walk."

"You have to walk or you won't be able to eat much and you need your strength."

"I don't want to eat, I want to die."

"No, you don't, I know you don't."

"You don't know me so don't suppose you know I don't."

"Look, just a small walk so that you can eat more. You have more treatment tomorrow and if you don't eat properly then the sickness will be even worse than now."

I think about it for a second and cannot justify making the sickness worse so I give in and take the small walk around the ward and back to my bed.

My parents arrive as usual and I see them talking to the nurse. They have brought a visitor that I do not recognise. I am curious now as the person has either very short hair or very blonde hair.

They finish talking to the nurses and walk towards me. I look at the stranger, totally intrigued, trying to figure out who it could be. As they get closer I see that she is oddly familiar. It is only when she reaches my bed that I see who it is.

"Callie, what have you done to your hair?"

"I shaved it off."

"Why did you do that?" I am completely astounded, as I cannot believe that she would ever choose to shave all her hair off voluntarily.

"To be like you. We were born identical therefore we should stay identical."

"Are you mad? You look dreadful!"

"No, I'm not mad. I'm the same as you. You wouldn't see me because I reminded you of how you used to look, so now I'm the same as you there's no reason for you not to see me."

I burst into hysterical tears and cannot stop. I see how much my sister loves me and what sacrifices she is willing to make to be with me in my toughest hour.

"I'm so sorry for being so mean but I just got so upset to see how I used to look, it was just so hard."

"I know and once I realised your reasons it didn't hurt so much. I just wish I had thought of it before."

In the year that has passed since I was first diagnosed I am on the way to making a full recovery, our hair has grown back and we look the same again, the rain inside my mind has stopped and spring is here again. I never thought that I could be so happy. The fog that clouded my future has lifted and as I sit here on a sunny winter's day my eye is caught by the endless blue skies above me. There was a time I never thought I would feel this free and alive again but I defied gravity. I fought against my disease because in the end medicine can only do so much, then the rest lies with you.

Direct to your home!

If you enjoyed this book why not
visit our website:

www.poolbeg.com

and get another book delivered straight to
your home or to a friend's home!

www.poolbeg.com

All orders are despatched within 24 hours.